I0723294

Contents

A Few Thanks

Joy's Grand Adventure started its life as a random picture I found when I had ten free images at Shutterstock and my best friend and bandmate, Tristan Edwards, and I were finishing an album we recorded during the COVID lockdowns.

This picture became the inspiration behind a concept album about joy, which is available for actual purchase (www.redwoodsmusic.bandcamp.com) if you didn't already get it in a pack with this book, which is why a lyric from each song appears at the start of every chapter. As the backgrounds behind each song became more fleshed out, I rather foolishly said that maybe I should write out what was happening in more detail for context; I *meant* to add "so that this informs the vocal and instrument performances" but didn't. Tristan said "yeah, it's about time you actually finished writing a book!" and frankly, I was too ashamed to correct his misunderstanding.

Writing a book is hard, even if it's not very good. I've probably tried starting about nine of them since I was eighteen years of age. Actually keeping the story going beyond the initial concept is very hard, it seems, and is not helped when you have children, or work, or ADHD, and I have all three.

It is important to me, therefore, that I acknowledge a few things first.

Much of this book progressed because Tristan sat in my tiny music studio- which can barely fit me on my own- for many evenings and refused to let me leave until I had written something new. On no less than six occasions I was prepared to abandon the project because it was taking about as much time as a university degree to finish and serves about as much use in my life at present. Trapped with both his encouragement and flatulence with no escape from either, the book moved ahead when I didn't think it would.

This book wouldn't have happened *at all* without Stacey Copas, to whom I first foolishly disclosed a nascent idea and whose unwavering belief in my meagre array of talents, despite all evidence to the contrary, made me in turn believe that a project that would consume almost three years of my life was not only worthwhile but also possible to be completed. Throughout this entire process she remained a source of wisdom and insight, someone I could bounce random ideas around with when I was wandering on my lunch breaks in the dim hopes of being struck down by a stray bolt of lightning so I could avoid having to return to work or, worse, finish this book. I'd not have finished it without her- not least because she is now, technically, a publisher. I am ridiculously grateful for you.
Also, shout-out to Terry and Lyn, for both being, and making, amazing people.

Tamara, my daughter who is about to turn 20 at the time I write this preface, served as an inspiration for quite a lot of Joy's personality. She also went through her first major heartbreak in the middle of writing and I am grateful for the opportunity she provided to observe the process up close. Amongst other things, I learned that saying "one man's trash is another man's treasure" is less encouraging than I thought.

Dr. Kevin Trinh, designer extraordinaire, assisted with my last-second book design request because I was out of time to write and had no time to fiddle around in Photoshop, and I owe him enormously as a result. Aside from (as of 2024) holding a PhD in design- it could have been break dancing since that's apparently an academic field now- he's also one of the most talented graphic artists I've had the pleasure of knowing. He's worth every penny I've never paid him.

James Belfrage, who kindly agreed to do a live reading playing the role of both Fear and the narrator, also supported the project from the outset and his interest encouragement to finish it helped more than I suspect he was aware.

Kevin McCove deserves a longer thanks and I ran out of space on the CD case where these belong. He originally hosted a musician Framework Friday group where I learned a lot about production, and then he made extra time to talk me through what to do with an album when you're mid-40s and don't tour, aren't Dave Grohl (which saves me having a secret second family) and will only have a handful of people ever actually listen to it. His practical advice and sharing of his time when he's already an in-demand musician and producer in his own right, really was something very special.

Ben, Jono, Aaron and Tommy, who have had to share me with this project over the years, are appreciated. They were great sports at hearing track samples and were always good sounding boards for the story's arc.

Anthony and Mandi Hirsch, who have always supported the project and indeed most projects I've ever undertaken, who were the first ones to put an order in when they heard it was pre-orderable, and whose friendship and support through the most challenging of times has been unwavering and deeply appreciated.

Lastly, but not least, my dad, who first taught me piano and who let me purloin an old guitar of his when I was 18 that I found in the garage. His early exploits in home recording on reel-to-reel 4-tracks and then early Roland MIDI devices kicked off the last twenty years of attempting to record at home.

Not only did he give helpful feedback as I worked on the tracks, but many of the places we lived in over the course of his academic life influenced both the surrounds of Pleasant Lane but also the landscape of Frieland. Moreover, there was an encouragement towards storytelling in our house and this is ultimately its practical outworking. Accordingly, if you hate this book, it's entirely his fault, and you should look him up and send him your disapproval.

If you love it, of course, it's aaaaaaaaaall me, baby. Buy a copy for a friend as a gift.

Given the limited nature of this story's release, I'll also take a final opportunity to thank you, whoever you are, for buying, reading, and listening to this adventure. For friends, family, and people I don't even know to take a chance on an unknown tale written by a strange guy in Western Sydney, well, it's pretty special. I don't appreciate it enough to return your money, but I'll be sure to think of you while both dollars of overall profit are spent.

Chapter 1

This Life

Waits for a dream to take his brain to some other place so far away

Joy Summerfield was born at 17 Pleasant Lane, which would have seemed prescient were it not for the fact that its name belied its reality. Pleasant Lane was a concrete jungle, a world of greys and blacks, concrete and asphalt; many of the houses were Housing Commission related and were uniform in their design, two-bedroom terraces with a concrete court-yard, designed for minimal maintenance and, clearly, minimal personality. Here and there, on odd balconies, there might appear a small spark of life: a hanging pot plant, a small flowerpot on the front landing with posies or other small and colourful flowers. However, these were stars in the black night sky, brief messages to a cold universe that life had not yet given up, but were also possibly light travelling from long-deceased gas giants gone nova many years before.

It fell into one of those "living mousetrap" categories. If you lived there, you worked, not at somewhere that paid enough for you to get ahead, but enough consistently that you could view those that didn't work as welfare cheats. You could always say 'there are people worse off than us' and feel reasonably certain that this was a true statement. Whilst some tenants came and trashed houses, they were not the norm. However, the residents were often the type who had hit a ceiling; they'd managed to get to a point where employment was steady and predictable but further progression was an impossibility, either due to skill or education or circumstance or their own innate view that greater responsibility required a different biological make-up than they were born with. After all, if you want to trap a mouse to keep, all you need to do is give it just enough food and water to get through the day with, and a door that only opens in one direction.

It was far enough from the city job centres that a commute was a chore, but not so far that the travel couldn't be justified, keeping the occupants just shy of moving to a full-scale welfare situation. Its costs were manageable in line with full-time work, but left most residents living paycheque to paycheque, except for the odd squirrelling away of funds for a holiday occasionally to a caravan park within the same state.

Whilst nobody would admit it, some part of you knew that if you lived there, you were going to die there.

There's a degree of contentment that comes with resignation, a certain warmth that comes with predictability on the slow decline towards the inevitable, a little like breathing carbon monoxide or developing hypothermia. It wasn't necessarily a bad thing; 'life's what you make it' was the familiar refrain and the surrender to routine did mean that the residents would build a small network of relationships within the complexes which became their own fortress against the world. Most people had similar family sizes, sufficient income to afford one or, at most, two children, and these children tended to be of similar ages. The kids on your street became the same circle of friends at the local primary school, and then there was the slow glacial drift of puberty and high school cliques, and the street would become quiet once again, back to the state that said that life could exist but, like the fast food specials pitched to the residents, only for a limited time. In those intervening years, kids would run in and out of each others' houses, parents would travel door-to-door for birthdays, occasional barbecues commemorating annual events like the founding of the country, the grand final of the key sports, or the long weekend in summer would bring everyone together in the middle of the street for food, connection, and salacious gossip.

It was not, if truly pressed, exactly *un*pleasant. It wasn't littered with junkies' needles, or home to screaming fights that spilled onto the street, or cars on blocks and the inevitable fortnightly police raid. It was three streets back but parallel to the main arterial road, meaning the residents weren't disturbed by the traffic but had only a short walk to go to the nearest bus stop. It was just one of those places, by design or circumstance, that functioned like a tar pit, sticking to you and becoming more dangerous the more you resisted.

Joy was named by her mother, somewhat hopefully, as if she might somehow bring meaning to the daily existence in which she operated; a chance to say, as most people in the street did, "I'm doing it to give my kids a better life" and "I just want my kids to be happy" and other platitudes that kept your hands busy and your eyes on the clock. It was never clear exactly what "it" was that they were supposedly doing for their kids, but it looked suspiciously like running out of ideas and alternatives and, in more than a few cases, Trying To Save The Relationship.

So it was into this unspoken tumult that Joy was brought, healthy and largely happy, an initial shock to a routine that then absorbed and enveloped her like lava around an errant mountainside house.

Carried along by the pendulum of the routine, her father would rise early and return after the street lights were out; with budgets tight and cash strapped, he would follow a simple mantra: keep your eyes on your work, provide for your family, don't rock the boat. The lessons gleaned from the failures of the families who had fallen from that precarious tightrope was that if you dreamed too big, or looked away, or forgot your place, then the wheels of the machinery would catch you and crush you and then someone very much like you would move into the house, the job, and the life of Pleasant Lane that you used to occupy. A simple man might not be able to solve *all* the problems, but if the blinkers could stay on then the bills would be met, a sad but willing trade made by many fathers before and, presumably, many afterward, in the interests of their families.

Joy could often hear him in the morning from her adjacent bedroom, his slow rise out of bed, his audible slow count from one through to ten, deep breaths, the process of dressing, picking up his lunch box from the kitchen, his boots clomping out the door.

Night times were their special times, when her father, weary from the day though he might be, would pull out crayons and large sheets of paper from the factory where he worked. He and Joy would then draw stories they would invent as they went, sketching out landscapes and strange characters inspired by school adventures.

"Did you know owls can turn their head all the way around til they can see their bum?" a six-year-old Joy had said in between furious colouring with her tongue sticking out the side of her mouth.

"I didn't know owls *had* bums," her dad had replied, finishing up a parapet wall for a city Joy had demanded, on the logical basis that there had to be somewhere to safely house the unicorns. "I thought they just had tails."

"*No,* Dad," Joy had sighed, "if they didn't have bums, how could they sit?"

"They don't sit, I think. Don't they perch?"

"What's that mean?"

"They hold on with their feet and tuck their legs in."

"Well, maybe. But they still need a bum to poo."

"That's a good point, honey."

"*Anyway,*" she'd carried on tersely and she tried to find a green crayon amongst the pile she'd hoarded on her side of the table, "they can turn their heads right round. All the way."

"Guess that would make it hard to sneak up on them, right?"

"Right. They'd be good on the parapet. They could watch all the bad guys."

"Do you even know what a parapet is, honey?" He'd asked, trying to change the subject from nocturnal avian anatomy.

"Yeah, Miss was talking about them in class this week. It's a bit of extra wall for people to hide behind so they can poke bad guys trying to climb up ladders and, like, walk around to see if anyone's coming," Joy replied brightly as her crayon navigated a complex curve in her drawing. Her dad had chuckled at that.

"A pretty good explanation, kid. Here, there's your parapet wall."

"Can I draw an owl up there?"

"It's your wall, you can draw whatever you want."

"He can watch the unicorns. You can't trust unicorns."

"Why's that?"

"Because they're wild and they're magic, Dad. They can do what they want. *They* don't know people want their horns for the magic, they just think they have murder horns."

"Murder horns?"

"Yeah, Dad, unicorns can stab people with their murder horns."

"But they make them better after, right?"

"They can."

"Oh good."

"But they don't."

"Oh. Right."

"So you have to watch your back. Which an owl could do."

"From the parapet?"

"Yes. Come on, Dad, you wouldn't want to be too close to a murder horn."

"I suppose not."

"Get with the program, Dad."

Her father had laughed at that. "Where'd you hear that?"

"*You* say it. To the TV sometimes."

Dad had looked at Mum, who had shrugged and nodded.

"So what's this city called, kiddo?" He had asked, making a deft topic change.

"Joytown."

"Not Unicorn Town?"

Joy had tutted. "*Of course not*, silly. I'm the one rescuing the unicorns, so the town has to be named after *me*. Unicorns aren't special."

"So why do you want unicorns?"

"Because then I can have a giant owl to watch them. See?" And she pushed the drawing addition back across the table, with a larger-than-human-sized owl standing on the parapet wall.

"Which way is he facing?"

"Any way he wants. He's an owl. He can always look around again." She'd paused for a moment, before continuing, "Owls are the *best.*"

Joy's mother, a jittery woman with unrealised dreams of stardom within the folk-pop music scene which she continued to doggedly pursue, had done her best to hold on within the life of Pleasant Lane for an admirable period. She had done what was expected, joined the play groups, fed and changed nappies and baked birthday cakes and tried her best to seem to those outside as though this small human had made things complete for her, much the same as other parents pretended. Once school had started, she had eagerly returned to work, in an office somewhere in the city where she had to wear a shirt with the company logo on it, and as Joy understood it, "helped people find who they were looking for to do a job." On weekends, she would find opportunities to perform in small bars and clubs, or would save for meagre time at low-budget studios to make demo tapes which would be sent out and returned unopened.

By the time Joy was seven, though, it was clear that Mum was not one of the people who could close out her dreams and just ride the machinery of the world. The grinding of the wheels skittered along her nerves, leaving her short-tempered, flinching at the sounds as kids ran in and out of rooms on weekends and back out to houses, every grudging daily step that required just to stay in the same place only increasing the pain with each shuddering footfall.

Joy never saw her parents fight about this; it was more of a note of discord, something errant that made it clear something wasn't right in the room, like an air pressure building up, invisible but undeniable. There was a restlessness, an unexplained circumstance where Joy would find her weekends mostly filled with time with her father alone, and she would orbit her mother when she could find her, trying to find a crack that would allow her into that world.

When Joy was aged nine, her mother was gone one day. The school had called her dad to come and get her when nobody had shown up, and there was a note at home simply saying "*I can't do this any more. I'm sorry. Goodbye.*" Her side of the wardrobe was empty, and that was about it, except for her guitar, which was left in the living room in its case. They had hoped for a few weeks that maybe she would return, having just taken a holiday to herself or joined a tour, but eventually the hope had waned as the unspoken truth became clear: Mum wasn't coming back. Joy was just old enough to know what this meant, whilst being too young to fully comprehend it. It meant, she thought, that she and her father weren't worth keeping.

Dad didn't speak about it again. To make ends meet, he had to take on additional hours, and in the absence of a solution to the emotional loss, had gone back to focusing on what he knew: keep your eyes on your work, don't rock the boat, provide for your family. The lack of discussion made a pressure cooker for Joy. In the face of the silence and the unasked questions which hung in the air, she wanted to scream, wanted to know why he didn't also demand the answers she longed for: why weren't we enough? How could you go? How come you couldn't even say goodbye? Why aren't you coming back?

Undercutting these questions, however, there was an accompanying fear that Joy had: what if *he* couldn't do this any more either?

So, as is often the case amongst perceptive young children, the over-arching fear became the daily goal: Make Sure Dad Is OK. Don't let him know you're upset, be helpful. They would still draw together in the evenings after work as a vehicle for their discussions, which stayed fairly superficial and related to the goings-on of the day. The finished drawings, however long they took to complete, would be taped to the wall, and then her father would go to bed without saying anything further.

They divided labour. Joy would make lunches for both of them for the next day; Dad would cook when he got home, somewhat inexpertly but capably enough for the two of them to get through. He would put the washing on when he went to bed; Joy would hang it on a clothes rack on the back patio before she had to get on to the bus. On the weekends, they would go shopping together in the morning at 10:30 and then he would mop the floors downstairs while she tidied the rooms upstairs. After a while, the unanswered questions became less pressing and the routine became dependable and survivable, and Joy didn't feel as much frustration towards her dad's silence on the topic. Besides, she had made a new friend to talk to instead.

Her friend was named Fear. He was, by and large, invisible to other people; tall, opaque, with black hair and grey eyes set against his otherwise pale features, and always seemed to be wearing a long black trench coat over a white shirt and a black tie, and pressed black trousers. Despite his name, he was actually not that bad of a bloke. He was a good listener, usually came with some decent advice, and was always ready to talk things through. He could be a bit of a wet blanket on occasion, sure, but by and large he was dependable, friendly, and genuinely concerned for Joy's wellbeing.

He'd shown up shortly after Make Sure Dad Is OK had become Joy's modus operandi. It was early days when the pain of the sudden absence of her mother was fresh and Joy had gone to her room to sit against the door and have a bit of a quiet cry. He'd walked through a wall, looked down at her, and then sat beside her on the floor without so much as an introduction.

"Hey there," he'd said gently. His voice was warm and fairly friendly, and despite his black hair and grey eyes, his features were gentle and not especially intimidating, given a nine-year-old had been sobbing alone and now seemed to be accompanied by what she assumed was a ghost.

"Hey," Joy had sniffed, her sadness too great to give way to shock, "what are you doing here?"

"Oh, you know. You looked like you could use someone to talk to."

"Should I be talking to ghosts?"

"Probably a bad thing to do. Though that might be rude of me, seeing as I've never met one."

"I have," Joy replied somewhat proudly between sniffles.

"What were they like?"

"I'm still finding out."

"Sounds fun. Can I find out with you?" he'd asked, exaggerating eagerness.

"Sure, I guess. I wasn't doing much else anyway."

"How do you talk to ghosts?"

"I don't know. People on TV usually have those boards and glass balls, but that's make-believe. I suppose you just ask them about their day."

"Could be a bit of a worry. What if they'd had a bad day?"

Joy hadn't considered this before.

"You think they would be mean?" she had asked.

"Maybe," Fear replied. "I imagine if you have a bad day when you have an infinite number of more days ahead of you, it could carry on a ways."

"Well, how was *your* day?"

Fear had shrugged. "Can't complain. There seems to be a lot of them. How about yours?"

"Terrible."

Fear had nodded sagely. "Probably the ghosts," he said. "Is that it?"

Despite herself, Joy had smiled and briefly chuckled.

"No, silly. I'm just sad. My mum went away."

Fear put a slightly see-through arm around her shoulder consolingly, which felt oddly reassuring for something she couldn't actually feel.

"You'll have to excuse my ignorance," he'd said, "but don't all mums do that? I see them going away every day."

"No, most mums come back. Mine isn't."

"Oh. I see. I'm sorry," he'd replied gently, concern entering his voice. "Why isn't she coming back?"

"I don't know. Maybe it's me."

"What's your name?"

"Joy. What's yours?"

"I'm Fear. I like your name, though. Joy, why do you think it's you that made her not come back?"

Joy had sniffed again, her voice cracking. "She was here before I was. And now she's gone and I don't know and I think she maybe didn't-" and at this point, Joy stopped talking and started crying again, her shoulders shaking but her noise suppressed. Fear had sighed.

"Right, up you get," he said matter-of-factly, standing up and walking to face her. He stood in front of her, and put his hands out. A little uncertainly, she had reached out with her own, and despite not feeling like *fingers*, as she gripped his hands she nevertheless felt a pull to her feet. He took her across to the mirror.

"There," he said, pointing at the two of them in the reflection, "what do you see?"

"I don't know. Us?"

"I see Joy. Nobody leaves because of Joy."

"It's just a name, silly."

"Ah, but it's *not*," he chided gently. "Let me ask you, do you and your dad do things together?"

"We draw."

"And is he happy drawing?"

"Yeah, but that's because he's drawing."

"Does he draw on his own?"

"No, I guess not."

"Does he draw with anyone else?"

"No."

"There you have it. He *enjoys* it because he's doing it with Joy."

"What if he's not enjoying it, though? What if *he* leaves?

"That's a good question. Why do you think he would?"

"I don't. But I didn't think Mum would. I thought that grown-ups just handled things. Isn't that why they're in charge?"

Fear laughed at this point, and it was a bit of a shock to Joy in what had seemed quite a serious conversation for a nine-year-old.

"Joy, if I may, I have to visit a *lot* of people. Grown-ups are often the *least* prepared or equipped to handle things. They make all *sorts* of bad decisions, especially when they're afraid. And I suppose I can't complain. It keeps me in the job. But *you* have a spark."

"A spark?"

"You didn't know? Watch this."

He lifted his hands as she watched in the mirror and lowered them slowly until they were just above her hair; as he did so, little fireworks leaped and danced, no more than an inch above her head, making an odd crackle like a discharge of built-up static electricity. Her eyes had widened and Fear smiled.

"I guess it's not for everyone to notice. But I did, while I was passing through."

"Why *are* you passing through?"

Fear looked sheepish.

"Honestly? I'm here to visit your dad. He's worried about you."

"I'm worried about him, too."

"Very sensible. After all, if he can't handle his things, who will look after you?"

"That's what I thought!"

"I know. See?" And here, his hand quickly darted into her ear, disappearing inside her head up to the end of his fingers. He pulled, and out came what looked like a thick worm, three inches long, purple and transparent and wriggling back and forth enormously, unwilling to leave its home without a fight. With a final flick of his wrist, the creature came away, a tiny head at the end trying to writhe back and snap at the fingers holding it. Fear held him up for Joy to see.

"See? He's grown big *fast*. He's been feeding."

"What *is that*?" Joy asked, quite alarmed. Fear had laughed pleasantly.

"Nothing to be worried about. You know how they say fear worms its way in to you?"

"Yes?"

"This is how. It's a Worm of Concern. But I'll hang on to this one for a while."

Fear reached into his pocket and extracted a large jar, not dissimilar from a marmalade jar, and deposited the worm inside. He held it up to look at it.

"You know," he said after a pause, "it's amazing how these guys grow and spread. They're really quite remarkable. But I'll take him and *this one-*"and his hand darted again, pulling another wriggling beast, a darker shade of purple this time, and popping it in with the first one- "because, my dear, you don't need to be afraid about these things."

"What was that one?!"

"That is the worry that you aren't enough for your mother. Sometimes, Joy, things become too much. Even for me, would you believe. That's sad, and it can be scary, and it can make it hard pick up your legs and continue onwards. But *you*, Sparky- if I can call you that?- *you*, are just fine."

"Really?"

"Really. Now, I'm taking these worms with me but if you need me again, well, just call me."

"I'm not allowed a mobile phone," Joy had replied in a bit of a stunned state. Fear had laughed.

"Just as well, since I don't have one either. You'll figure out how. I won't be far away. You just look after your dad, and he'll look after you, and you both'll be OK."

"We will?"

"I promise."

Fear took her shoulder and turned her to face him, cupping a finger under her chin so that she looked up directly into his eyes, and then put his fingers either side of her head. She ought to feel afraid, but she didn't.

"Joy Summerfield of Pleasant Lane, whatever else you might be, you will never be alone. Here-" and she felt a slow flow of cold leave her body, a bit like a warm draught but going from her rather than past her- "I'll take some of these feelings with me along with the fears. I can always return them later if you want them back. You just ask for me."

Joy's sadness had stopped. The empty, hollow feeling that had gnawed at her was gone. She felt a wave of exhaustion hit her, as if the sadness and fear had been holding back a tide that suddenly washed back into the vacant place.

She looked at fear.

"Thank you," she said gratefully. "Is this something you do a lot?"

"Almost never."

"Only almost?"

"It's the 'never' you need to be thinking of. Never's a long time. 'Almost' is only a *tiny* bit less than that," he replied, and started walking through the door before leaning back and touching his forelock which meant that only his head and arm were visible.

Joy smiled. "Bye, Fear."

"Goodbye, Joy. We'll see each other again, I'm sure."

Chapter 2

Hello, Yellow Brick Road

I can feel my feet, they're lighter than they've been.

It was not a typical Thursday afternoon.

Joy was now in her final term of her final year at high school, and it could be argued that the relative predictability and monotony of her life in Pleasant Lane meant that it wouldn't require much to make a day atypical, even for a young woman with an invisible friend. This Thursday, however, was unique because of the boat.

Firstly, Joy hadn't had any experience with boats. She was aware that there were people who boated, or messed about, or whatever the description was for people with far more money than her family and who could afford such recreational nautical pleasures or, for that matter, recreation.

Her home was far from any natural waterways, and even her school camps to date hadn't included so much as a canoe.

However, her journey home at the end of the day comprised of a bus change which required a few blocks' walk between the stops for the relevant routes, starting on a major six-lane road which had a concrete canal running below it to manage stormwater overflow locally and also served as a repository for errant shopping trolleys wielded by young men with limited futures. What flowed in it most days could *charitably* be described as water, in much the same way that drug dealers could be described as urban entrepreneurs, but entry into it was, at best, a dare and, at worst, a guaranteed way out of final exams. Due to recent storms, it was moving along slightly faster than its normal turgid flow, which often sounded like an old woman eating particularly sticky caramel as it sucked its way along the canal walls.

Today, as it bubbled along, an old rowboat was visible, flecked with old paint in a few places but otherwise weatherbeaten timber, although it looked fairly solid despite this.

The second thing she noticed was that it almost seemed as though it was following her. It just listed along, never passing them and never falling behind.

Fear stopped walking, leaned against the railing and remarked about this.

"That's something you don't see every day," he said.
"A boat? Surely most people see them, where they're supposed to be," Joy replied.

"Well, *is* it supposed to be there?" Fear asked.

"I don't know, maybe someone's washed away? Come on, we'll miss the bus," Joy said dismissively, starting to walk off.

"What, out of a garage and eight blocks along into a canal? That's a bit far-fetched isn't it?"

"How would I know?" she shot back testily. "I'm here talking to the invisible personification of Fear."

"Anthropomorphisation, please."

"Oh, whatever, Fear, you know what I meant. So, what exactly don't we see every day?"

"Well, I've not seen a boat bobbing *against* the current."

Joy had stopped walking, in spite of the need to make the connecting bus at the next stop, and walked back to have a look again. The current affair, as it were, hadn't been immediately apparent to her.

"Okay, I'll say that's odd," she conceded grudgingly. "But it's not going against the current, it's sitting still. Maybe it dropped an anchor?"

"No anchor visible," Fear replied. "Plus it was moving along with us, and now it's not."

"Maybe it's got a chain underneath and it's getting winched?"

"Who'd run a winch along a canal?"

"Look, we'd better get the bus. Or I had. You seem to travel however you want, I've never figured it out."

"I like the bus. Everyone's worried about something. Gives the worms a chance to grow."

They'd started walking again, against the current flow below, until she heard the ongoing slapping of water against wood. She stopped again and leaned against the rail.

"I think the boat's following us!" Joy said at last. "Look, it's stopped again!"

"How can a boat follow someone?" Fear asked innocently.

"I don't know, how can you walk through walls one moment and then lean up against them the next?"

"Touché. Maybe there's only one way to find out: you should get in."

"Do you *really* think that's a good idea?" Joy asked suspiciously.

"Depends. Are your tetanus boosters up to date?"

"Fear, shut up!"

"Don't forget Joey McArthur at school, who lost his toe last year."

"Oh, you always imagine the worst."

"Your point being...?"

"Just watch."

Joy walked five paces forward and stopped again; below them, the little boat moved up slightly and came to a rest. She walked again, and stopped again. The boat mirrored the activity. She then sprinted the other direction, and the boat floated backwards with the current until it was level with her.

"Looks like you've got a pet," Fear remarked with a grin. "Got space in your room for a pet boat?"

"Ha ha," Joy replied sarcastically, "you should try stand-up."

"Maybe it's a ghost ship!" Fear continued, clearly enjoying himself the more ridiculous the suggestions became.

"What, a rowboat in the twenty-first century in a country that doesn't have pirates?"

"Well, for a very lonely or irritable pirate. Maybe he was just starting out. Or he was short and didn't want to be on a Tall Ship."

"Should I talk to it?"

"I don't see how it could hurt. You're having a conversation with an invisible person, so yelling instructions at a haunted rowboat is hardly the craziest thing you've done in public."

"Wow, thanks for putting it that way. If you think it looks weird, why do you always start talking to me first? Come to think of it, why follow me around at all?"

"Because nobody's looking at *me.*"

"Oh, thank you *very* much," Joy said with a moderate amount of rancour. She increased the walking pace. The boat continued to bob along, not hurrying or racing, against the current and right on the edge of the canal until it was level with them again, and then floated in place with the water slapping softly against the hull. Joy leaned over the rail and flicked a hand at it.

"Shoo!" she half-yelled, half-called. "Go home!"

The boat continued floating in place.

"What do you want?" she called again, acutely aware of her voice bouncing off the concrete walls of the canal, drawing attention of the passers-by. Inside the boat, an oar moved slightly, but it could have been just due to the water's ebb. "No! Go home, I'm not rowing you!"

A boat has no physical features to look disappointed with, but nevertheless it gave the impression of a dog being told that today was not Walk Day. After a few more moments, it started dropping back from them, carried a distance by the current but not quite at the same pace. Joy watched it until it was perhaps a hundred metres behind them, and then resumed the journey to the bus stop. It hadn't yet arrived, based on the number of strangers waiting, so they were in luck that it was slightly behind schedule. Joy and Fear took their place in line.

"If you want to keep it, you have to understand it's a big responsibility," said Fear in a fatherly impersonation as they waited amongst the crowd of other passengers, waggling his finger. "You'll have to feed it and take it for regular swims and don't be surprised if it tries to sleep in your bed. You'd probably think that was oarful."

Joy hated when he'd do this, trying to make her giggle without explanation in a group that couldn't see him. Fear knew this, so did it at every conceivable opportunity. They boarded the bus, Joy snickering slightly and Fear giggling gleefully, and continued the journey home.

"Italy," Fear said, lying on his back on Joy's floor with his legs going up the wall.

"Rome," Joy replied from her bed.

"France."

"Paris."

"Dubai."

"It's an emirate and a city. It doesn't have a capital per se."

"Good! Thought I'd get you with a trick one. Azerbaijan."

"Urrrrrrrrrgh... oh, come on."

"You know this one," Fear said encouragingly.

"You suck. I hate you."

"Yes, very convincing. Sounds like 'achoo'?"

"Baku! On the Caspian sea!"

"Got it!" Fear said with a delighted clap of his hands. Joy scowled at him.

"I still don't see why you can't just give me the answers in the test. It's not like anyone can see you," she said grudgingly. "Finals aren't that important."

"Well, aside from the fact that I'll be working, thank you, you've got better things to do than become a cheater," Fear chided.

"What's the worst that could happen?"

"Well, you could avoid learning anything at all, become unemployable, become a smack addict, live in a box."

"What, all because of geography?"

"Stranger things have happened."

"Well, I guess that's what happens when you ask the personification of fear anything. What about if I pass?"

"You could work, save, travel to these places, become unemployable, smack addiction, box. But at least you'd know where that box was, you know, geographically."

Joy laughed, despite herself. "What are you doing in the exams anyway?" She asked. "Seems a bit ghoulish to me."

Fear just shrugged on the floor. "I'm there every year. There's always something for the worms to feed on. 'Didn't I study that?', 'I shouldn't have been on social media so much', 'my parents are gonna be so mad'. That kind of thing."

"What, you're always at my school?"

"I'm in every school, Joy," Fear replied. "I'm everywhere. Just sometimes, I'm also here specifically."

Joy sighed. "Must be nice, to travel all the time," she said wistfully.

Fear considered this. "I mean, I've been around a long time. Sometimes it's nice to stay away and then visit to see what's changed," he replied.

"Have you been to Baku before?"

"Sure. The Cold War was very good for my frequent flyer miles."

"What's it like?"

"Depends on the time of year. For the longest time they were either worried about the cold, or, you know, the Cold War. If you remove the random terrorist attacks and power centralisation with the oligarchs, it's quite a beautiful city. Lots of old buildings, wonderful carvings, and the kidnappings are smooth as glass."

"Fear!"

"What? The last thing you want when you're working is to get stuck in human traffic."

"You're a terrible person."

"Thank you."

"For saying you're terrible?"

"For calling me a person."

Joy paused for a moment. "Fear?" she asked eventually.

"Yes?"

"What happens after exams? I mean, to me? And you?"

"Why, are you worried about it?" he asked gently.

"No. Yes. A bit. Why?"

"The worms might be hungry."

Joy threw a pillow through him. It made her feel better, in spite of the lack of efficacy. "Seriously," she said. "I mean, you're like the only person I really talk to."

"It's a cross I have to bear as the most interesting person to ever live," he replied, throwing a hand theatrically across his forehead. "Oh dear! Joy might have to have a conversation with a person!"

"It doesn't help," she retorted, "that every time I start meeting someone new, you tell me they could be a murderer. Or a gym teacher."

"It's worse when they're both."

"*Fear!*"

He sighed. It looked like Joy was serious. He put on his serious face, which was very similar to his messing-with-Joy face, and only he could really tell the difference, or so he told himself. "You want to see the world?" He asked.

"I don't know."

"I can shoooowwwww you the wooooorld…" he started singing until another pillow went through his head. He turned to look at her.

"You're not asking about me, really, are you?" he said gently. "You're asking about your dad."

Joy sniffed and seemed a little smaller.

"I'm never going to leave Pleasant Lane. I mean, what would he do without me?"

"What did he do before you?"

"You know what I mean, what we have is each other and that's been enough!"

"Has it?"

"Oh, you *know* I hate it when you do that!" Joy huffed. Fear dropped his legs down, sat up, and put his hands out.

"Joy, look at me."

"I don't want to," she replied, looking at the bedspread instead.

"No, really. Look at me."

Joy raised her head to look him in the eyes. Suddenly, his hands were either side of her temples, and there was a flash behind her eyes, and the next thing she could see was a circular bay at night, a city on its edges, three wavy towers lit up in different colours and the rest of the city awash with light, sandstone structures casting long shadows, with gardens and greenery along the bay waving slowly in the evening breeze. The smell of the ocean filled her nostrils, and down below she could hear the sounds of traffic that had a curiously familiar and yet foreign feel. The Caspian Sea stretched out in front of her, looking like it reached to the edge of the world. Carved stone arches and cobbled streets flew by as she was brought down to the city level. There it was, Baku, the capital of Azerbaijan, a strange mix of old and new, a man-made canal lined with willows and shrubs moving ponderously between modern office buildings, the Old City at the side like a strangely teleported excavation.

Joy gasped suddenly and the picture disappeared as she sucked air into her lungs.

"This place isn't forever, Joy," Fear said carefully and earnestly, his usual sarcasm slipping away for a moment. "I don't know what you're afraid of- well, I mean, I *do*, of course, but I mean metaphorically- *but* it's important to understand that fear of the unknown can be worse than fear of the cage. You can make it as comfortable and well-furnished as you like, but at the end of the day, if you *can't* leave, then it's a prison. The bars might be of your own making, even."

Joy swallowed. "Well," she said after a moment and with a small mustering of bloody-minded anti-authoritarianism, "if you can just magic me into a memory, why leave at all?"

"Memories are better if you make your own," Fear replied. "Like the memory of the capital city of Denmark."

"Copenhagen."

"Well done."

The school year meandered onwards; assignments came and went, practice exams took place, finals approached, and throughout this time, Joy found herself developing an increasing restlessness, starting in her feet. Time would be lost in a daydream and her feet seemed to wander automatically past travel agencies, newsagents with postcards, buildings with paintings of destinations she wasn't familiar with; beaches, strange cities' markets at night, deep green forests of massive redwoods stretching up mountains, snow-covered ski runs, cities circling bays in the tropics, almost ethereal reefs, sunsets setting over the savannah, glistening towers thousands of feet high.

The trudge home seemed like blowing into a balloon, an ever-increasing pressure that was slowly but surely seeming to reach a point where all available surfaces were stretched. Joy wondered if her mother had felt this way; as much as she resented the circumstances resulting from that fateful day, and the role forced upon her, there was a curiosity as to whether this wanderlust was a genetic thing. She'd never really wondered about travelling beyond her world, in part because there was so much to do, and in part, she supposed, because her only real friend went wherever she was anyway; would scenery change that experience?

Every few weeks, as she walked the gap between her connecting buses, she would glance into the canal and see if the boat was back. In her head, she'd named it Steve, because somehow that didn't seem as weird to her as admitting that a boat was alive. On a few occasions, she was certain she could see it farther down, a small object on the edge of vision, but it could have been anything; a shopping trolley thrown in while the water was low, or a small stolen car crashed and left behind. However, as the end of the year approached, the dry seasons set in and the canal eventually became a man-made creek, barely able to float the refuse that fell into the canal, deep enough to wet a shoe but certainly nothing that would bestow buoyancy. Nevertheless, her feet felt heavy in these areas, as if imploring her to stay in the middle of this strangely barren concrete mockery of nature, surrounded by cars fighting to get home, the only colours being bestowed by the changing traffic lights.

"I know what he's afraid of," Fear said to her quietly one afternoon, a week before finals.

"Who?" Joy responded, snapping out of a daydream and glancing over the hand rail. Still nothing.

"Your dad," Fear replied.

Joy frowned. "I thought we had agreed you weren't allowed to tell me stuff that he was thinking."

"I don't know what he's thinking. Just what he's afraid of."

"Why are you telling me? I mean, you could be sneaking me an early look at the exam questions."

"Because you might think it's important," Fear replied calmly.

"Yeah, well, a good education is important too, they tell me," Joy replied sullenly. She had been enjoying the daydream and, frankly, talking about her dad made her feet more restless. In the evenings she'd taken to very brief conversations with him, enough to keep him satisfied about her goings-on and then she would excuse herself, ostensibly to study. She knew it was a lie; any more time in the room together increased the feeling of pressure within her. So far, she was pretty certain he hadn't picked up on it; he'd wish her good luck and goodnight, sit down in the single recliner in the living room adorned with the paintings and drawings they'd done over the years, and turn on the television. It had been a long time, she reflected, since they had created anything together.

"A good education is *not* me helping you cheat. What do you learn from that?" Fear remonstrated.

"Well, I'd *like* to learn that exams I don't care about can be made easier and that my friend cares about my success."

"I do care about your success. That's why we've been studying," Fear countered.

"*Ugh.*"

"So do you want to know?"

"No, I *don't* want to know. I don't *need* to know. I'm not obligated."

"All you had to say." They continued walking for a few moments. Then Joy let out a knee-sagging sigh of exasperation.

"*Uuuuuuuuuuuuuurrrrrrrrrrrrrrgh,*" she complained dramatically, "*why do you do this?*"

"Well, I was trying to be a friend."

"Do you *know* what it's like having to care for someone? Someone who doesn't have anybody else?"

"It sounds familiar."

"Hey, you can go any time. I don't *ask* you to follow me around."

"No, you don't. But neither does your dad."

"He doesn't *need* to ask. But he looks after me and I look after him and that's something that Mum should have done and because she didn't, I can't just go leaving because then the only person he has is himself!"

Fear walked along quietly beside her. "You know, I get your point," he said after a moment, "and it sounds tough. But it reminds me a bit of this guy way back in the Wild West."

"Who?"

"His name was Billy Flynn. The railroads were crossing the country and that made for a lot of attention from highwaymen and others. Risky business; trains could be carrying marshals, or everyone could be armed, it being the days where the carriage of pistols was pretty ubiquitous, and trying to get on to a few tons of rapidly moving iron is a bit more work than the movies suggest. Something you really need a team for. Anyway, Billy's farm runs into a drought and the animals die, and money has to come from *somewhere*, but Billy's no gang member. Robbing a train full of rich folk seems mighty appealing, but that's a bit much for a one-man job. Unless, he figures, he can bring the train to a full stop first and deal with the driver.

"But what's the best way to get the train to stop? If you block the tracks with rocks, then there's going to be an indication that something's up, and armed people might be wary. Ah, but what if it was a person who was in need? So he came up with his grand scheme: he would pretend to be tied up on the tracks, as if he had been accosted, and when the driver would dismount to check on him, he would slip his ropes and capture the driver and use the opportunity to rob the train. Of course, he forgot the first consideration of any successful enterprise."

"What was that?"

"Location, location, location. The closest railway point to his farm lay at a bend coming around a number of rock formations. Consequently, he wasn't to know that the driver's vision was limited. The train ran over him and never knew he was there.

"What was worse for him, however, was that while his parents had been digging in search of aquifers to manage the drought, they had discovered that their land sat upon a modest but significant oil reserve. Certainly more than enough to secure the financial well-being of the family for some time to come. Whilst he had been planning and preparing for his grand debut, he had missed the opportunity to talk with his family about what had been going on, and filled with the notion that he could become its saviour, hadn't bothered to share the family news.

"Nobody else knew why he was on the tracks tied up in the end; some assumed that bandits had gotten word of the family's windfall and had intended a ransom. His devastated parents couldn't imagine how and why he would have formed an enemy. But what was most significant in all of this was that he died a pointless death simply because he took on someone else's problem alone, without actually having a discussion with them about it."

Joy rolled her eyes. "So you think I should tell my dad that I want to leave after exams. Or I'm going to tie myself to the tracks like this idiot?"

"Well, Billy's devotion to his family did him credit. But you know what he was afraid of?"

"What?"

"He was afraid to hear the despair of his parents. He was afraid that if he asked them what they were going to do, as their animals died and as banks approached for loan repayments, that the people he loved and idealised, already at breaking point, would collapse. He was afraid of suggesting that they do anything other than what they had always done. But even more than that: he was afraid that they couldn't do it without him. And in the end, that fear is underwritten by a greater one: what if they *can*?"

"What do you mean?"

"What if they *can* survive without you? Guardian against harm, filling the role of the dutiful child, taking one's place in the family destiny? What does that leave you to do?"

"So what's your point, exactly?" Joy asked testily.

Fear stepped in front of her and looked her in the eyes. "I mean, look, I'm the anthropomorphisation of fear. And I'm telling you: the best antidote is to go and look what you're afraid of right in the eye, or you're going to be like Billy, tying himself up on a random stretch of railroad to be the saviour you don't need to be. Because as much as you're afraid that your dad might not be OK without you, you're also worried that he *might*, in fact, do just fine."

"*Or*," Joy countered lazily, "you could take my fear away and I wouldn't have to worry at all."

"That's true, but you know the rules," Fear replied. "If you really want it gone, you have to say it. Not just suggest it."

Joy gave it a moment's consideration.

"I'll leave things for now," she eventually said, "it might be good for me to spend some time thinking about it."

In true teenager fashion, Joy did *not* think about it. Instead, she pushed the situation as far as possible from her mind and avoided contact with her father at every opportunity. She found they passed each other a little like neighbourhood cats, with an enormous gap between them but acutely aware of the other's presence and location, gesturing sufficiently to maintain the status quo. Exams remained the ostensible excuse, but eventually these came and went in a flurry of final cramming, summary sheets, and when all else failed, outright invention of 'source' material. Fear had maintained his strict no-cheating-assistance rule, but Joy had had taken the opportunity to have him extract some of the worms of concern from her mind prior to the actual sitting of the papers, adding them to the ever-growing jar he kept for her. Whilst Joy might feel, on occasion, under-prepared, she never felt afraid, even as the final paper came and went, and she left the exam in the school hall with the strange realisation that this was really the last time she would walk through those doors, hallways, and gates. The day was grey and lonely, the kind of day an orphan in a musical would sing about to suggest a simple approach to resilience and squash any suggestion that they would bear lifelong trauma from their near-death experiences. Grey clouds were giving way to almost-black clouds, threatening imminent storms. Joy paused at the gates to say farewell to acquaintances, with all the usual empty promises to stay in touch which she knew that she had no intention to keep and was fairly certain the others would not either. They had been soldiers in a trench together for the past six years, but now it was time for the war to end.

Joy wondered if she should have become closer to some of them, as there was usually some expectation that school years would form one or two lifelong friendships, but it somehow hadn't happened. Maybe it was the inherent risk posed by the social strata of teenage girls, where a friend one day could switch camps and reveal every personal detail you had shared the next, or perhaps it was the workloads between school and her home, which she used to justify limited availability, or maybe it was because it all seemed so very *pointless* with people whose daily concerns were so far removed from the circumstances she found herself in. Fear was usually so blunt- to a fault- in his conversations, in part because he knew nobody else would be listening, and in part because that was just his personality, and Joy had begun to find it frustrating interacting with people who were so vague or circuitous about what they wanted or what they thought.

Whatever the myriad of factors which had led to that moment, Joy waved what she knew would be her last goodbyes to the school, its students, and her old routine, and began the final trip back home on the first bus. Traffic whizzed past them as the storm clouds became darker.

"Well, you did it!" Fear said from the seat beside her while she rested her head on the window. "Want to go throw your back pack off a bridge?"

"Why would I want to do that?" Joy replied softly, her eyes still locked at the view, as if encoding it for future reference.

"You know, I'm not sure. I've seen a lot of people do it, though."

"That's littering."

"Nah, the books are good for the fish. They use them all the time."

"They do?"

"Of course they do. They're always in schools."

Joy pulled her forehead off the window in order to look at him and roll her eyes. Fear just grinned.

"I can't believe you got me," she said as they dismounted at the highway stop near the canal. Fear looked smug.

"Often imitated, never replicated, little lady. So, what now?"

"Now, I'm going to go home and sleep. For a week."

"No boat today," he observed.

"Apparently not. Guess it's too dry."

"Shame, with this being your last trip."

"I guess so."

"You talk to your dad yet?"

"No, he's going to ask me what I'm doing next, and I still don't know. He probably wants me to get a job until the exam results come back."

"Not a bad idea. Could save up for a trip too."

"Still with that?"

"Still avoiding it?"

The bus arrived right as the first raindrops started to fall. Its brakes hissed and is doors opened, a time when Fear usually liked to get his last word in, because he knew Joy wouldn't be able to respond in front of people without appearing to be a few years and a cardboard box away from being one of those women who screams at invisible people in the street and hoards stray cats, with no consideration given to their state of aliveness at the time of collection. As he often said to Joy, after a few hundred thousand years, sometimes it was the little things that got you through the day.

"Well, the good news is, you'll have pleeeeeeeeenty of time to talk to him about it now. This rain looks like it'll be around for a while and, after all, it's not like you've got to focus on exams any more. Lucky you."

Joy cast a look at him which, if not shooting daggers, at least threw cutlery emphatically.

Fear was right about one thing, though. The rain set in like it had arrived from vacation and was just getting unpacked for a lengthy stay. It was torrential, soaking everything and everyone for days on end; some houses in Pleasant Lane started seeing water runoff from the street seep under their doors as the stormwater drains struggled to cope, but thankfully Joy managed to avoid this. Her father would leave in the morning, stepping into the downpour with a three-quarter-length raincoat with the collar turned up, and would return home in the evening soaked, sniffling, to settle into their almost-silent evening routines. Oh, they'd try to make small talk, but Joy wasn't ready to consider all the implications of what the future did, or could, hold, so the conversation withered and died before it could get to anything significant.

Mid-way through the second week of the rain, her father sat down at dinner with her as he usually did, but started the conversation off in an unexpected way.

"I got you something a little while ago," he said.

"You did?"

"Yeah, I guess I figured you'd want to talk eventually about what you want to do. Maybe I figured wrong, huh?"

"Not exactly," Joy replied sheepishly, pushing her food around her plate and avoiding eye contact.

"You know," her father continued, "your mum always had big dreams. I don't know if I've said this before, but big dreams aren't a bad thing. I mean, sometimes you have to find a lane and stay in that lane, because that's life. And sometimes you don't. You've gotta decide. And, well, I mean I guess I'm saying this wrong, but I don't want you to live and die here."

Joy was shocked. Her father took a deep breath, and continued, "I guess if I've been afraid of anything, it's that you'd stay here."

"I thought you'd be worried that I'd leave!" Joy exclaimed. "Or that I'd be like mum or something!"

"Well, the only thing I wanted was for you to be like you. But you'll never find that here. I can see that."

"But I *like* being here!" she protested lamely.

"Oh, please. You've barely had a conversation with me in almost seven months and you tried to tell me it was about exams. I might not be the smartest guy, but I'm not *that* stupid." He stood up and went to a cupboard, and pulled out a brand new backpack. He wandered to a drawer and pulled out an envelope.

"This is what I got for you as a graduation gift. It isn't much, but it's a start of an adventure. Your adventure. And maybe that'll bring you back to Pleasant Lane, but God I hope not. Cos if I do one thing right for you, kid, it'll be to give you an opportunity to do more than I did."

Joy opened the envelope. There was a loose collection of cash notes that amounted to thirty-six hundred dollars; a fortune for their household. Her father smiled weakly.

"It's not a huge amount, out there in the world, but it's enough to get you started. You can figure it out from there, I'm sure. Two hundred dollars for every year you've been alive. It's all I could save."

"Dad, I don't know what to say," said Joy, overwhelmed. "What about you?"

He laughed. "Oh, kid, I'm a grown man. I can take care of myself."

"But I don't know if I *want* to leave!" Joy protested, knowing that it was a lie. Her feet were telling her so; throughout the conversation, it's like they had awoken and they itched to pull her in a direction away from the house. Her father looked at her kindly.

"You're always going to have a home if you need it, kid. But eventually, home is going to be somewhere I'm not, and you might as well get started seeing where that might be. Otherwise, before you know it, you'll have to start a job, and then it'll get harder to really get away from things, and the next thing you know, twenty years will have passed. I love ya, kid, and I'll be damned if I'm going to miss the signs and leave you stuck just existing like I did."

"When do I leave?" Joy asked, with a mix of excitement and concern.
"Well, I'd not have it in me to kick my own daughter out into the rain. So how about we agree that the adventure begins when the rain stops?"
"That soon?"
"Pffff, I *wish* that was going to be soon!"

And he was right, as the rains continued for another four days. Joy began a slow process of packing her bag, talking to Fear, trying to come up with a plan. There was enough money for a plane ticket, but she wasn't sure how long that amount of money would last out in the world itself. She could probably make it last longer if she travelled around the country herself rather than going overseas, and it was hard to decide which was the better opportunity. The biggest issue, however, was with her feet. With each day, the pull that came from them intensified, to the point that the destination and the plan became less important than relief from the incessant draw beyond the house. She just needed to *go*.

With the issues between Joy and her father now aired, there was freedom to reconnect, and she spent her next few evenings sitting again with him, talking as freely as they had years before, sketching and laughing and sharing strange visions on sheets of paper and spare canvasses. Joy became more aware of how much she actually enjoyed these moments, as the time to leave neared.

On the fifth day, the clouds became greyer and the rain had finally eased and stopped in the late afternoon. Joy's bag was fully packed, and she was in the kitchen cooking up batches of lasagne and casserole to freeze for her dad. The only thing she had prepared for herself were half a dozen cheese sandwiches as a starting point, and a water bottle which she put into the designated receptacle on the side of her new backpack.

She knew she was procrastinating as she fiddled around the kitchen, stalling for time but restless simultaneously. A hand fell on her shoulder. She turned around from the stove, and her father was holding her bag. He smiled at her.

"Now's as good a time as any, kid," he said.

Joy felt tears begin to well up. "Promise I can come back?"

"Always. But only so you can go again."

"You're just saying that so you can pee with the bathroom door open."

"Shows what you know. I do that now. You *have* been distracted," her dad replied as he helped load trays into the freezer.

"Dinner's on the stove."

"I know."

"Don't eat it all at once."

"I know."

"It'll last you the next five days if you're careful with it."

"I *know*."

"Don't use too much salt, or it'll-"

"*Joy,* I bloody *know,*" he said, exasperated. "I'm a grown man. Go on, if you leave it any longer you'll be out after dark."

She took a deep breath, and held both his hands to reassure herself. "We can do this," she said to him. Her father nodded.

"We can," he replied, "and we will again. Goodbye, kiddo."

"Goodnight." She put her arms around him, under his armpits, feeling his large hands on her back as he held her close and kissed the side of her head. Eventually he pushed her away gently.

"I'll be here," he said reassuringly. "I mean, where am *I* gonna go?"

"On your own adventure?"

"Oh, I've been on that for eighteen years. Maybe it's time I had a break." Joy laughed, feeling lighter all of a sudden as the weight of the months passed and gave way to the feeling that her feet were barely touching the ground. There was only possibility ahead, she told herself. Fear appeared beside her ear all of a sudden.

"Yeah, the possibility of being stabbed under an overpass," he whispered. He was helpful like that.

Joy swung her pack onto her back and headed out the front door, finding it hard to let go of the handle as she pulled it closed. She stayed at the top of the stairs, willing her fingers to release, and stepped down onto the sidewalk, heading for the bus stop, because that's where her feet wanted to go. Fear walked alongside her, humming to himself.

"Told you I knew what he was afraid of," he said smugly. "Imagine the stress and tension you'd have saved if you just let me be right."

Joy grinned wryly. "If that's the trade-off, I'll pay that price any day."

"I don't doubt it. Where are we going?"

"This way," she said firmly, turning left.

The adventure was underway.

Chapter 3

Float

Up and up, and away...

Joy's feet clattered over the city pavement as she made her way to the bus stop as fast as her legs could carry her. Fear wandered along at his own pace, as he technically didn't need to touch the ground to get any traction. Her feet seemed to be giving her instructions as she went.

It was her standard journey in reverse. Make it to the end of the road. Turn right. One block uphill. Reach the main road intersection, cross on the lights, turn left and head past the terrace houses with shopfronts downstairs that had long been vacant, except for the 24-hour convenience store which stood on the corner next to the bus stop. Take the 419 bus to the eighth stop and exit beside the canal. By the time she got there, the sun was starting to set.

"This doesn't look like the way to an airport," Fear mused as they walked beside the guardrail, traffic blowing its way past them.

"What's your point? It's not like I could buy a ticket right now anyway," Joy shot back. "I don't have a passport."

"I feel like this is going to be like one of those sagas when you're six and cranky so you tell a parent you're going to run away forever, and pack yourself a cheese sandwich and a single apple because you're really good at thinking ahead. Then you get to the end of the street and it gets a bit cold and you remember that your mum makes good hot chocolate about now, and running away can wait until another day," Fear continued in an annoyingly smug tone.

"Ha, joke's on you then, my mum never made me good hot chocolate! Also, how do you even know what hot chocolate tastes like?"

"Fear needs to use all the senses."

"Who fears *chocolate?*" Joy asked, incredulous.

"Diabetics. Vegans. Dogs. Celebrities under contract with Jenny Craig."

"Really?"

"Well, dogs, no. But they should. The others, well, depends when you catch them. Where are we going?"

"I don't know! Anyway wasn't this your big idea?"

"Actually, I think you'll find it was your father's. Now, do you even *have* a plan yet?"

"No," she said, "I'm following my feet."

"Seems a bit haphazard."

"Maybe, but they seem to know where to go."

They made it to the canal, the street lights starting to come on and casting a shadow owing to their position away from the top of the wall, turning the water into a deep black not too dissimilar to how it looked in sunlight. From further below, there came the *schlup, schlup* noise of the water lapping against wood travelling the entirely wrong direction.

Joy peered over the hand rail separating them from the concrete edge of the canal. The temperature differential had caused a low level of fog to sit above the water, but she could make out the shape of the boat.

"Steve's back!" she said, nudging Fear with her elbow. Fear groaned theatrically.

"Oh *no*, if you name it, you'll go getting attached!" he said.

"Very funny," Joy replied flatly, rolling her eyes.

"Well, what are your feet telling you to do?"

"I don't know, I feel they want to go where the boat's pointing."

"Well, then. Can't hurt; we have three cheese sandwiches each so we'll be right for at least twenty more minutes."

"*And* an apple."

They walked on another three or four hundred metres, hearing the boat bob along below them, until they came to a gap in the handrail which led down to a set of galvanised metal stairs, some form of maintenance inspection access presumably, and ended on a small metal grate platform, presumably to allow the passage of surplus water in the event of heavy rains exceeding a nominal existing height. As it happened, this platform was still sitting a foot above the water, and the boat bobbed along to a stop directly beside Joy, at just the right height for her to step in, if she chose to do so. She stared at it.

As before, it was weather-beaten but sturdy, the few remnants of blue and white paint that remained keeping a death-grip on the sun-bleached wood. Two oars sat in their rowlocks, the paddle end sitting inside the boat itself. No name was visible on the outside. For an inanimate object, it looked surprisingly expectant.

"I think we should get in," said Fear.

"What?" Joy responded without looking at him, eyes fixed on the boat which was doing its best impression of being friendly and outgoing. "Since when are *you* suggesting doing something risky?"

"Well, firstly, your feet seem to have stopped."

Joy reflected on this for a moment. Her feet certainly did not still feel the restlessness they had done before; they seemed to be telling her to take one step more alone. "Got any other reasons?" she asked after a moment.

"Well, it's a boat in a one-way canal. If you don't like it, you can divert it to the side pretty easily before you get sucked out to sea and eaten by pirates."

"Do pirates eat people still?"

"Maybe not, most of them have flatscreen TVs but that's not the point."

"What, they eat the televisions?"

"*No*, if they want to be entertained by the demise of humanity, they can watch reality television. But if this is where you need to go, it's not that hard to get back out, is my point. I mean, it's a canal. It only goes one way."

"We've seen the boat can go two," Joy pointed out.

"Even better. This can go against the flow of the water, so all you need to do is make it go backwards if you don't like going forwards. Worst case scenario, it takes you almost back home."

Joy thought about this.

"You know, this is the first time you haven't told me something would go horribly wrong."

"Oh, it can. Let's circle back to the pirates and their televisions later."

Joy took her bag off her shoulder and put it into the boat. The boat stayed in place.

"Can only go forward or backwards, right?" She asked Fear. "How bad could it be?"

"Courage is not the absence of fear, but rather the assessment that something else is more important than it," Fear quoted.

"Who said that?"

"Franklin D Roosevelt. Which was ironic because he was scared to enter World War II until it was almost halfway over but what matters is the sentiment."

"You really think I should do this?"

"I really think you need to follow your feet."

Joy stepped one foot tentatively into the boat, which rocked slightly but stayed remarkably still. She lowered the other in. Fear jumped in, making absolutely no change to the buoyancy whatsoever. The boat began drifting from the metal platform and reached the mid-point of the canal's width, remaining stationary as the water ebbed past. There they remained for a few minutes.

"Well," Joy said at last, "that's one thing we didn't anticipate."

"What?"

"What we'd do if the boat didn't go forwards *or* backwards."

"Maybe you need to use the oars?" Fear suggested. Joy grabbed them, pushing the handles down so the paddle end came up and rotating them in their rowlocks until they sat in the water. She pulled and felt some traction, but the boat didn't seem to move forward at all.

"Hmm, try pulling harder?" Fear suggested. She circled the oars again, feeling the water resistance and a sensation of movement that wasn't met by a change in the distance from the platform. She tried again. And again. And again. It started getting easier.

"It feels weird, I'm moving *something*," she said to Fear.

"Oh, you're moving something, all right," Fear replied, looking over the edge of the boat. Joy peered over to see what he was looking at. The boat was now about three feet above the water, its keel entirely above the surface. Joy and Fear looked at each other. They shared the same thought: jumping *into* the water, with its mix of unknown pollutants, was possibly worse than jumping out of a flying boat onto the ground. At least a fall could mean certain death; it was *uncertain* death that was truly terrifying.

Whatever she had started, however, continued and the boat began rising and rising. Soon they were level with the top of the canal, parallel to cars that were rushing along the arterial road with their headlights on, paying no attention to the mysterious spectacle occurring in the shadowed area of the canal. Up and up, slowly but surely, it rose above the trees and the streetlights, then above all the roof-tops, and continued rising until it began pointing to the east and finally started moving forward.

There was an eerie calm as the boat climbed gently over the city. Without much else to do, Joy had continued rowing, before she realised that the oars were serving about as much purpose as a municipal council, and she had pulled them back into the boat.

Whilst she had never been on an aircraft, she was aware that they were extremely noisy machines; instead, in vehicular silence, she was treated to the sounds of the city that faded in their own time as the boat rose higher.

"This is a bad idea," Fear said to her, leaning back in the seat directly opposite. "Do you know what hypoxia is?"

"What? This was *your* idea!" Joy protested.

"Ah, it's setting in already!"

"What's hypoxia?"

"A lack of oxygen to the brain at certain elevations."

"Are we going to die?"

"No, of course not," he said reassuringly.

"Phew."

"*I'll* be fine, I don't need oxygen."

Joy shivered. She dug in her back pack and pulled out a heavy jumper as the boat hung in the night sky, moving past the city's edge. Oddly enough, she didn't feel a lack of oxygen to her brain. She didn't feel much of anything, really. She knew she ought to be scared- boats could be many things, but the one thing they were *not* was aircraft- but there was a part of her telling her that this was safe, and another part telling her that it was just a dream, and a third part telling her that she was up in the sky and hadn't had to spend a dollar, so it might be rude to look a gift horse in the mouth.

The boat stopped rising and started moving forward. Joy looked at the time; it had almost reached midnight.

"I'm tired," she said to Fear.

"That's a sign of hypoxia!" He said, with altogether too much excitement. He saw her expression and took a more serious tone. "You get some rest," he continued, "you could hunker down and use the bag as a pillow."

"What about you?"

"Oh, I'll be fine here."

"You won't leave me, will you?"

"I might have to step out for milk and biscuits."

"Oh, ha, ha, very funny. Come on Fear, I'm *so* tired."

"Don't worry," he said a bit more gently, "I'll still be here when you wake up."

And so Joy took her bag, pulled up her jumper's hood, wrapped her arms around herself, and lay down at the bottom of the boat. A few minutes later, there was a rustling in the bag, as if someone was reaching in and extracting a cheese sandwich. After that, however, there was silence, as the boat sailed through the night.

"Well, that isn't good."

There are noisier alarms to be awoken to, but as phrases to regain consciousness to go, it's certainly one of the most effective. Joy jerked awake. She couldn't see the ground any more, not because of the height, but because of the cloud density. Her clothing was damp from the hanging condensation, and before her sat enormous black storm clouds, like an angry bruise in the sky. She grabbed the oars and rowed backwards desperately, and the boat, to her surprise, came to a stop just in front of the storm cloud. It did its best to seem both impatient and a little concerned; the oars hung down like expectant eyebrows.

"Good morning," Fear said, a sandwich in his hand. Joy looked at him blearily.

"You couldn't wake me sooner?" she asked groggily.

"Oh, of course I could have. But you managed it in time."

Joy's eyes narrowed as she looked at Fear's hand. "*How* are you eating my sandwich?"

"I asked myself the same thing. It tastes terrible."

"Where are we?"

"Hmmmmm... somewhere over the Pacific Ocean. Speaking from experience."

"What are fish afraid of?"

"Bigger fish."

Joy looked at the clouds. The boat hung in the sky, and the clouds loomed before her, lightning flashes illuminating parts momentarily, giving the mass a sinister depth that its original shape belied. Joy sat on the bench in the middle of the boat.

"Can't go backwards?" She asked Fear.

"We probably could, I guess. We could try. But do we know where we're going?"

"I thought you knew everywhere."

"I'm not a GPS system. But ahead looks dangerous."

"I know, I don't want to be soaked *and* electrocuted!"

"Don't forget frozen. Or hailed upon. Or hit by an unseen albatross."

"*Fear*! I'm worried enough as it is!"

"That's reasonable, in the circumstances. What are our options?"

Joy considered this. "We can't row down," she said at last.

"No," Fear agreed, "I guess we can't."

"We can go back. But the boat has kept us safe so far."

"We can, and it has."

"Do you think it would let us go home?"

Fear stopped and thought about this.

"Is home where you *want* to go back to?" He said at last. "This is, after all, your adventure."

Joy gave this suitable consideration.

"I've waited so long. I don't want to go back, just when we're starting. I think we need to go on, but I'm worried that if I panic, it could be the end for both of us."

"No vagueries. You know the rules. You gotta ask."

Joy took a breath. She always felt weird when this happened.

"Could you please remove my fears?"

Fear nodded, and reached his hands into her forehead again. He brought out a small fistful of vividly coloured wriggling creatures, purple and green and yellow, and Joy felt serenity overtake her again. She looked at the clouds and felt... nothing. They were just an object, despite their imposing size and threatening rumbles. Fear put the worms of concern into a jar within his trench coat, which he somehow concealed again.

"Well," he said delicately, looking again at the clouds before them, "this is your choice. There is one bit of good news though."

"Which is?"

"Whatever happens, I'll still be okay. I know you were probably worried about that."

Joy laughed, out of her newfound serenity.

"I'm not scared of dying. If something goes wrong..."

"*Everything* could go wrong. But then, everything can *always* go wrong." Joy paused, and took three deep breaths to clear her mind. She looked up, resolute, and took hold of the oars.

"I guess that we're doing this," she said, and pulled hard at the oars. The boat, giving the impression of excitement, moved slowly forward into the storm clouds.

The experience inside was strange. The boat moved forward slowly, the cloud swirling around it like mist, curling away and then rushing back to fill the void as it moved silently forward. Distant lightning flashes illuminated odd chunks, casting bizarre shapes like a shadow puppet show performed by a family with no forks in their family trees and altogether too many digits on each hand.

Occasionally thunder rumbled, but it didn't sound like when she was on the ground; it rumbled through her body, finishing with an almost metallic sound, making the oars buzz in their holders each time and vibrate in her hands. Fear was standing at the bow, one foot at the very point of the boat, a hand held up to his forehead, like great explorers of the past.

"Well," he said cheerfully, looking back at her "at least we don't have a huge metal rod sticking up from the rowboat!"

"So we won't get hit by lightning?" Joy asked hopefully.

"Honestly, I don't think it would make a difference. I said it more for moral support."

"You're the worst," Joy grumbled, pulling at the oars in an attempt to speed the boat up.

"I wonder if this is how insects feel near a vape pen."

"You wonder weird things, Fear."

"I'm just naturally curious," he sniffed.

They sat in silence again as the Sturm und Drang continued around them.

"Where do you think we're going?" Joy asked after a while.

"I know where we're going," Fear replied. "We're going to Frieland."

"What the- you *know?*" she spluttered, narrowing her eyes and with venom entering her tone.

"I know everything, don't I?" he said smugly.

"Wait, wait, wait- do people have to go through these clouds to get there?"

"Oh, yes."

"Then there was nothing to worry about! I can't believe you made me think this was so dangerous, and then you just casually tell me people come here all the time!"

A sudden bolt of lightning struck beside the boat, as thunder rumbled past. Joy yelped, jumping backwards in her seat. Fear sat down and looked directly at her.

"Most of them," he said slowly and deliberately, "die before reaching it."

Joy was silent at this. It took her a few moments to find her voice. "*And you still let me go?!*"

"There's no freedom without choice, Joy. And with that choice comes consequence. That's how this works."

"This?"

"Life." He slapped the side of the boat twice with the palm of his hand, making a satisfied and hollow thump.

"But," he continued cheerfully, "the important thing on a perilous journey is not the will of the adventurer, it's the quality of the vessel carrying them. And Steve here seems to have done a marvellous job."

"How can you tell?"

"*That's* how."

Fear pointed ahead. The darkest, purple-black portion of the cloud swirled around them, enveloping them for a few seconds, until a glow appeared at the bow of the boat and grew brighter as each oar stroke landed. It wasn't long until the storm clouds had given way and beyond them lay a sea of whiteness upon which rested a platform of earth, as if it had been cut out of the ground by a giant's shovel and hung in the sky. There was a jetty, leading to a road, which led in turn to city walls, with verdant fields and mountains behind it. The sun was rising above it, and at that very moment finally reached its apex above one of the city's spires, bathing everything Joy could see in a warm glow and soothing her freezing hands which she hadn't noticed until the warmth had entered her body.

Steve reached the moorings. He gave the impression of being smug about it.

Chapter 4

Frieland

I know that I have never been here, but it seems I'm back again.

As the warmth of the sun slowly melted away the last of the mist hanging around the moorings, a light breeze carried the scent of cinnamon and fresh bread from behind the city's walls. Joy, who realised that by this stage her carefully planned food rationing system had been beaten by both her limited degree of foresight and her poor choice of travelling companion, felt her stomach growl.

It was helpful, she thought to herself, that she had money, but then what currency does a mystery city in the sky use? She hoped it would be hopes and dreams, then regretted that, as she wasn't entirely sure at that moment if she had any on her. Also, maybe swapping a dream for food was short-sighted; the value in having the desire to play the piano at Carnegie Hall, for example, seemed a strange hope to give up in return for a sandwich.

"Thinking about trading hopes for food?" asked Fear.

"Yup."

"Every time. Come on, then."

Joy clambered out of the boat behind Fear, steadying herself on the jetty. It had been curiously reassuring when a sea of cloud had ebbed and flowed around the base of the jetty's pilings. Now, as that mist had risen and dispersed, Joy's quick glance down the gap between the boat and the pier revealed a few thousand feet of nothing, and her stomach did an unexpected somersault. She desperately hoped that bathrooms were a thing up here.

She and fear walked along the wooden surface which moved and creaked as though tides were moving below it, impossibly long for an unsupported structure jutting into the void, until they reached the cobbled road that led to the city gates. The walls were twenty feet high and made out of sandstone. Joy wondered where it had come from. She assumed that trying to load up heavy blocks into a floating boat would be some level of cross-purpose, but perhaps now was not the time to consider the impossibility of things, having just flown through a storm on what seemed to be a sentient boat with an invisible friend.

The city gates were closed, large ten-foot oak panels hung on huge iron hinges, with an enormous knocker in the middle at almost head height. They stood in front of it, staring up.

"Should we knock?" Joy asked after a bit.

"What's the worst that can happen?" Fear asked in return.

"Hey, I usually say that!"

"I know. And the answer is: arrest, slavery, toothlessness, forced scientific experimentation, being made to walk the plank, wanton sky piracy, or being forced to eat vegetables."

"You always say the worst things!"

"I know, the worst part is finding something to do with the wheelchairs afterward."

"Not cool. What about if we *don't* knock?"

"Hmmmm. Starvation, dehydration, succumbing to the elements, falling off the edge, and being caught pooping by someone eventually patrolling the top of the wall *right* at the moment that you've finally satisfied yourself that nobody is going to look and you definitely can't wait any longer."

Joy reached up and grabbed the handle of the knocker, and banged it hard three times. Fear leaned against the wall with an expectant look on his face. Joy stepped back, crossing her fingers and squinting her eyes against an imagined response by an armed constabulary, giant, aggrieved unicorn, or other unknown and/or imaginary threat. After a couple of minutes of nothing happening, she turned and looked at Fear. He shrugged.

"A bit anticlimactic," he said casually. "I was hoping for something pointy."

Joy grabbed the knocker and banged it again. The result was the same. She ruled out the city being empty; the sounds of commerce in the morning were filtering over the wall's edge, in addition to the smells that signalled the start of the day, often far more pleasant than the accumulation of the ones that signal the end. Feeling a little impatient and feeling a pressing need in her lower stomach region, Joy put her palms flat against the left-hand side of the gates and pushed hard. To her surprise, it swung open deftly and smoothly, not even making so much as a creak.

Behind it was a covered arch area and waiting there was a man in a top hat and tails, but wearing fairly normal britches and practical leather shoes. He had a moustache and the overall effect suggested he *should* have a monocle as well, but lacked it. He had a clipboard under one arm and a cane in his other hand; Joy got the feeling that he was the ringmaster of a circus that was small enough to only require his position part-time, but wanted to be ready at a moment's notice.

He strode up to her and looked her up and down. "Hmmm," he said after a few moments, "Early, I see. I thought you'd be late."

Joy was speechless. Fear nudged her with his elbow. "This is a first," he said smugly, "just ask your teachers."

The man stared at his clipboard for a moment, and then put it under his arm. "You'd be Joy Summerfield then, correct?"

"Um, yes?"

"You're not sure? Who else would know?"

"No, I mean, I am, but- I mean, um, you're waiting for me?"

"That's my job. This way, please," he said as he guided her forward.

"I thought you might work for a circus," Joy said as she nervously grabbed at her bag and started walking.

"Only part-time."

"I'm sorry, *who are you* exactly? Where are we?"

"Oh, of course. How rude of me. I've barely completed the paperwork for you. They call me The Great Benevolenza and *this,"* he said as they stepped out of the arch and Joy's eyes adjusted to the light, "is Frieland."

The city opened up in front of them. Wooden carts were being pushed past with a variety of produce in wooden crates, stalls were set up in the marketplace, recently-lit fires was burning down to coals under cooking surfaces, small children ran in and out of stall areas with friends and ene-mies which were, as is the way with children, quite often the same person.

Joy stopped walking to take it all in for a moment when the clipboard was shoved under her nose.

"Sign here," Benevolenza said, proffering a pencil. Joy looked down at the form, totally confused.

"Wait, *wait,*" she said, "I don't know what's happening here!"

"Bit presumptuous to go pushing down the door then," her guide replied with a sniff.

"It was open!"

"And here you are. Still, you're free to have done so, whether you were ready or not. That is, rather, the point."

"The point of *what?*"

"Everything?" he replied, as though talking to a child who had just been caught eating paste. "This is Frieland."

Joy had had enough. "*Listen,* that doesn't mean *anything.* It's just a general statement. If I gave you a cat, and you asked what it was, and I said it was a cat, and you asked what it did, and I replied again that *it was a damn cat-*"

"Sounds like a perfect description to *me,*" muttered Fear beside her.

"...then you'd be quite within your rights to shake me by the shoulders until my brains managed to restart!" Joy finished, shooting an angry look at Fear. "I'm tired, I've been damp, I'm hungry, I need the toilet, and this is impossible! If I don't start getting some straight answers soon, I'm going to find someone to punch very hard in the throat!"

The ringmaster brightened. "Ah, yes," he said. "*Frieland.*"

About a half hour and a hurried bathroom stop later, they were sitting down at a table whilst a cup of hot chocolate and fresh buttered bread with eggs was brought out for Joy. The Great Benevolenza only had a glass of ice water, because his throat was sore.

"Sorry," Joy said, as she swirled her cup around. The ringmaster tugged at his collar and cleared his throat.

"No problem," he said a little hoarsely, "you're free to do so. That's what Frieland is, really."

"Explain it to me- *gosh* I could drink this hot chocolate all day- like I'm a kindergartener."

"You *could* drink it all day, you know. You're free to do that too. You see, Frieland is a place to find yourself- or your happiness, really- and we don't do things like rules."

"But your throat is sore now," Joy pointed out.

"Yes, yes it is. I'd certainly be happier if you didn't do that again."

"*I'd* be happier if you answered my questions."

"Then it seems we're equally unhappy. But I'm getting to that. You're in Frieland city, and if you review the paperwork I gave you, you'll notice that your welcome comes with a handy map. Our land provides an opportunity to find your happiness in a state of true freedom, and there are many cities and towns that pursue this quest differently. You can meet some if you want; they come here to exchange their goods as well as their ideas, and let me tell you that the slam poetry can get pretty intense."

"Slam poetry doesn't make me happy."

"It doesn't make *anyone* happy, except when it stops. Swings and round-abouts."

"Okay, I think I have it."

"You are here as a visitor. We allow our guests to stay for three months to find their happiness. If you can't find it by then, then unfortunately, you will be made to leave and our security representatives will remove you."

"How will they know where I am?"

"How did you get here?"

"On a flying boat," Joy conceded.

"Then let's not try to pretend too much is impossible, shall we? Don't test the theory, though, please. They are *quite* zealous about their work."

"Arresting and evicting people?"

"Hey, it makes them happy."

Fear was sitting at ninety degrees to Joy, with a scowl on his face. He did not like the ringmaster, in part because he had an innate distrust of anyone wearing a top hat, and in part because he always found people used bureaucracy to try to control fear with imaginary guidelines, which made his job not only harder, but far less interesting. Mainly, however, the hat. "Punch him again," he muttered near Joy's ear. "*That'll* give him something to be afraid of."

"You'll be given modest supplies before you leave and you can use the money changers here to obtain local currency," The Great Benevolenza continued, "and of course it is up to the towns to decide to share their goods with you. If it makes them happy. There's three main gates out of the city; you are, of course, free to choose where you start."

"What's outside the walls, besides the other towns?" Joy asked.

"Oh, various woods and forests. Some mountains and streams. The kinds of things that you find in nature."

"I'm not sure how often they're found a thousand feet in the air," she replied pointedly, "so perhaps assume that I'm not going to take anything for granted."

"Well, there's the Tall Woods, the Deep Woods, the Dark Woods-"

"The Nobody Woods..." muttered Fear.

"... Settler's Field, Fairy Meadow, Winding River, and Random Mound."

"Why's it called Random Mound?" Joy asked. The ringmaster just looked at her pityingly.

"Let's just pretend you didn't ask that. Otherwise I might not think you were entirely ready for this journey."

"I mean... I still don't understand *any* of this!"

"Very well. You are Joy, correct?"

"Yes," Joy replied, knowing at this point it was about the only thing she was still entirely certain of.

"And did you, or did you not, experience an existential quandary of a significant nature, questioning the very purpose and place of your life in the grander scheme of a cosmos billions of years old, spinning endlessly towards entropy?"

"Well... no?"

"Did you have a problem at home and feel unclear what the future held?"

"Yes!"

"Basically the same thing. Well, the forces that control Frieland like to find, occasionally, the unique sparks of the world and give them the opportunity to find answers to the most important question of all: am I free to be happy, and am I happy to be free? What happiness or, for that matter, freedom means is quite up to the person to discover, but Frieland is a place for impossible things to become entirely reasonable."

"I... guess that make sense," Joy said slowly.

"Then you're already taking the impossible in your stride," he said, and leaned forward with a serious expression. "That's a handy trait to have, because there's one thing I need you to understand, Joy: other people's happiness comes from many places. Some you may not enjoy. Frieland may be free, but that's not the same as saying that it's *safe*."

"Yeah, here we go," Fear whispered, "this is the part with the murderers and people wearing flesh suits and sickos eating cauliflower and stuff."

"Is it *un*safe?" Joy asked the ringmaster.

"That, my dear, depends entirely on your perspective. We are careful who is brought here. Few are able to make the journey. We don't recruit the ignoble, the unimaginative, those who would find it easier to murder and take than to build and craft. But there is no freedom without risk, and no choice without consequence, and it's something worth being aware of."

"Well, how did you get here?" she retorted.

"I was a Chartered Accountant."

"See?" Hissed Fear in Joy's ear, "That's even worse!"

"Numbers make me happy. *Order* makes me happy. Turning chaos into order makes me particularly happy..."

"Oh, please, he'll probably say *forms* make him happy," muttered Fear.

"And you'd be surprised the happiness that a properly completed form can bring," the ringmaster continued.

"Called it!" Fear said whispered triumphantly. "What a sicko."

"Well," Joy said, ignoring Fear, "I appreciate you taking the time to explain. And what happens if I *can* find my joy in three months?"

"Ah," Benevolenza replied sagely, "I knew you were a smart one. Not enough people ask that question. Well, the good news is that then you're free to stay if you so choose, although that does *mean* staying. We are not a place for a regular commute, if you get me. Or, you can take your happiness and leave."

"What if me staying makes me happy and you *un*happy?"

"I refer you back to slam poetry. I feel, however, that you're wasting your three month window already. It's less time than you think."

"Yeah," muttered Fear, nudging the back of Joy's shoulder, "before exams, *you* thought it was enough time learn three whole subjects you'd ignored the entire year."

"Hey, I studied!" Joy hissed back. Fear leaned in to her peripheral vision, slowly so she could see his obscene grin and groan inwardly. Sometimes having an invisible friend was the absolute worst.

"Let's not make liars out of both of us," he said. "It is indeed amazing what you can do with a couple of weeks."

"So!" the ringmaster said brightly, "let's get you kitted out."

"I've already got my bag," Joy said, pointing at the hiking pack. "I really just need food."

"And it's pleasing to see you care so little for shelter," he responded flatly. "I'm sure you'll find joy in no time flat. Come this way."

So the afternoon was spent visiting vendors, acquiring the kinds of foods that lasted without refrigeration: jerkies, jams, pickles, a few loaves of bread, some unripened fruit, and she took the opportunity to fill her water bottle again. The stallholders were pleasant, their children playing in the courtyards behind the stalls, the interactions friendly and welcoming. The Great Benevolenza would extract, from his otherwise-empty hat or from behind an ear, a coin for the children at each stall. It was clear he enjoyed entertaining them, and it enabled Joy to converse with the stallholders and get directions to the money changers. Joy had decided against getting a tent, given that it would become too cumbersome over distance. This meant a little more planning was going to be necessary.

As the afternoon sun reached its zenith and began its descent towards the horizon, she sat down with Fear for a final meal for the road- roast chicken and fresh bread- and they pored over the map to work out a journey which would limit the number of nights where sleeping rough would be necessary. It wasn't clear if there was transport between cities, but Fear suggested that making an assumption for walking allowed for safer planning than hoping for faster travel to reveal itself. Unfortunately, it didn't leave a lot of options immediately available.

"The closest place seems to be Gloomhaven, but that's *got* to be a misnomer, right?" Joy said to Fear. "For a place that's about happiness, maybe it's the equivalent of Pleasant Lane? You know, named the opposite?"

"I mean, maybe," Fear conceded. "Like a hidden treasure? If I had a delicious lunch I didn't want anyone else to eat, I'd call it a Fartburger or something like that. Stankwich, maybe."

"I could see that working. I wouldn't eat your stankwich if you paid me."

They stood and looked at the road. By the map's scale, it would take four to five hours to walk, but the closest alternative looked like it would be closer to seven.

"If it's not ironically named," Fear said cautiously, "then perhaps there's better alternatives."

"Not before nightfall, and we don't want to be getting to places after the accommodation closes," Joy replied as she folded the map back into her bag and gathered the rubbish to put in a bin. "Besides, what could possibly be depressing about being free and searching for happiness? They'd have to be trying to keep the best place secret, for sure."

"You know, maybe you're right!" Fear said with suspicious optimism as they started walking. "Probably going to be the best place on the whole trip."

Chapter 5

Bad Habits

You can say that you'll be happy in misery, but I see through the smile you're fakin'.

The winding cobbled path seemed to have gone forever; it went over small creeks, through verdant fields, and eventually into the woods, which loomed large and created a canopy through which the afternoon's sun struggled weakly to penetrate. Joy was pulling apart the insides of a long baguette and telling herself that food eaten while walking contained zero calories, while Fear was performing one of his favourite activities, proclaiming the worst things possible at every odd noise or shifting shadow, just because he could. It was like a poor man's remake of the haunted forest in *The Wizard Of Oz*, except Joy was wondering how to lose company rather than gain it and nobody was wearing footwear stolen from a corpse.

It seemed that hours had passed; Joy was sure the sun would be setting any second.

"How long's it been?" she asked Fear.

"About thirty minutes," he replied. "I wonder what bugs will try to drop out of the trees as we pass?"

"It's got to be longer than that!"

"Mmmmm, I don't think so. I was counting the seconds. Tick, tick, tick, tick…"

"I *know* how seconds work."

"Oh, I wasn't counting seconds just then. I was counting parasitic insects."

"You're absolutely no help *at all*, do you know that?"

There was an earthy, damp and mossy smell to the forest, especially on the sides which got the least sunlight. Occasionally in the undergrowth something small would rustle and scamper out of the way as it lost its nerve from the approaching footsteps, but they were never seen. Old fallen timber mouldered quietly, occasionally a bird would make a sound, and all the while the trees themselves rustled their leaves peacefully in the afternoon breeze. For a girl from the city, it was an incredibly pleasant change.

"So, what do we know?" Fear asked after the silence had become uncomfortable but no easy conversation topic had presented itself.

"Not much. I mean, the town's called Gloomhaven. It's on the map. No population details, no real details at all. It's like they've never thought about producing a tourist guide," Joy replied.

"Yes, how bizarre that a floating landscape only able to be accessed by a flying rowboat doesn't consider the regularity of visitors and future investors," Fear replied dryly.

"You asked."

"You're probably on the ground floor of this idea. When you get back, you can set up some kind of pyramid scheme, maybe."

"You suck."

"I can't wait for you to tell the publishers. Quick, get your notebook out. Point one: effective catering when travelling to flying cities. I'm sure there will be a terrible rush to be the first to sign you to a contract."

"Shut up, you! You know, whenever there's a few seconds of silence, I swear you start something just so that you can begin teasing me again."

"Not at all. Sometimes I wait to see how long you can go trying to avoid sneaking out a cheeky fart."

"*Fear!* Stop being gross. Ugh. Anyway, I thought you'd been everywhere."

"I thought I had, too. Maybe these guys aren't afraid."

"Isn't everyone afraid?"

"It's possible that that's just marketing I use to get pay rises every year," he said conspiratorially,

"Who from?"

"Media organisations are very generous sponsors of my work."

They continued around a bend as the light stooped low on the horizon, and the last rays that were still golden disappeared, leaving a weird half-light still hanging around unwanted and unrequested, like a mother-in-law three hours after Christmas lunch. It was in that strange, desaturated and frankly tired illumination that Gloomhaven first came reluctantly into view.

It had grey stone walls, unadorned with anything especially noteworthy or eye-catching. There were no gardens. No curated blossoms or elegant arrangements. Even the weeds that cluttered the gate and the base of the wall looked like they were half-hearted about it. The gate was a large wooden circle, about six feet in diameter, and was in a state of some disrepair.

The streets beyond were paved, but were slippery with a green fuzz which grew lightly on the surface.

It could have been the evening mist rising as the warmth started to leave the ground, but there was a haze in the air, as if the smoke from the town's activities had lost all motivation shortly after exit, and was now hanging around in the hope someone would let it back inside.

As Joy and Fear walked through the gates, lanterns had started being hung outside the town's central evening venues, an ale house and a covered late-night market for those last-second items or street food. Maybe twenty or thirty people were still out, moving between the tavern and the market building in pairs or families with little noise other than murmurings. The breeze blew the odour of stale beer and burnt meat. Fear turned to Joy.

"On the up side," he said, "we don't have to bring a law suit for false advertising."

"Oi, you two!" came a gruff and slightly irritated voice behind them. It was attached to a man in an ill-fitting jacket, a grey scarf thrown over his shoulder and fingerless gloves, looking a bit like the old caricature of the Artful Dodger whilst simultaneously failing appearing either artful or capable of dodging anything of note. "You're late! You should be locked out, door closes at five o'clock!"

Joy turned and looked surprised. "I'm sorry," she said, "nobody told us. What time is it now?"

"It's just on six!"

"Well, the gates were still open."

"Yeah, but you oughtn't to have come in!"

"Well, isn't someone supposed to be shutting them?" Joy retorted somewhat defensively.

"That would be me," the man replied sullenly.

"Well, I mean, is it wrong because I walked in, or because you didn't lock them?"

"Look," the man said testily, "no-one expects this job to be done on time. Use some common sense."

"Then no-one expects to need to *be* on time, right?" Joy countered. The man glared at her.

"None of your lip, miss! You could spend a night in the cells, got a good mind to call the sergeant over, I have, then we'll see-" Unbeknownst to the man, but observed by Joy, Fear had laid a hand companionably on his shoulder, leaned close to his ear, and began whispering.

"If the sergeant comes over, he'll be cranky at being disturbed, and then he'll ask why you didn't close the gate, and then people will stop giving you gate monitoring money, and you won't be able to buy a drink with a friend if you had one," he whispered straight into the man's subconscious. Joy could see the thought patterns change across his face. *"Whereas,"* Fear continued, *"if this stranger is here to spend some money, everyone might be happy that you let her in, and nobody will ask about gates."*

The guard's mind was made up for him. What was odd to Fear was that he did not appear to be resolute, or even relieved. He just shrugged to himself, as if the alternative was only vaguely worse.

"I'll be nice this time," the gatekeeper said gruffly, "but try it again, and see what happens."

Joy decided to push her luck, because she was eighteen and female and absolutely *had* to have the last word.

"I suspect," she said sweetly, "that I'll be let in again."

"Name!" The man barked, flourishing a clipboard. She wrote her name down carefully. He looked at it equally carefully.

"I can sound the letters out for you," she said with false helpfulness. "Just let me know if you need help."

He let out an exasperated sigh and turned around. "You can get lodgings at the tavern, or you can sleep on the ground, I don't care. Lodgings is two coins a night, breakfasts included, hope you don't mind your bread being a bit stale. Now, get on with you!"

Joy decided the pram of her luck had lost a wheel now and was no longer able to be pushed, so moved on. Fear sauntered beside her, humming to himself.

"Oh, yes," he said to Joy as they walked through. "I think this is going to be my kind of place! Miserable and surly? Could be the most fertile grounds the worms have ever encountered!"

"They don't seem very happy," Joy said with some concern.

"Well, that's just one guy. And a guard, at that. If your only job is to open a big door and then close it again a few hours later, you're probably not going to be in the best frame of mind. Are your feet tired?"

"Yeah, I didn't think I'd have to be quite so mobile."

"Well, to be fair, it's hard to know how mobile you're going to be when you don't have a plan, Sparky," Fear chastised mildly.

"Well, let's go find somewhere I can sit down and get some dinner, and maybe get a room for the night. There was a tavern that looked promising. Things are bound to improve."

Two hours later, Joy was stationed in the tavern nearest the window that looked out towards the market, having experienced the worst service of her entire life. Her efforts to attract the attention of the innkeeper had been largely in vain until she had physically walked behind the bar and manhandled the barmaid, who seemed largely bemused by the interaction. Yelp didn't exist in Frieland, but Joy got the impression that even if it did, a threat of a scathing review and a report to the Better Business Bureau might be met with laughter and spit, possibly simultaneously, which would have been quite a feat. The bar itself didn't even have the joi-de-vivre of a state funeral, something that was bothering Fear more and more with every passing second. He was becoming twitchy, like a squirrel who had accidentally fallen into a vat of energy drinks before doing a line of cocaine, eyes darting and his fingers drumming every surface they came in contact with. He had gone through the room, dropping worms and whispering in ears like a creepy Santa Claus, but nothing was getting a reaction whatsoever.

Joy wasn't entirely clear about what went on in a tavern, and perhaps the idea of carousing and singing were a little far-fetched, but the glumness of the patrons who sat around the room looking introspectively into their drinks, which were consumed in silence, seemed at odds with the whole point of a tavern.

She was given a warm flat drink that should have probably been cold and sparkling and may, in fact, have been so at some stage before it was left on top of a boiler. She couldn't identify exactly what it was, but she *could* identify that she would not be drinking the next sip of it.

Food was a lacklustre affair. She had often, along with her peers at school, made jokes about the quality and tastelessness of fast food but now she longed for a patty made out of old Chinese newspapers flavoured with salt and last year's tallow. The items on the plate had substance and texture but beyond that, identifying them was a challenge. There was a white pile that could have been mashed potato but could also have been an exploded sinus. She presumed the roughly oval-shaped grey item was a meat of some description, but there was every chance it was the tongue of a boot that had been boiled for a few hours just to bring out the tenderness. It was clear the chef had not felt the need to wash the plate prior to service. Not this service, but possibly the one a week beforehand.

Joy felt a wave of homesickness wash over her. Back home, they might not have eaten fancy meals, but they were things she and her father took the time to resource appropriately and at least indicated some degree of care and affection and desire to continue living; if this dish were a message, there was every chance it would be a suicide note. At a compound. In Waco.

Fear, by comparison, remained fidgety and restless. His eyes were darting from side to side and he would tap his foot impatiently every minute or so, then get up, go check the window, and return to the table. Joy was tired, and hungry, and disappointed, and therefore irritable. Having a public conversation with a vacant chair was something she tried to avoid for the potential issues it raised, but after an hour had gone by and the untouched plate had been removed, presumably to be sold again to someone else, largely representing how the day itself had gone, she hissed "what *is* your *problem?*"

"Something's super wrong here," Fear replied. "There's no concerns in the minds of *anyone*. It's like a totally barren field. You've seen those drought pictures where the ground is all hard-baked and cracked and nothing grows?"

"Yes?"

"It's like that. I can't see anywhere for the worms to grow *at all*."

"Oh, diddums. Worried it'll catch on and you'll be out of the job?"

Fear looked at her seriously- something he didn't do regularly. He was usually full of swagger or silliness or mischief or, occasionally, all three, but these were entirely absent.

"You don't understand," he said, "it's like someone's conducted a mass killing on their imaginations. The worms are important, they help fertilise the fields and make you aware of things you might otherwise miss. But... it's like everywhere I turn, every mind has a wasting disease and its muscles have atrophied. A grown man just filled his underwear with his own nefarious home brew, so to speak, and shrugged it off. And it's so bizarre because there's no way *in*. I've never seen this."

"Maybe it's just something tonight?"

"Maybe. We'll have to see. But I'm worried."

"Why are *you* worried?"

"Because people who have no fear can do anything, and 'anything' encompasses a *lot*."

Joy was quiet and circumspect while she considered this. Despite everything else, Fear's concerns usually kept her pretty safe.

"Well, the town wouldn't be here if it didn't bring joy to *someone*, after all," she said quietly. "Let's talk to some people in the morning. I'm sure a good night's sleep will improve the mood for us as well as everyone else."

"Put it this way, kid. If your food was like *that,* what do you think your *bed* will be like?"

"Oh, come on, how hard can it be to make a bed up?"

Six hours later, as a burning itch took full root across almost the entire length of her body, Joy regretted asking the question. It seemed someone had sent an invitation out to the entirety of parasitic insectoid creation to a street race across her skin; one of these must have been Bed Bug Vin Diesel and anyone he deemed 'family'. Maybe they were stealing microscopic DVD players and running from the police, because even her *scalp* was on fire, and she dreaded what her skin would look like when the sun finally rose.

The room had been fairly sparse and the mattress had been made of hay, a fairly significant change from her experience back in the city, but she had assumed as she lay down that despite some of the less spinally-supporting designs, its relative softness compared to the oak floorboards or the tiles outside the room would at least facilitate a state of restfulness, if not entirely peaceful slumber. Her assumption was entirely incorrect.

The mattress must have served as a halfway house for down-on-their-luck bed bugs, each presumably with their own unique plethora of diseases acquired through their hard lives down by the bed bug railyard or something similar. What little fitful sleep Joy was able to clutch in between the random bites and itching was filled with visions of bed bug preachers, handing out bed bug soup and bread and sharing the news that they needn't be slaves to their bed bug addictions any longer. However, the potential redemption of these microscopic souls was of little comfort to Joy, so at 2am she had surrendered to the inevitable and gone to sleep on the floor, head resting on the bag, a lone blanket over her after shaking it out as best she could.

She was awake just after dawn, shoulder aching from the floor and entirely irritable. Gloomhaven would not have a lengthy visit, she decided, but what irked her was the fact that there was little explanation for the abject misery that the town produced, in a land dedicated to freedom and happiness.

She went downstairs to the innkeeper, a rotund man in his late forties with a blank expression on his face.
"You'd be wanting breakfast, then?" he said as she approached.
"No, I want to talk about that room," Joy replied firmly. "That was the worst sleep I've ever had. There's *creatures* living in the bed, and bedding."
"Well, why did you expect a good night's sleep?" the man replied simply. "Didn't say anywhere it would be comfortable."
"Perhaps I imagined it would be reasonable because I'm *paying* for it?" Joy fired back.

The innkeeper sniffed.

"You haven't paid yet. For all I know, you could be one of those that does a runner first thing in the morning. No point trying to make the bed if people mightn't pay. That's just logic."

Joy was surprised at this.

"So... if I *don't* pay, because the stay was horrible, you won't be surprised, because you didn't expect that I *would* pay, and so didn't make it worth staying in?"

The innkeeper sucked at his teeth. "When you put it like that, it sounds about right."

"But surely," Joy countered, "you'd like me to pay, and it would be in your interests to make the rooms at least something someone wanted to pay for?"

"Dunno about that," the man replied while he jotted a few things down in the ledger at the front. "But that'll be two coins for the night, thanks."

Joy bristled. "I had intended to pay, but I'm not paying for a room to be eaten alive by bed bugs. That's crazy."

The man shrugged in resignation. "Good thing I didn't bother changing the sheets, then," he replied simply.

Joy was flummoxed. She needed at least one more night's stay, because there were investigations to do in the town now, to see if this was the attitude throughout, but there was no way she could manage another moment in that room.

"Look," she said by way of negotiation, "I'm *not* paying for last night. *But,* I'm prepared to pay three coins for tonight, *in advance,* if you can make up a room I can actually sleep in. Something more comfortable than that mattress, and absolutely no creatures."

The innkeeper thought about this. "Seems like a lot of work for no good reason," he said. "It's not like there's anywhere else for you to stay, not really."

"I'd rather sleep in woods," Joy replied firmly. "At least it's softer than the floor. Come on, think about it. How are you going to pay your suppliers if no money comes in?"

"Oh, I'm behind with them," he shrugged. "But then, nobody here pays on time. That's probably why they don't bother supplying me with anything good or fresh. And the ladies that do the cleaning and the rooms, well, they don't do much and so I don't always pay them, either. But then, I don't pay them right cos they don't do much. Nobody's disappointed."

"*I'm* disappointed. Tell you what, *four* coins. If you agree to put a half-decent effort into breakfast, I'll give you two coins now, and if you get your ladies to set me up in another room and get some fresh sheets on the beds, I'll give you the rest of your money in advance. This evening. We go look at the room together, I give you the money, and we can shake hands."

The innkeeper thought about this. It was hard to see how he could be let down on this basis.

"Alright, miss," he said cautiously, "just this once, I'll give it a crack. You give me the first two coins now, I'll put a bit of effort into the breakfast."

Twenty minutes later, Joy was sitting down, as the sole diner, to a plate of somewhat-underdone eggs next to somewhat-overdone bacon, on blackened toast, that was at least recognisable and edible. She was famished and the food was at least edible, so she dived into it. Fear sat down beside her.

"Looks a little better than last night, at least," he said. "I think I've got a handle on this place. I spent a bit of the morning around the town, trying to find why there'd never been any work here before."

"Mmmf," Joy replied with her mouth full and gesturing with her knife. "Foundf good. Whaf'f you find out?"

"It's a mystery to me how you've stayed single for so long. The town seems to have decided that expectations are the cause of unhappiness. If they expect something good, well, they're able to be let down. But if they expect the worst, well, then they're never disappointed, and so can't ever be truly let down. Thus, they find a weird kind of happiness, in their minds."

"'Scuse me, miss," came the innkeeper's voice from the partition that led to the kitchen. "Just thought I'd see if things were to your liking?"

There was an odd note of hopefulness to his voice. Joy didn't want to quash it.

"It was decent, thanks," she said. "A little longer with the eggs, a little less time with the bacon and toast, but I really enjoyed it."

"Really?" the innkeeper replied happily. "Haven't had much cause to cook before. Usually we just heat up something from the night before if people wants breakfast. If you don't mind me saying... actually enjoyed myself a bit."

Joy pulled out an additional coin from her money bag and passed it to him. She had local currency notes as well, of course, and it was hard to get a real sense of the exchange rate, but given this was worth half the cost of one of the inn's rooms, it seemed to her to be generous.

"Back home, when people give a bit extra to us, we give a bit extra to them. It's called a tip. I appreciate the effort."

The innkeeper looked the coin over. "You know, that gives me an idea," he said.

Fear looked bemused.

"Well, that was surprising," he said with a grin. "Look at you, changing the narrative. But it's a bigger problem outside these four walls."

"How come it's a problem?" Joy asked. "I mean, I get it. This place is the worst. But why are *you* so bothered by it?"

Fear took a deep breath. "You know, I don't know if you've ever really fully understood how important fear is. Fear of losing something means you value having it. Fear of disappointing someone whose opinion you value helps people excel with mentorship. It can bring your attention back to what's important when other distractions have gotten in, it makes people feel alive. It forces innovation to protect the people you love, like worrying about getting through winters and summers and making refrigerators, or storehouses, or electricity. I do what I do because I want to help humans, not because I like making them upset. Most of the time, anyway. But this town... nobody is actually living. There's no meaningful change between life and death, ultimately. There's *vague* things I can sense, a concern or a discordant note of some sort, but it's hard to get anything tangible."

"What does that mean, though? For the townsfolk?"

"It means that absolutely everything is about them. They can't think of others, because others could be a disappointment. They can't try something new, because nobody expects anything positive to come for the effort. It's a stagnant pond, really."

Joy forced optimism for a moment; if this was really true, then surely there was something she could do about it.

"Well," she said, cramming the last piece of toast, egg, and bacon into her mouth, "it'ff about time we faw efferyfing. Let'f go ecfploring!"

"After seeing that, how could I refuse?" Fear replied.

They spent the morning going through the village; market place, main shops, past blacksmiths and weavers and carpenters, live animal auctions and trade exchanges. It remained a gloomy and lackluster affair, and its denizens put little effort into conversation generally, least of all to a stranger who they wouldn't be seeing again. Where pressed as to their attitude or the lack of pride in what they had produced or were selling, the responses would come the same as the innkeeper: it was simply easier to expect a poor outcome than to see that effort go unrewarded. It seemed to have left the city trapped in the middle ages, and Joy reflected on Fear's point about the stifling of innovation by this flattened populace. Joy was terrified about the prospect of buying anything, food or otherwise, when disinterest was so high and expectations were so low.

"You're right," Joy said to Fear as they walked, "I can see why you were so surprised by the lack of reaction. It's all so..."

"Flat?" Fear suggested. "Nothing changes here. On one hand, nobody *expects* change, because they assume that nobody else wants to do something well. On the other, nobody *wants* it, because it could be worse."

"This isn't a place I think I'll find joy," she replied. "Maybe we get on the road tomorrow?"

"Sure. There's bound to be somewhere we both might be needed."

They were wandering back through a moderate crowd when someone pushed past Joy and grabbed her purse from her hand on the way by. Joy cried out as he did so, but the crowd assembled only turned the odd head and then returned to whatever other business they had. It was clear that crime, when it raised its head, was just accepted as something to expect, and intervention would probably just result in one's injury. For Joy, on the other hand, this was everything her father had put away, years of his work and struggle, and it was disappearing on the third day since she had left home and only the second day of her adventure. The whole incident seemed to be in slow motion; she'd barely had time to register the bump when she saw the fleeing hand holding her purse, and she had just enough time to feel her stomach drop as she registered what had happened and call out "no!"

The thief managed a to run a few feet before Fear appeared in front of him and shot out a hand which went straight through the top of the man's head and into his brain. The thief froze on the spot, his eyes rolled partially until only the whites were showing. Fear's hand was partially opened as if he was carefully holding a snow globe. He used his free hand to reach inside his trenchcoat, and Joy saw him extract her jar of fears, which had been added to over the years and was now a writhing mass of Worms of Concern, blue and purple and yellow and green but all fat and lively. All the terrors, doubts, and avoidances of the last nine years, from school failure right through to the fear of dying in the clouds, snugly contained in one glass receptacle. Fear brought the jar up to his face and flipped the lid open with his chin, then dumped the entire contents into the helpless man's head. All the colour drained from the thief's face and he went rigid; in doing so, he dropped Joy's purse as his fingers started flexing and relaxing of their own volition. Fear took a half step back, his face dark with fury and his grey eyes darkening to almost black with rage, and then whispered into the man's ear out of Joy's hearing: "*Nobody, **nobody** in this God-forsaken town is to lay a hand this girl, or the next place you will be found will be in a six foot hole. You think you have nothing to fear, and let me tell you how very wrong you are. Nobody expected anything from you in your life and so nobody will mourn your death, but believe me when I say there are so many ways to lose your life that you don't want to discover. Think on that.*"

Fear pulled his hand out of the man's head, who let out a shriek and then sprinted away, hands covering his ears. This reaction caused a small disturbance in the crowd, who had only seen him stiffen, drop the item, and scream, a level of curiosity as the unexpected situation had had a positive outcome, but the entertainment had been short-lived and investigating further clearly invited more potential negatives than positives, so their attention to their normal activities resumed.

Joy was still reeling from the shock of the situation; she had not seen Fear take such an interventionist approach in her life, much less so dramatically and, frankly, aggressively. She stepped forward and picked up her fallen purse; Fear was still watching the thief's retreating figure in the distance. "Thank you," she said softly.

"I *told* you to be careful in a town that only expected the worst from its inhabitants," Fear remonstrated angrily, spinning to face her. "Honestly, Sparky, you can't just wander about, flashing your wallet, as if you were invincible! What if something happened to you?"

Joy had not seen this side of him before, and as she looked at his thunderous expression, she felt terrified. Even in his angered state, Fear still noticed this, and he softened immediately.

"Hey, hey," he soothed, putting his hands up "don't be scared. Not of me. I'm sorry. I just... I don't want to see you get hurt. And I *tried* to warn you last night: if people only expect the worst, then the worst of human behavior can be pretty terrible. It's much easier to take what you want than it is to work for it, especially if nobody expects anything better of you."

"What did you *do* to him?" Joy asked, horrified.

"Well... nothing he didn't deserve. I figured if he was *already* expecting the worst, I'd have to up the ante a bit. He'll be fine... probably." Fear brightened for a moment. "And hey, look at the positives. We know now that fear is just a question of volume."

Still feeling shaken, and with the afternoon getting colder, Joy returned to the tavern. Her walk was a little more suspicious, watching strangers for stray glances. It was disappointing, she thought, how the town's outlook had taken an optimistic girl and made her mistrustful in so short a time.

She returned to the tavern, and found herself pleasantly surprised. The innkeeper had corralled the barmaids and the bar area had been cleaned up.

Tablecloths had even been laid on the large timber benches and a sign had been erected at the entry to the bar: "Give A Bit More, Get A Bit More."

He brightened when he saw Joy approaching, hopping across the room. "'Ullo there, miss," he said with more enthusiasm than she'd previously seen, "how's about we go see to your room?"

He led her upstairs to a different room than the one she had previously occupied, and there was a marked change; a daffodil had been inexpertly plucked, partially crushed in the process, and put into a small vase on a dresser, and the bed, whilst it still appeared to be a palliasse, it looked neat and clean and serviceable, with fresh sheets visible even if they were tucked in poorly.

"Washed 'em myself," the innkeeper said proudly, "guaranteed to be serviceable for you, miss."

In the gloom of this town, this small gesture- in particular, the lone mangled flower, a small burst of colour in the otherwise drab room and a tiny bit of effort that spoke to care on the part of her host- was overwhelming. Especially in view of her afternoon, she felt a few small rays of hope for humanity. Joy felt compelled to reward this properly. She opened her purse and pulled out a low-denomination note, worth approximately ten of the coins.

"I love it! Thank you. I'd like to offer this to you, in return for the night's accommodation, a serviceable meal, and would there be any way to secure this room?" she asked.

"Why, something happen today, miss?" the man asked, concerned. "I mean, I can do that, but I've always just assumed a lock wouldn't serve much purpose if someone really wanted to get in eventually. Why not save the door a bit of damage, right?"

"A man tried to rob me in the markets," Joy replied bravely. The man looked at her impassively, as if this was everyday news.

"And then what happened?" he prompted.

"That was it!"

"And that upset you, miss?"

"Yes!"

"Well, here, you could save your money and keep your bags with you, but I'd be happy to spare one of the lads to keep an eye on your room if that's what you want. But you know, I get robbed maybe once a month. It's probably young Darren Brendish, he hasn't ever really done much useful with himself, and that's how he makes his way; we never really expected more of him than that. Can't say it's ever ruined my day, as I never keep much for him to take. I just assume every day that someone's going to rob me, and every day they don't, it's a good day!"

He said this quite happily, as if imparting sage-like advice for Joy, who was aghast.

"Do you guys arrest people who do these things?" she asked.

"I mean, sometimes, but I guess we kind of figure they're just going to do it again. What's the point of worrying? We have to pay to house them and feed them if we build a jail; we might as well pay them a little bit when they rob us to feed and house themselves. They're happy, and we're happy, and we've cut out the middle man."

Fear stood in the middle of the room, shaking his head.

"Not everything can be changed overnight, Sparky, and not all minds *should* be changed all at once," he said, which would have been wise- if deflating- advice, except that Joy was naturally a contrarian. She bristled visibly and decided to double down.

"Let me ask you this," she said to the innkeeper with her back to Fear, "This guy, nobody expects him to achieve nothing, and so he achieves nothing. If you townspeople expected more from him, would anything change? Like, if you punished the bad behaviour, but gave him a chance to try something where you told him you thought he could do well? And if he did improve, he could try a little harder the next day? You know, everyone comes through the tavern eventually; you could be the catalyst for changing their minds! Imagine, he'd be so grateful and *you* wouldn't get robbed any more."

The innkeeper, positively disposed at present, subjected this to due consideration.

"Hmmmm. You've got a point, there, miss," he said eventually. "Well, let's see what we can do about that. In the meantime, I'll get someone to watch out for the rooms and will fix you some tea. I have to say, I didn't think I'd have such a good time back in the kitchen again! But if you'll excuse me..."

"Oh, of course."

"Give the lad a chance, you say," he mused as he closed the door behind him. "Well, you've been right so far!"

A few hours later, Joy was sitting in the tavern with a plate that contained an identifiable pork chop, apple sauce, and mashed potato that wasn't actively trying to crawl off her plate. As with breakfast, it was not high art, but for the venue, it was chalk and cheese. The patrons seemed to have noticed the change; the room atmosphere was lighter, and the improvement in both the food and the drink, which was now at least served in glasses that had been carefully washed, seemed to open people to conversations. The barmaids must have had a talking-to and they approached guests with a smile and a few words, which had a downstream trigger on the openness for discussions in the room. No longer feeling like a funeral, the old inn was starting to show early signs of life.

The innkeeper had put out a tip jar with a rough explanation of how tips worked, given that Gloomhaven had no concept of this before, and the improved mood seemed to open the pockets of the guests; by the middle of the evening, it had already been filled, emptied, and replaced once.

Joy was, of course, happy to take credit for the change in the habits. In fact, this happiness started to border on smugness as she finished an edible meal and the room atmosphere continued to lift.

"They'll probably make a statue of me," she gloated quietly to Fear. "Changing hearts, changing minds. The woman who brought joy to their town."

"Oh, for sure," Fear replied sarcastically. "Nothing could possibly go wrong."

"Of course you'd be snarky," Joy said haughtily. "*You* thought that people couldn't change, but here we are."

"I didn't say they couldn't, I said not all minds should be changed. And you were the one who said you might be better off leaving the town, after all."

"Well, here we are, making a difference. Maybe this is my calling. To turn Gloomhaven into Joytown. All I'll need is a parapet wall!"

"I wouldn't get ahead of myself," Fear warned. "There's the law of unintended consequences.":

Ignoring him primly, Joy finished her meal and retired to bed. She woke up in the middle of the night to drink some water and use the facilities, and noted that she could hear the footfalls of the guard outside her room, walking up and down the hallway. The service had definitely improved, she thought to herself; clean sheets, a secure room, a place people felt comfortable. Few things felt as good as a pleasant night's sleep and the wonderful feeling of potential canonisation by a grateful citizenry, and Joy looked forward to both.

She awoke the next morning feeling refreshed and happy. Her room was untouched and her bags unmolested. After checking her belongings and counting her money, Joy dressed and packed and opened her door to an empty hallway; it seemed fair that further patrols were not necessary. All in all, a reasonable trade in the cost for the outcome. Whilst her rates may have been generous in Gloomhaven terms, the local pricing clearly reflected the poor expectations, and the whole experience had cost her less than twenty-five dollars of her home currency, including the meals.

There was an angry commotion taking place downstairs, so Joy headed down to see what was going on. The innkeeper was stuck behind the front desk and five angry middle-aged patrons were in the middle of serving him a piece of their minds. Joy couldn't hear through the commotion, so she yelled out "Hey!" loudly, and the guests stopped and looked at her.

"What's going on?" she asked. "How come you're all so upset?"

"We've been robbed!" one of the men replied, short and squat with a long black beard and thick hair going from the backs of his knuckles, under his shirt, and sprouting across his shoulder like a chia pet. "Here, miss, what'd you lose?"

"I didn't lose anything," Joy said. "I checked first thing. But I don't understand, the innkeeper had his staff patrol last night to make sure everyone was safe."

"Point of order, miss," the innkeeper said, "I had the young man patrol to keep *your* room safe."

He looked at the others. "What?" he added defensively. "*She* paid for extra care. You lot only paid two coins a night, *and* I still made the beds up special."

There was a murmur of approval from the guests; the beds had indeed been an improvement.

"Well, who did you get to patrol?" Joy asked. "Maybe he saw something."

"I did like you suggested, miss. I gave that young Brendish boy a chance. I told him in very clear terms: you're not to steal from this room."

"Wait," Joy said, confused, "you hired a known thief to watch peoples' rooms? What did you expect him to do?"

"Yeah!" agreed the hairy man. "I even tipped downstairs last night because I liked the change, but then you go and hire the Brendish boy? He robbed me just last week!"

The assembled crowd started arguing again in indignation, forcing the innkeeper to raise his voice.

"What did I expect? Listen to yourselves!" he said defensively. "I did what *she* said. She said that if we never expected more from him, he'd never be more than a thief."

"Oh, so it's *her* fault?!" shouted the mountain gorilla, rounding on Joy. In unison, the other four turned on her. Joy started backing away towards the door, her hands held up placatingly.

"Fear?" she whispered with a tremor in her voice. "A little help?"

Fear started rolling up his sleeves theatrically.

"All right, but isn't this where they make a statue out of you? I'm sure that's what you said. Changing hearts and minds, that's the ticket!"

"Is now the time to be right?" she hissed.

"It's always a good time to be right," he replied.

He stood between Joy and the patrons, ready to unleash unseen fury if they crossed him, and Joy continued walking backwards out the door until she bumped into someone. She spun, and looked into the face that had tried to rob her the day before.

The arguments stopped, and the patrons looked shocked. Even the innkeeper was surprised. Young Darren Brendish stood there awkwardly, tugging at his collar and clearing his throat.

"Um, hello," he said nervously. "Mister Simmons here, he paid me yesterday to keep a room safe. And I did, but you all left your rooms open, and so, I kinda figured, you know, since I'm going to rob you guys anyway, I might as well do it at once and save you the future inconvenience."

Oddly, the assembled crowd nodded in agreement, despite the anger. If robbery was to be expected, well, then it may as well be slightly more convenient.

"But then," Darren continued, "I got thinking. Like if Mister Simmons is paying me, I don't need to rob you. And, like, I know other people who steal, and I figured since I know them, I can do a better job stopping that here. And so thought that if you want to pay Mister Simmons like this lady did to stop people from stealing from your rooms last night, then he can pay *me* to stop them, and I can give you your stuff back, and, well, then I won't be robbing you, 'cos you'll be paying me not to."

"But we could stay and not bring our valuables with us when we're drinking," countered one of the men helpfully. The crowd murmured in agreement again.

"You could," said the innkeeper, "but wouldn't young Darren here then just rob you out in the street later?"

"Oh, yeah," said the man. "That's a fair point."

There was an awkward silence while the parties considered this impasse. Darren was the one to break it.

"Tell you what," he said, "I always thought nobody would give me a chance. Mister Simmons did. So I'm going to give you a chance, too. How about I give you all back your stuff? Then if you want to take a chance and pay Mr. Simmons for having me secure the rooms last night, he can keep me in a job. Or, like I could wander round at night and make sure you're *not* being broken into at your houses, if you wanted to pay me to do that."

With that, he pulled open his bag and walked to the front counter, placing the purloined goods on top and stepping back. The assembled crowd seemed hesitant. It was a good chance to get their things back *and* keep the money, really, and it seemed to be just sensible for this young man to have learned not to expect altruism from other people. Preparing to be disappointed was the surest way to avoid it.

Joy broke the impasse by stepping forward and facing the young man, and slapped him firmly across the face. He raised a hand to his cheek as the terrible threat Fear had placed into his subconscious rose to the fore: this was not a woman to touch, or he would never be heard from again.
"That was for trying to rob me yesterday," she said firmly, before pulling out an additional coin and placing it in his hands. "And *this* is a tip, because you guarded my room last night very well and never left your post. Except to go into these fine peoples' rooms," she added as admonishment.

There is a saying that when one person does something crazy, they're a lone nut. When two people do something crazy, they're just a couple of loons. But eventually a third person will join, and a fourth, and once you get to five, well, now you've got a movement. This is true, right up until someone mentions a refreshing drink of Kool-Aid on a hot day in your long white robes.
The innkeeper pulled out a coin, and gave it to him as well.
"Your wages for the night, lad," he said with a respectful nod. "If you work for me again, you aren't to touch *any* guest's belongings, though, you hear?"
The hairy man pulled out a half-coin, and grudgingly flipped it towards Darren. The others soon followed.
"Dunno if we'll stay here again," the last man grumbled as he surrendered his half-coin. "You can have this, but I ain't adding a tip!"

The five men, having recovered their goods, exited the premises. Joy exhaled a deep sigh of relief. Mister Simmons, the innkeeper, tapped her on the shoulder.

"Didn't know if that would work, miss, but it's better than nothing.

"I'm so sorry, I didn't mean-" she started, but Mister Simmons held up a hand to cut her off.

"Never tried something new. Got a bit burned, but we did well last night. But Miss, sorry to say, you're trouble. Best you were on your way. I've made you a roll with bacon and egg for your breakfast, and the roll had hardly any mould on it and all. Can't say fairer than that."

Joy considered her options. Fear was nodding furiously.

You're right," she eventually said. "That's very fair. I was leaving anyway. But thank you for your hospitality."

"You're very welcome. Young Brendish here might work out; I'll be sure to expect him to. But one more trick like that, lad, and I'll leave you to those guests," he warned, looking at the young guilty man. The innkeeper extended a hand to Joy, who shook it, and that was that.

So Joy took her bag and wandered down to the town gate. The gate guard was nowhere to be seen, but that wasn't a surprise. It wasn't clear that he had ever actually closed the gate; he may have just assumed nobody was going to get up early enough to check. In reality, it didn't seem that anyone was ever going to be desperate enough to get in, as much as being desperate to get out.

Fear was whistling smugly as they started on the road

"*That* was close," he said as the town disappeared behind them.

"Shut up."

"Good thing I was there."

"You didn't *do* anything!" Joy protested.

"No, but I was about to. And technically speaking, neither did you."

"I changed one person!"

"Maybe. Maybe not. That innkeeper is now worried he's going to lose guests who now have to assume they're not going to be stolen from."

"Oh."

"*But*, on the up side, the Brendish boy is scared that if he steals from someone, he'll feel like he did when he stole from you. He'd rather have a job. That's a win for me. Changing hearts and minds."

"I hate you."

"You can hate my statue."

They continued bickering about who had had the bigger impact, because it was a nice day for a disagreement and this kind of thing had formed part of their banter historically, and the sound of their argument floated up through the trees causing birds to scatter as they wandered back through the forest to their next destination.

Chapter 6

Something Happens

Baa Baa, black sheep, here's exactly what you need.

The unpaved, sandy-soiled track through the forest started to transform from a winding path into a straighter, intentionally-made path. As the trees began to dwindle and fields emerged, the road became paved and Joy started seeing more traffic moving along. The landscape became pock-marked with farms and farmhouses, large well-appointed brick affairs with white lintels and tree-lined dirt driveways, flattened and hard by its regular traffic. The road itself widened as other smaller paths joined it, and increasingly there were other travellers, well-dressed and all engaged in excited conversations, heading towards a city.

Gone was the quiet, cool breeze and shadowy path filled with birdsong, and in its place was the warmth of the sun shining down, an unobstructed vision of the horizon, and what could only be described as a throng that made its way to the city outskirts. The city had no walls, but did have a ring of large multi-storey buildings with warehouses at the ground floor that effectively functioned as the same thing. Twilight was starting to set and a large illuminated sign carved into white stone with black painted lettering declared proudly that they were entering Luxoria. Beyond the commercial buildings that functioned as the town's barrier, at what looked to be the centre of the city, there was an enormous pillar of light shining upwards. As the crowds began to approach the boundaries and created a traffic jam, there was an excited tittering amongst all the people.

In contrast to the experience in Gloomhaven, the sense of positivity and purpose in the air. Despite the long journey, the crowd's energy brought out an electricity in Joy's body that made her shift her weight between her legs to the rhythm of a mystery beat playing in her head. Everyone was dressed so neatly and she became aware of both a latent odour and the shabby state of her clothes, which was hardly a surprise given she'd flown through a storm, walked across townships, slept on a torture device disguised as a mattress, and not once in all that time managed to find a shower.

"What I need," she said aloud, half to herself and half to Fear, "is to get somewhere I can do some washing."

A hand from behind her tapped her on the shoulder, and she turned to see a nervous but smiling young woman who appeared to be a similar age, with dark brown hair and a perfect complexion. She was a few inches shorter than Joy but was carrying a pair of high heels which would have put her almost at eye level if she wore them, and was dressed in a pastel pink skirt suit with a white shirt and a very clean pair of practical shoes occupying her feet, presumably until the high heels would be swapped in.

"Um, hi, excuse me" the stranger said, "is this your first time visiting Luxoria?"

How friendly, Joy thought to herself. *Definitely beats the last town.* "Yes," she replied with a smile, "I'm kinda new to this whole place really. I just came from Gloomhaven and-"

"Oh my *gosh*, isn't that place just the *worst?*" The woman said emphatically. "Like, ugh, we get it, your thing is being sad, never enjoy anything, blah blah blah."

"I'm not sure being *sad* was their point, but-"

"But this place is *so great*. Honestly, it's my happy place." Joy's ears picked up. This sounded promising.

"What's your name?" The woman asked, keeping up the Labrador-level friendliness and enthusiasm that left little room for an actual response. "Avaritia always says 'a customer is a friend you're about to win over, and a friend is a customer who always comes back.' She's such an inspiration."

"Oh, uh, my name's Joy, Joy Summerfield, but who is Avar-" Joy tried to say.

"Oh my gosh!" The unknown woman interjected enthusiastically. "I literally *love* your name, it's *so great*! Did you choose it yourself?"

"Good heavens," Fear muttered over her shoulder, "have you ever seen a Coke bottle with a Mentos chucked in? This woman's overflowing! Quick, throw a ball and see if she runs off to catch it, or bring out something shiny and see if she just follows the sparkly colours!"

"No, my parents gave me the name," Joy said, pretending to shift her bag on her shoulder so she could elbow Fear in the process. "What's yours?"

"My name is Cupidity Cooper, fashion doyenne and owner of She's The Man, power clothes for power women!"

"Oh, really?"

"Because if you want to leave your mark in a man's world, you might as well make it in lipstick!" Cupidity continued effusively, before lowering her voice conspiratorially. "Avaritia says you can't define yourself if you haven't defined your brand. Make a statement to the world about who you are every day and business will follow!"

The massive queue was slowly making its way through the boundary of the city and Joy was getting jostled closer to Cupidity in the throng. Joy felt a flash of annoyance at one of the bumps and whipped her head around to find the culprit, but when she looked back into the beaming face of Cupidity she wondered if her temper or road-weariness was getting the better of her.

"People are a bit rude, aren't they?" Joy said, seeking some solidarity. Cupidity just kept looking enthusiastic.

"Oh no," she replied, "I think it's just *so great* that everyone's coming to the Launch tonight!"

"What launch?" Joy asked.

"Oh! That's right, silly, I forgot you're new here," Cupidity responded, smacking herself on the forehead with her palm. "You picked the best night to come! Avaritia is going to come and give her motivational talk and do her Product of Now presentation. You can see her in person!" Cupidity frowned as she looked Joy up and down. "Oh, but you can't come like this, oh my. That wouldn't be great *at all*."

"Yes," said Joy, suddenly embarrassed, "I haven't had a chance to do any washing yet. Is there somewhere I could do that?"

"Oh no, silly, *nobody* washes in Luxoria," Cupidity laughed. "That's what I was going to tell you before I got distracted. But my shop isn't far from here and you can just buy some new clothes! Your frame is just *so great*, I think I have the perfect things!"

Fear was wandering among the crowd, taking the opportunity to seed and harvest some worms, but on his way past Joy's shoulder going the opposite direction to the flow of traffic he muttered sarcastically "and I *bet* Avaritia has something to say about washing?" into Joy's ear.

"Avaritia says that chores should be outsourced or embraced only by the brave-hearted souls seeking mundane adventure!" Cupidity enthused, and Joy had to struggle to keep a straight face.

"I mean, I need to find somewhere to stay and have a shower, probably, before I get clothes," Joy continued. "And I'm trying to watch budget a bit; I mean, all I need is some soap, water, and somewhere to dry the clothes after."

"Oh, don't be silly," Cupidity responded. "You can stay with me. I have a spare room and I live above the shop so you can have a shower and then come and try things on! And you won't have time to make it to the Launch otherwise, which you absolutely *cannot* miss. Like, literally why would you come to Luxoria and *not* see Avaritia in person, am I right?"

Fear caught up to them in time to mischievously whisper "Skin suits made from incautious customers! Guaranteed!" in Joy's ear and she had to fight down a chuckle. But why not take the offer up? If she saved on accommodation then she might have enough money for the clothing, so it probably balanced out. Also, she was tired, in the middle of an adventure, and she had never once seen James Bond or Lara Croft or even Darth Vader stop in the middle of their activities to scrub a stain out in the sink, although this was probably why Darth Vader always wore black. Perhaps Cupidity was right; was she seeking mundane adventure? No, she was not. The clothes could go, and she would have more time to find her happiness. She had money. There was no down side whatsoever.

"Look, I'd love to," she said. "Thank you so much! By the way, what does it mean to be a fashion doyenne?"

"I think it means to be like a groovy chick or something," Cupidity responded. "I heard someone say it once and thought it was like, *so great* and absolutely was me. It sounds like someone has cool hair and one of those French cigarette-smoking things they hold with white gloves when everyone else runs around doing what they told them, right?"

"I mean, yeah, it sounds cool, but should you be using a word you don't know in your job description?" Joy asked.

"Of course! It's about how the word makes people *feel*, they feel like it's important and French probably. I don't think people know what it means either, and it makes me sound more smart and photosynthesis."

Fear heard this up ahead and his head whipped around as he started a wide-eyed grin that almost reached his ears; he looked like the Cheshire Cat after finding a whole bag of cocaine hidden in a tree. This was a gift that kept on giving to him, and Joy could see a thousand jokes start to line up at the poor woman's expense. Even *she* wasn't certain she could survive them, and bursting out laughing at someone who has offered you a bed and a shower is a very quick way to lose both. Besides, a minor quibble to be levelled at someone friendly, positive, enthusiastic, and generous seemed to be terribly unappreciative. Before Fear could speak, Joy said loudly "I'd love to come to your shop, Cupidity. Thank you so much. I think your title is-"

"*So great*?!" Fear muttered.

"Perfect," Joy finished, ignoring him.

It took about twenty minutes to get to Cupidity's shop, during which time Joy got an understanding of the city layout. Right in the centre was the stadium where they would later go to attend the mysterious Launch event, and radiating out from this were the various trades and stores by order of prestige and importance. The most popular and sought-after product designers and makers were close to the stadium, and as the distance increased from the epicentre of the town, the prestige reduced. On the outside of the town were the warehouses, smelters, slaughterhouses, and granaries, allowing the goods and raw materials to be delivered to and dispatched from the city expeditiously and then allocated within the town as needed. These were volume businesses that then supplied the nucleus of the city; if your shop was on the outer radius close to these, you sold practical goods to the families operating the requisite trades. The further you moved in, the more specialised the markets became. More fashionable, more costly, seeking fewer units with greater margins but having to have an endorsement of the greats to survive. Cupidity's shop was only slightly closer in than the bulk manufacturers and blue-collar goods, aspiring to make its way slowly inwards to the city. The shop design, however, eschewed its humble surroundings and pointed its nose squarely towards the tastes of the mover and shakers, and Joy wondered if this area was a sort of dead-man's zone where sinking or swimming was the law of the land. It did its best to say: I may be from here, but I'm not staying.

The shop itself was quite lovely and well-appointed. It was clear that Cupidity had made a substantial effort, with tasteful lighting and soft colour pallets that made the clothing options stand out in the small room. Joy followed her behind a shopkeeper's curtain and took a left turn up a narrow staircase, which led to a fairly simple and bare two bedroom apartment. Armed with a towel, a robe and some basic directions, Joy found the shower, changed out of her road-worn clothing and stepped under hot water, offering a silent prayer of thanks for the invention of indoor plumbing and boilers. She felt her muscles, unused to long days of travel, relax as tension melted away. She could feel herself coming back to life again; she felt clean and fresh and a sense of positivity that had been drained out by the energy vampires of Gloomhaven.

Fear had always maintained a respectful approach to his involvement with Joy, or at least insofar as it came to changing and showering; he religiously avoided bathrooms, saying whatever fears they held were for the occupant alone, and if he ever entered Joy's room in the morning, he did so with one hand over his eyes. As a result, the whole shower experience was a rare moment of total peace and as Joy stepped out of the stall into the steam-filled room, drying herself with an incredibly soft and fluffy towel, she wondered if this would be the place she'd find happiness. She'd already made a friend, apparently, and whilst it was almost against her will, maybe Stockholm Syndrome had its perks, she thought.

Feeling thoroughly human again, she tied the towel around her head and stepped out of the bathroom wearing the nominated robe. Whatever Cupidity was going to charge her, she decided, it was worth it.

"Oh my gosh, that looks *so great* already!" Cupidity enthused, looking up from the small round dining table in the kitchen when she caught sight of Joy walking down the hallway.

"I mean, I'm not going to be wearing just *this* to the Launch, am I?" asked Joy nervously.

"No, silly!" Cupidity laughed. "Come on, I'm supposed to be closed today but as Avaritia says, 'Open Doors Open Hearts' and we should always be open to our friends! Leave your old clothes in the bathroom, and let's find you a style!"

As they wandered back down to the shop front, Joy wondered how many sentences Cupidity said that *didn't* have exclamation marks involved. There was an intensity to her enthusiasm that was relentless, although Joy had to give credit where it was due: Cupidity seemed happy about *everything*.

"The Launch is *the* event here, so you have to bring some style, girl!" Cupidity said as they walked around the room, grabbing a tape measure and randomly measuring waists and hips legs and busts and then scanning the racks of clothes. "We have to say something about your brand. What's your brand about?"

"I don't think I have a brand?" Joy replied with her arms outstretched as the tape measure went elbow-to-armpit and being enormously aware, even if her kindly host was oblivious to it, that she was an errant tug away from full-frontal nudity. "I think my main brand is not to be naked in front of people?"

"Tch, everyone's naked under their clothes," Cupidity said dismissively, "nothing I haven't seen in a mirror myself! Now, let's say power! Let's say this is a high-value boss girl out there to slay like a queen!"

"How do we do that?"

"With grey!" Cupidity enthused. "But the right *kind* of grey. Normal grey is for dull people with dull ambitions. I think we do an Elephant Foot Grey skirt, pair it with *this* blouse, maybe add a scarf or a cravat... package the whole thing in a fine trench coat, black epaulets, maybe a nice set of heels..." she fussed and bothered through the racks, pulling out item after item in search of the pieces she was imagining. She continued talking but Joy wasn't sure if it was to her or just out loud, and the words got half-muffled the deeper in the racks Cupidity went. "Gotta say that you're no-nonsense, powerful, but keep it feminine, you know, really own that energy, practical, but not absorbed, we can use the scarf colour to then really *pop* your face..." and all of a sudden, an arm was thrust out from the sea of clothing clutching six or seven coat hangers, including underwear, skirt, blouse, and coat. "I'll get you the scarf in a moment," Cupidity said, "but go try these on."

Joy took an armful of the clothes and was half-pushed, half-directed to the change rooms by her excited companion. She managed to get a brief glance a Fear leaning up against the wall with one foot behind him, a bemused expression at the whole ordeal and process. The door was pulled closed by Cupidity but Joy could see her feet outside moving excitedly.
"Let me know how they feel!" she called out.
It all seemed a little over-the-top to Joy, and she worried that the items looked to be expensive, but out of courtesy to her new friend she obligingly put on the ensemble.

Good heavens, she thought, *I've never felt **anything** like this.* The prospect of high quality clothing was, in the context of Pleasant Lane, something of a dream to be distrusted. In a world of practical people making do and trying to get by, clothing was handed down amongst children, sought from thrift stores, or purchased cheaply from basic chains and felt a little like a sandpaper handshake.

By contrast, the blouse felt airy and smooth, still breathing but hanging lightly against her skin, and the skirt had some kind of silken lining but enough elasticity to both hug her form and allow her legs to move, thanks to a careful split to allow full a greater range of motion. The trench coat still managed to narrow at the waist and then splay out at the rear, following her frame rather than just hanging off her shoulders. She looked at the mirror in the change room, and thought *that's a high-value girl boss that's out to slay like a queen, alright!* She looked older, more mature, but she had to agree that things seemed a little bland despite the comfort. She opened up the door and started saying "these feel really great, but I'm not sure about the price, what do yo-" before being cut off by the excited shopkeeper.
"Oh. My. *God!*" Cupidity exclaimed, "you're an *icon!*"
"I am?" asked Joy nervously.

"You're perf! The world is gonna know you! Here, let me just put this on..." Cupidity said as she reached up to pop up the blouse's collar and drape a multi-coloured scarf that faded between reds, yellows and oranges. She stepped back to look at Joy critically, hand on chin, marvelling her own handiwork. "How does it *feel?*" she asked.

"It feels incredible!" Joy replied. "I've never had clothes like this before. They fit so well! But I don't know if I can afford all of-"

"What you *need* now, is a pair of shoes to tie the whole thing together," her friend said matter-of-factly. Something to make the legs pop, to put you on eye level and show you mean business." She bustled off to an area behind the counter which had an assortment of large pigeon holes containing boxes of shoes. Fear came across and looked Joy up and down.

"Well well, it's a bit like Undercover Boss, but instead the employee is dressing up as the manager?" He said.

"Shut up, these are amazing!" Joy retorted haughtily.

"Hey, it's not a bad thing. Don't they say fake it til you make it? You certainly *look* the part, Sparky! I was about to ask if you could sell me some real estate."

"Oh, you're just jealous that the trench coat steals your look," Joy fired back.

"Not at all. *My* trench coat is black. They tell me it's good for *all* seasons. Weddings, funerals, Halloween, Christmas..."

"Why would you wear a black trench coat for Christmas?"

"Can you imagine the fear of someone in a black trench coat turning up during a festive season? People think the government is after them."

"I thought nobody could see you, though."

"They can't, but they can *imagine* it happening, and that's fear enough. 'Merry Christmas, we're here from the tax office! Please hand over your youngest child's kidney. This is the season for giving and receiving, so you give, and we'll receive, thank you very much.' Anyway, I haven't seen any prices on these things. How attached do you want to be if you can't afford it?"

"I don't know, she won't ever let me finish asking her how much it costs," Joy hissed in reply.

"Look at the time!" Exclaimed Cupidity all of a sudden. She rushed across with a box of gunmetal-coloured high heels. "Put these on quickly, we'll be late for the Launch!"

"But I haven't paid for them yet, do you-" Joy started, but Cupidity had already rushed upstairs, grabbed her own pair of heels, and started back down.

"Come *on*, silly! We can deal with that later. Besides, you'll need a change of clothes for tomorrow."

"But I just got thes-"

"Come *on!*"

Cupidity dragged Joy by the arm out of the door and onto the street, and they started to make their way toward the Stadia. The shoes were not exactly the most comfortable things in the world, but they fit well and whilst they weren't as familiar as her old walking shoes, on the paved sidewalks they felt solid and functional enough. The streets were well-lit and well-signposted and after a few blocks they reached a tram which had a line running straight to the city centre. It was a tasteful wide boulevarde, with mid-sized trees lining the way, alternating with street lights. Shops with residences above, similar to Cupidity's, lined the way behind the sidewalks. The last vestiges of twilight were visible on the horizon but night had mostly fallen and the long lit road toward the Stadia sparkled like a jewel.

The tram was almost full and three others were queued behind it to manage the volume of people making their way in; Joy and Cupidity managed to make it in but missed seats and so had to hold on to leather straps attached to the roof. There was a buzz of excitement in the press of people, energetic conversations and Joy could make out a lot of people responding that something was going to be *so great*.

Caught in the standing crowd, Joy found it difficult to ask anything of Cupidity. Fear seemed unperturbed, having somehow found a space of his own to loiter; although people *could* walk through him, they somehow tended to move around him, as if some primordial instinct picked up a sense of fear and danger.

"Do you go to this every month?" Joy half-asked, half-yelled to Cupidity.

"No, silly, every week!" Cupidity replied.

"And you wear a completely new outfit for each one?"

"Of course! Everyone who's anyone does!"

"Doesn't that get expensive?"

"Well, Avaritia always says, 'debt is nothing to be feared; it is the sail with which the visionaries move mighty vessels to their vision's end,' and who doesn't want to be on a big boat?" Cupidity replied, but looked somewhat furtive as she did so. Joy got the sense of some stress and discomfort, but the tram was not the environment to follow this up in conversation.

They disembarked at the Stadia, a colossal structure in concrete and glass into which thousands of people were still milling, like an ant farm that had a bit more geometric sense. Cupidity was tugging at Joy as she went; they crossed the forecourts and Cupidity started pulling off her walking shoes and putting on her heels. Joy commenced doing the same, but saw Cupidity throw the walking shoes into the bin.

"Hey, won't we need these later?" She asked. Cupidity waved dismissively.

"Returning won't need the rush, and we can always get more shoes. We can't be seen *carrying* items which detract from our first impressions, can we?"

"Well, I guess not-"

"*And,* look, everyone else has, too."

This was true; the bin had dozens of pairs of shoes, all appearing reasonably serviceable, some of which appeared to be entirely brand new to the naked eye.

"It just seems like a waste, you kn-" Joy started to say, but Cupidity was already tugging at her arm.

"Come *on*!" She said with a small note of frustration entering her usually sunny tones, "we'll miss the seats if we wait any longer!"

Stumbling in the new shoes and unfamiliar with the height of the heels involved, Joy allowed herself to be half-led, half-dragged through the bowels of the Stadia and down to an entrance tunnel that led through to the seating. As they reached the other side, Cupidity was visibly dismayed to see the higher seats already taken, probably many hours beforehand. These went from far above the stage to a point of being level with the stage; it was clear the less desirable seats descended below the performance platform, allowing the viewers to still see the speaker but limiting the speaker's ability to see them, and casting shadows down to the area. Although she was temporarily deflated, Cupidity nevertheless was resolute and took Joy down the concrete stairs to two available seats right next to the staircase itself. Cupidity took the seat farthest in, leaving Joy next to the stairs and beside a handrail. The position was about six feet below the stage, but there were many empty seats even further down with plenty of people still coming through the gates, and Joy could see her review the situation in her mind and decide that, whilst not ideal, the positioning could have been worse. They had a good view of the stage itself, even from the lower position. Joy settled back for the first time in what had been a number of rushed hours, and took in the room.

There was a susurration across the crowd, hushed and whispered conversations by thousands which sounded like the rise and fall of the ocean at night. Joy could make out small snippets of chats- what was Avaritia going to choose today? What was Now? What was Then? Do you remember the last one- and Joy had no idea who they were talking about- who is now running the largest shop in the Mall? Sure, but what about the other one who crashed and burned after a month because they were never able to catch lightning in a bottle again? How does Avaritia stay so on trend? Is today going to be our turn? Or the turn of someone we know? It created a strange kind of hungry pressure in the air, and Joy felt her heart rate start to quicken. Fear stood near the handrail on the concrete staircase next to Joy, scanning the crowd, and tapped her on the shoulder.
"Looks like a bit of work has come up," he said, "I'll be back."
Joy nodded, knowing it would be a hard thing to explain any dialogue to her hosting companion.

Cupidity was shifting in her seat, excited and nervous. "I'm sorry if I took too long to get us here," Joy said apologetically, even though everything had felt like a rush to an unknown finish line since she had met Cupidity outside the gates.
"Oh, don't worry about that, silly!" Cupidity bubbled, having returned to her default setting of Labrador-level enthusiasm. "Avaritia always says 'the place we deserve and the place we get are rarely the same, and the only way to align your destination is to believe in your heart that you deserve to be there, whatever it costs.'"
There were a thousand questions pressing on Joy's mind; who was this

Avaritia *really*? There was a level of fanaticism that Joy could see in Cupidity matched only by terrorists and Taylor Swift fans, but it wasn't even entirely unique. The same sense was palpable within the crowd, albeit to varying degrees, an undercurrent of barely-held-back mass hysteria that was waiting for the flashing lights to come on and say "cheer!"

"Do you know what a Pavlovian response is?" Fear asked, wandering back down the stairs.

"Uh-uh," Joy tried saying to herself with a slight shake of her head.

"Well, this guy, Pavlov, decided to train a dog by getting food, having the dog smell it, ringing a bell, then feeding it the food. Then he stopped giving it the food but would ring the bell and if the dog heard it, it would start salivating even if there was no food present."

"Mmh, hmmm," Joy responded.

"Which does beg the question whether every time *he* heard a bell, he thought about feeding a dog," Fear continued, "but I only mention it because-"

But before he could finish explaining the thought, all the lights suddenly cut out and the stadium went dark. A roar emerged from the crowd, not just the cheer of an audience, but the battle cry of a bunch of Scots in a Mel Gibson movie. It was like someone had found the exact point of Beatle-mania where the hysteria led to several windows being shattered, and dialled it back by exactly three and a half per cent. Then *wham!* The spotlights suddenly lit up the stage, and along the walkway came Avaritia, wearing white linens and some flowing half-scarf-half-cape thing that Joy had never seen before. The crowd's cheer remained, but was joined by a slowly building clap in unison, building up in intensity for each step their idol took towards the centre of the stage. The clapping's crescendo became a rabid applause right as Avaritia reached her podium, and beside

Joy Cupidity was smashing her hands together so hard that Joy was worried they'd somehow combust from the friction. Avaritia stood there for a moment, hands on either side of the podium, looking around the room and taking in the adoration. She slowly raised her hands over her head like a conductor, and then made a quick circular motion to signal for quiet. Silence descended so suddenly that it felt like a vacuum that had sucked all the air and noise out together; Joy felt her eardrums ache.

"Citizens of Luxoria," boomed Avaritia at last, "it's *so great* to see you all!" The crowd responded in unison, almost as liturgy, *"So great to see you too!"*

"Friends, do we worry about the past?" Avaritia called.

"There is only the now!" The crowd chanted.

"Friends, are you satisfied with today?" Avaritia almost sang, as her voice intonation slid upwards.

"There must be more tomorrow!" roared the audience.

"Friends, let me ask you this. We are together tonight. We are one. I have seen tomorrow, and do you know what it looks like?"

"Show us!" Came the crowd's shrieking response, a certain desperation now mixing with the excitement, and Joy noted the mastery and ease with which Avaritia had taken the assembly to the very edge of fever-pitch without tipping them over the edge, like a tight-rope walker who's got the wheelbarrow pushed halfway across.

"Friends! As you know, I'm just like you! I get tired, I get run down. I go from place to place and stretch myself too thin. And I know all of you out there know what I mean!"

"Yes!" The crowd cheered.

"To be at my peak, I consulted with my personal performance coach, because living your best life means getting help. She said I needed to juice cleanse, so my body could absorb more of nature's bounty, and that my sleep could be improved if I was going to manage the creativity I needed to turn visions into reality! So I went out, to find the best products-"

"Oh, dear lord," Fear said while Avaritia started revealing products on plinths lighting up one spotlight at a time, baskets of fruit and vegetables from named grocers, sleepwear and masks, a juicing machine which could fit a large pineapple or a small baby, "this is like one of those Instagram influenzas back home."

"Do you mean influencers?" Joy hissed quietly.

"No, I said what I said." Fear replied. "Because I swear it's catching, and a whole generation is filming themselves in their cars for some reason."

"... and yes, I can confirm that these wonderful suppliers will be offering a discount to you good people this week," Avaritia continued. "But being your best isn't simply about *feeling* your best. No, friends, you are not wilting flowers. You were destined to shine! And to shine, really, you need to ask yourself: is the radiance I adorn myself with, matching my inner beauty? If a picture is worth a thousand words, can you tell someone your life story with a glance? I believe that you can; no, friends, I believe that you *must*. And so-"

Joy tuned out again and Fear leaned across and whispered "you know, the strangest thing I've ever experienced is a unifying fear, and that's sometimes happened at places like Pompeii, or during those Japanese Tsunami events, or when people hear that supermarkets are out of toilet paper and then suddenly only want to buy toilet paper, you know, big cataclysmic events. There's panic and chaos but in amongst the minds of *all* the people there's just one unifying thought and it becomes just so big."

"And?" Joy whispered while keeping her eyes on the stage.

"Well, that's all I'm getting here. This entire crowd is afraid, but it's weird. They're not scared of something external; they're afraid that this woman won't like them somehow. I mean there's thousands of people and she couldn't possibly know them all, but the entire focus of their being is to please this woman. They want her to tell them how to live, what to wear, what to feel happy about, but all of it is because they think it'll make them visible to her, and she'll see they're living correctly, and like them for it. But if *everyone* is doing the same thing, how does anyone ever stand out enough to get her attention? It's like a snake that eats its own tail."

"I don't like it, it feels weird being here," Joy said.

"Well, you're not exactly a follower, you know," Fear said and then paused.

"Then again, you have to meet people to follow them, I guess."

"Oh, shush."

"Well, nothing's keeping you here, is it? Are you finding joy? Are you sitting down here still because you want to sit, or because everyone else is?"

"I don't know, maybe I'm scared people are going to look at me."

"Want that solved?"

"Sure. Fear, please take away my fear of being stared at by this crowd,

Fear reached across and plucked a Worm of Concern from her forehead.

"There," he said, dropping it into a new jar, "you now have the confidence of a massage oil salesman with Diddy's personal phone number. So, do you want to get out of here?"

Joy considered this. She didn't want to seem rude to her new friend, but she found Avaritia grated on every nerve she had. If there was one thing Joy hated, it was being told what to do. Cupidity was still staring at the stage, enraptured, so Joy nudged her and made a gesture indicating she was going to be getting up. Perhaps Cupidity assumed it was for the bathroom or something else, but she just signalled "OK" and returned her attention to the stage.

Joy stood up and stepped on to the staircase. On the stage, Avaritia must have noticed movement like a T-rex; she made a slight gesture and all of a sudden, a spotlight landed on Joy and every eye in the stadium turned to her. Fear, turning around, started laughing uncontrollably. Joy wanted to be mad, but at that point the dazzling brilliance was calling her like a moth coming across a search light.

"You!" called Avaritia from her podium. "Join me on the stage, please, friend."

It was not a quick trip to the stage access, and required going up the stairs and across one of the walkway rows while the whole room watched. The journey was filled with the whispers of the crowd on her way past felt like being called in front of the whole school assembly for farting out of turn, except the school had ten thousand people in it and the principal looked like a well-dressed serial killer. Looks of jealousy and curiosity caught her eye as she made her way to the final staircase that led to the stage, and as Joy reached the final approach, she hesitated. Fear, who had managed to gather himself together, came and stood beside her. Oddly, with the concern over people looking at her having disappeared, Joy merely felt uncomfortable and a little awkward. She took a deep breath.

"Hey, I'm right here," Fear said reassuringly. "And you don't have to go anywhere. We can leave right now, if you want."

Joy said nothing, but began climbing the stairs for what seemed like an eternity. Avaritia was standing before her, tall and imposing; she must have been three or four inches taller than Joy, exuding grace and elegance. Her smile to Joy was warm, but her eyes were an ice field, betraying no emotion at all but running rapid calculus second to second. It seemed like a computer, processing thousands of points of data, darting around sections of the room and returning prompts to the owner behind the eyes. She stepped forward and held out a hand.

"And you are?" she asked.

"Joy. Joy Summerfield," Joy replied nervously, extending a hand to shake. Avaritia raised it high and used it to twirl Joy around.

"That's *so great*. And tell me, Joy Summerfield," Avaritia continued, "*whom* are you wearing tonight?"

"Um, I got these clothes from Cupidity Cooper, at her shop, She's The Man?" Joy replied nervously, but still taking the opportunity to promote her newfound friend. Avaritia dropped her hand and spun away from her to address the audience.

"Friends!" she said enthusiastically, flinging a hand up dramatically, "there is someone here who understands what it means to project your true essence, your *brand*, your inmost self through your outward being. Someone who knows you need to leave a mark on every room you enter. Joy Summerfield, this radiant creature, stood out in the dark and I'm sure, as she caught my eye, that you can too! These clothes-" and here she paused, getting maximum crowd buy-in, "these clothes aren't today. They aren't *now*. They are *tomorrow*. They are *not yet*. And I tell you tonight friends, that I will be visiting She's The Man tomorrow, and encourage you to come and see me there!"

Avaritia flung her both hands up and the audience erupted into applause.

She then walked across to Joy, clapping as she did so, encouraging the audience to continue. When she got close to Joy, she put an arm congenially around her and waved to the crowd as photos were taken, leaning close and muttering through a smile that never left her face, "you might look good, but *nobody* walks out on me, girl. You got that? I make and break you hopefuls every week. Get back in your place and don't let me see you pull this kind of stunt again, or so help me I will turn this crowd against you so fast you won't be able to do up the buckles on your ridiculous shoes."

Joy felt a stone drop in her stomach, but stayed smiling as she looked around the audience. In her peripheral vision, she was keeping an eye out for Fear, whose face had darkened into a wrathful glower again. He had begun to move close to Avaritia, with his hands held up above her head, when she suddenly stepped forward to the podium and motioned to the crowd for silence.

"I'm afraid that's all we have time for tonight, friends! Go home safe, I can't wait to see you all again!"

And without even another glance towards Joy, Avaritia turned and walked off stage; music started up and the spotlight followed her out across the runway and through the curtains at the end. Joy was left to move awkwardly back to the staircase, as the enormous crowd started draining like a toilet being flushed.

Cupidity was standing at the bottom of the stairs, being bumped by the crowd but hopping up and down with excitement.

"Get ready for a very loud, very long vowel sound," Fear said to Joy as they made their way down the stairs.

"*Eeeeeeeeeeeeeeeeeeeeee!*" Cupidity exclaimed as soon as Joy was within arm's reach, grabbing her hands and jumping up and down. "I told you! You're an icon! This is it, it's finally happening! The future is going to be all about us!"

Joy was getting more disturbed by the second. She wasn't sure she *wanted* a future about "us"; internally she scolded herself for breaking her rule of never making proper friends. All she'd wanted was a shower, a bed, and a chance to wash some clothes, and now she had apparently fallen afoul of the most powerful person in the city *and* become a spokesmodel for clothes she'd never worn before today.

Joy felt lost and barely remembered the trip back to Cupidity's shop again; she was conscious of lots of excited and effusive words from her offsider, but it came at her like an underwater conversation. To be fair, this didn't seem to slow Cupidity down at all. Before she knew it, they were back in the apartment above the shop, with Joy sitting at the small table and Cupidity pacing as she nattered.

"...and I can't even *sleep* thinking that Avaritia herself is coming to *my* shop! Oh, my gosh, I'm going to have to get things ready, I can't have her come in if things look-"

"Uh, Cupidity?" Joy interrupted. "I'm really sorry but I'm *super* tired, would it be OK if I went to bed? I'll help you set up in the morning if you want."

"Oh, my gosh, I'm sorry!" Cupidity responded, as if snapping out of her trance. "Sure, yes, of course, I mean did you want anything to eat?"

"No thanks, I've lost my appetite," Joy replied.

"OK, well, you go get some rest. We have a big day ahead of us tomorrow!"

Joy brushed her teeth and when she went into her room, there was a new set of silk pyjamas on her bed, still in their plastic wrapping. She changed, keeping a mental note of the number of items she would have to pay for, and lay down in the dark, one lone window allowing a sliver of moonlight into her room.

"Fear?" she asked after a few moments had passed.

"Yes?" he said, emerging beside the window.

"What were you going to do to Avaritia?"

"Can't tell you."

"Why not?"

"Because it's not what I *was* going to do. It's what I *am* going to do."

"I don't think I like it here."

"Say the word and we're gone. But where will we be going?"

"Good point. I don't know, yet. I think on the main road there's a split between Securis and Aureus Creek, but then there's a diversion along the plains and I saw a couple of towns on the map there too.”

“Well, we’ve only been here for part of a short while. Maybe we can pick a destination tomorrow or later in the week, when you’re ready. I could use a couple of days here, though.”

“Why?”

“That’s private.”

“Well, good night, I guess.”

“Night.”

The bed was soft and pleasant enough, but Joy’s sleep was still fitful and she found herself awake as the sun started to rise. She could hear Cupidity downstairs already, moving things around and generally fussing. She hoped that Avaritia would not actually follow through on any of her promises; meeting that woman twice in twenty-four hours seemed like it may be a bridge too far.

Unfortunately, amongst whatever list of vices Avaritia had, tardiness was not among them. Joy kept a close eye on the street out her bedroom’s window. By eight-thirty, there was a throng outside the shop, a small red carpet laid out and a security team standing by. At 9am on the dot Avaritia arrived, flanked by a small team of attendants. She paused to be photographed outside the shop, and then swept inside, where Cupidity was waiting. Joy left her room and moved to the top of the stairs to eavesdrop.

“*Darling* child,” Avaritia said to Cupidity as she swept across the room, gesturing around the store, “how have you kept a jewel like this hidden?”

“Oh, ah-ha, it’s not really hidden, your grace,” bumbled Cupidity. “I wrote to you a few times and sent some samples, because I really live my life by what you say-”

“*Tom!*” Yelled Avaritia. One of the attendants, a similar age to Joy, came forward. He had mousey blonde hair and was neatly dressed as one would assume all the people in Avaritia's orbit would have to be. "Tom, *how* have this one *genius'* missives been going astray? Surely if a devotee has taken the time to correspond, you would have made me aware."

"My lady," Tom replied in a flattering tone, "you receive thousands of letters a week. Indeed, it does you credit how you respond to the people as often as you do."

"Of course it does. My question was not about my own capabilities, Tom. You are paid to ensure that the cream rises to the top, are you not? And yet this *gem* here was allowed to go unpolished."

"I'm sorry, my lady, there's only so many things we can-"

"Enough! We do not need more excuses for your failure. Leave us, this artist was about to work her magic."

Tom dutifully walked away, having taken the blame, and took himself to the back of the shop where he sat on the stairs until summoned again. Joy felt a pang of pity, and wandered down the stairs to sit next to him.

"Well, that was something," she said.

"Oh, no, that's nothing," Tom replied. "She *gets* the letters, and there's not a single product she hasn't opened. It just helps her brand if she's seen as always attentive to responses, but she never reads them and doesn't ever really reply unless there's a paid sponsorship. Those get sorted separately and get short-listed for the Launch events."

"Really?" Joy asked, surprised. "I thought she actually sampled products before the day."

"Oh, heavens no!" Tom replied with a chuckle. "Keeps, sure, but actually comments on? No, endorsements cost money; nothing's free in Luxoria! Unless you're Avaritia, of course."

"So why do you work for her? Is it just the money?"

"Oh, no, she doesn't pay me. I have to work on the side but I do get to keep products she doesn't want, or menswear items that are sent to her that she can't use, if they fit. You know, some general benefits. And if people know you work for Avaritia, they look after you."

"Doesn't that get tired?"

"Of course it does. But don't they say it's better the devil you know?"

"Than?"

"I don't know, honestly. Maybe knowing the devil makes him nicer? 'My, the brimstone is lovely today,' that kind of thing? Anyway, how much did it cost *you* to get up on the stage?"

"It didn't cost me anything, I just got here yesterday."

"What?" Tom asked, genuinely flabbergasted. "You know that kind of exposure is worth a *lot* of money."

"I mean, the clothes weren't even mine, my friend just gave them to me because mine were dirty-"

"Oh, yeah, nobody washes clothes in Luxoria," Tom replied sagely.

"... and yeah, you know, I was sort of swept up into the Launch and then was going to go and she spotted me and then..." Joy trailed off for a moment. "Here we are, I guess."

"If that's what happened, Avaritia must have been worried you'd take the attention away from her product spotlights. I have to admit, it's a smart pivot in the moment; if she acts like you were always going to stand up, then you're just part of the overall show instead and everyone will assume it's a clever plan."

"I guess," Joy conceded.

"But whoever dressed you must have been gambling on this," Tom continued, "because I mean, you stand out. Not to put too fine a point on it, but the blonde hair, the white top in the grey coat, the flash of colour in the scarf, plus I mean, not to be too bold, but you're *very* pretty. It doesn't matter if you're going to be sitting in the darker area below the stage, you stick out like a sore thumb. It's not exactly an accident. I don't know your friend myself, but unless she's the luckiest amateur in the world, I'd say she was banking on *something* drawing attention. After all, Avaritia's most well-known phrase is 'once you have their attention, you have their heart, and you should never share either.'"

"Is it really?"

"Look, Avaritia is the best marketer you'll ever meet. She's made this town what it is; there's so many cheap products because you'll *always* have a sale the next day. But she's an awful, *awful* person. And if she's got you marked, you should watch out."

Joy felt a sinking feeling. Had she been used? Did Cupidity actually like her or was she just a tool to get onto the stage?

"Tom!" Came Avaritia's voice. "Stop fraternising and come earn your money!"

Joy got up and walked through the curtain, in time to see Avaritia's entourage gathering boxes up and preparing to leave the shop. Tom followed her and hurried to the front counter to pick up anything that couldn't fit into arms of the existing staff members. There had to be thousands of dollars worth of clothes, Joy thought; nine or ten whole outfits, plus shoes. Avaritia saw her, and gave her a withering glance. "Still in the same clothes as last night, I see?" she said, turning to Cupidity. "You might want to upgrade your model, young lady. Tomorrow becomes yesterday with barely a warning, and I will *not* be seen wearing anything that *was*."

"What?" said Joy, but Cupidity bustled past and said "Thank you, thank you, Avaritia! I'll get her ready straight away!"

Cupidity turned to Joy and hissed "*Why are you wearing this again? Get rid of it and put on the clothes I left upstairs on the kitchen table.*"

Joy hadn't seen anything on the table, although she had primarily been in her room until Avaritia arrived and must have walked past it. Cupidity seemed much snappier than the previous day, although Joy could appreciate the stakes. She meekly agreed and went back up the stairs, where two boxes were on the table with clothes that looked, for all intents and purposes, the same as the ones she had worn the day before; slightly different cuffs, or a pleated line in a different location, but not substantively different. She could hear Avaritia downstairs saying to Cupidity, slightly muffled but clearly enough, "Darling, let me give you some free advice. An uncut diamond is always a good find, but if you want to stand out long term, roughness is going to be a problem. Either polish her, or cut her, but if you want to make your brand Number One, then *you* have to come first. Always. Otherwise you'll polish that diamond up and it'll try to outshine you. A word to the wise."

Taking some umbrage to this, Joy was about to come back and share a piece of her mind, but before she could make it down the stairs she heard Avaritia sweep out the shop and as soon as this happened, chaos descended and hundreds of shoppers crowded into the store. Joy put aside her feelings for a second, and entered the shop floor again, eager to help Cupidity. In amongst the bustle and the hubbub and the throngs of customers, she sweated and measured and watched the power of the king-maker sweep inventory right off the floor and into Cupidity's bank account.
Cupidity was frazzled, but delighted. At the end of the day, she said to Joy, "this is what things are going to be like forever now!"

And for a week, she was right.

Chapter 7

Love Me Like It's True

I hold my breath on every word from you

In the first week of frenzied trade, it seemed pretty clear that Cupidity had indeed "arrived". It was her time and she was ready for the limelight, blasting through inventory and enjoying the local newspapers that declared her brilliance. She enthused to Joy at the end of each tiring day of trade how *this* would be just the start; she had her eye on one of the main shops right near the Stadia, would deck it out with plenty of crystal chandeliers and deep red carpets and the feeling that when you were inside, you were royalty.

The days were so busy that Joy noticed Cupidity hadn't done any designing, as they eventually collapsed after dinner into well-earned exhausted slumber. Joy was happy to help her new friend, and Cupidity continued to provide fresh clothes each day, although Joy retained the items rather than throwing them out, much to Cupidity's chagrin.

Joy stayed home during the next Launch event. Cupidity asked her to come along, but conceded that she didn't have any 'now' outfits for Joy to model and, although she would not admit it to Joy, was aware that lightning was unlikely to strike twice and Avaritia did not offer spots on stage for free. It seemed she was actually, relieved that Joy stayed home.

On her return that evening, Cupidity said there had not been any new fashion items in the spotlight, and seemed relieved.

In the second week, a large amount of replacement inventory arrived. Joy was concerned at the quantity, but Cupidity explained that they were on their way to the top of the fashion field and needed to meet their loyal fans' demands. Joy wasn't sure how many loyal fans there were after a week, but it wasn't her business, she decided, in both senses of the word.

Trade was quieter, but still with fairly heavy patronage. Joy felt there was a bit more time to breathe compared to the suffocating crush of the first week, and found herself during the day chatting away with Cupidity about her dreams and plans. Cupidity's certainty of her success and her incredible optimism was matched with a lack of caution that Joy felt found refreshing. It enabled quick and bold decision-making to be taken in the moment and Joy was so busy keeping up that it was only ten days after the first Launch event that she realised she had hardly heard from Fear. She wasn't especially worried; in fact, she was surprised it had taken her so long to notice the absence. Maybe it was a good thing. He seemed busy elsewhere, and at her request had stayed out of the shop during business hours so that Joy could focus on her work and support her friend's rise to success, which didn't lend itself to a lot of crossover moments for the two of them,

She wondered if this was the secret to joy- not having to over-think things, being the darling of the moment, anticipating the next new thing that would replace an old thing, a world of constantly changing experiences.

On the third week, however, foot traffic had dropped to a crawl. On Wednesday, right at the end of trading hours, there was a knock at the door. Joy opened it up and in swept a member of Avaritia's entourage, a stern-looking woman in her early thirties with a severe-looking outfit, the kind of power clothes reserved for high-profile lawyers and the sort of accountants who either know where the bodies are buried or are in the process of burying them. She invited herself upstairs and sat down with Cupidity and Joy at the kitchen table, although she never once looked at Joy directly throughout her visit. In even-toned, dispassionate voice, she matter-of-factly noted that Avaritia's generosity had elevated She's The Man to the main stage in a single instance, but that grace had limits. For continued promotion in the future, she explained, it was incumbent upon Cupidity to prepare an entirely new product set before the Launch that Saturday, and pay an endorsement fee of twenty-five thousand dollars.

Cupidity was shocked. Up until now, she truly seemed to have been convinced that these were genuinely merit-based endorsements made out of interest and support for the innovations of the citizenry.

"That's more money than I made last week!" Cupidity protested as Joy brought tea to the table. "I won't be able to afford to make new clothes if I can't buy materials!"

"Well, these are your choices," the woman replied calmly, unmoved. "You're still making money now, yes? As Avaritia says, if you aren't investing in you, you can't expect a dividend. I'm sure you can find a way; extend your credit perhaps. Defer the terms with your suppliers. Or you can always remain the small business that never really managed to *become* what it was destined to be."

"But I can't possibly complete a whole range of clothes in two days!" Cupidity protested. "Even if I *could* get the money!"

The woman sipped her tea.

"Young lady," she said firmly as she put her cup down on the saucer, "the terms have been provided to you. Their fairness is not our problem. They are set. Friday night for the products and the payment. If your dreams are worth it, you will make it happen. Good day to you."

She pushed her chair out, but left her cup where it was, and let herself out.

Cupidity looked absolutely panicked. It was the first time Joy had seen her without her sunny disposition, and she excused herself to use the bathroom but assured Cupidity that she would be right back. Once inside the bathroom, she whispered for Fear, who walked through the door with his hands over his eyes.

"Take your hands off your eyes, idiot, I'm not actually using the bathroom!" she hissed. "What's she going to do? There's no *way* those terms are fair."

"Of course they're not," Fear replied with a shrug. "But what's fair got to do with it? You think they don't know this is an impossible ask? This is a shake-down. Your friend has had a taste of the good life, but can't hang on to it, and the blood is in the water. The sharks are going to come and take everything she's made and she'll run herself into the ground trying to hang on to the last vestiges of her dream. Even if she makes deadline this week, it'll be the week after, and the week after that."

"Do you think Avaritia does this to everyone?"

"I couldn't say. But if I were to hazard a guess, it probably depends who you are to her; the larger businesses are a bit like sheep, which she can shear regularly. They'll have teams working on the products and the impact of the fees won't be as hard to manage, so she'll look for longer-term partnerships. The smaller ones, like your friend, are more like gazelles; you run it to ground and then you feast. That woman you met? She's a lioness, and she's out on the hunt. You should see her mind; it's like a knife, cold and refined for a single purpose, no emotion, no concern. She's probably a bit more motivated to crush it since you're involved, too."

"What's with all the animal metaphors? Have you been watching nature documentaries again?" Joy asked.

"There was a good one on World's Most Dangerous Predators before we left. I was only watching to see if Epstein was mentioned, but he wasn't."

"So what do I do? I should tell Cupidity they're out to ruin her, right?"

"Yeah, great idea," Fear said sarcastically. "Your friend, who thinks she has a winning lottery ticket, is *absolutely* going to listen to advice to abandon her dream after a couple of weeks of the sweet life. She'll ignore everything she's built her beliefs on over the years because of the redemptive power of friendship. They'll make a movie and a heroic dog will be involved. Ryan Reynolds will probably even voice it."

"Well, what do *you* suggest?"

Fear shrugged nonchalantly.

"Let her make her own mistakes. Let her *own* her own mistakes. She's terrified of losing it all, but I mean, the popularity was artificial rather than organic. As a consequence, it's either going to be given away, or it's going to be taken. Better not to be part of the process, really."

"I can't do that!"

"Well, I'm glad we had this talk. It was absolutely worth the time."

Joy emerged from the bathroom, to see Cupidity already sitting down at a pad and scribbling furiously. There were already crumpled-up balls of paper littering the floor.

"Hey," she said gently, "maybe you can tackle this tomorrow when you've had a chance to think about it?"

Cupidity looked up with a crazed look in her eye, properly frazzled for the first time Joy had seen her.

"If I order materials tomorrow and they arrive on Friday then I can sew all Friday night and into Saturday to get them down to the Launch!" she enthused madly.

"Sure," said Joy soothingly, "but wasn't the deadline Friday night regardless?"

"They'll have to be flexible!" Cupidity replied sharply. "They want me, they'll have to work to my time table!"

"I mean, that woman didn't *seem* very flexible to me," Joy replied doubtfully. The frenetic activity continued, so Joy tried appealing to reason, which is the first mistake in an emotional situation. "If you think about it, if you *do* pay the money, and got the clothes made in time, do you then have to do this every week?"

"I don't know!" said Cupidity, exasperated and flinging a pen down. "Do you know how long I've waited for an Avaritia endorsement? You saw the crowds! I have a lot of work to do and you're not helping!"

"I'm just saying, if you're giving all the money you worked for to Avaritia to promote your work, does it actually help you to-"

"Oh my gosh, *shut up*!" snapped Cupidity angrily. "She's giving me a chance, you know how many people want that? She's doing *me* a favour, and it's up to me to earn it, and what she said was right, so I'm going to do this and it's going to be *so great*!"

Joy was taken aback by the harshness of the tone. Fear had been right, which was frustrating, and so she resolved to say nothing about the incident in order to at least deny him the opportunity to crow.

Cupidity didn't sleep in the next day. The quietness of the store opened up some time for her to rush to her mannequins and sewing machines and put her concepts together, after darting around suppliers for fabric and additional materials. However, it seemed that the pressure was wearing and she often undid hours of work, cursing as she did so, or attempted to repurpose existing items. Joy tried again to get a breakthrough the following afternoon.

"Hey, these look *so* great," she said admiringly about the half-finished items, bringing in a sandwich and a glass of water for her friend who hadn't eaten anything that day.

"No, they're not enough! They're not going to suit Avaritia!"

"I mean, look, you already gave her a full wardrobe of clothes and things, do you really need to pay her and do it again? Surely she could use one of those and still take the fee? People are still coming in today, too; maybe you don't need the latest endorsement?"

"You don't under*stand*," wailed Cupidity, "if you're not current you don't exist. People have, like, seen the styles in the store already. This is my break and I'm going to take it, and I can't waste time talking to you about it again!"

"Well, I mean, do you want me to wear the clothes instead?"

"No! When I saw you I knew you'd be right for the designs I already had, but I need to make Avaritia *pop* now and that has to be *perfect*!"

Joy took this information in without changing her expression. Had her new-found friend just picked her at the gate hoping to get attention at the Launch? Had Tom been right, and all of this was self-serving? Cupidity continued muttering to herself and working away and so Joy left her alone;

she wanted to tug at that thread but at this point in time a whole curtain would unravel.

As Friday came around, Joy couldn't find Cupidity at all. She ran the shop on her own, and customers still trickled in, but it was easy to see why her friend would be worrying about popularity and why being current was so important in this town. There was a slight uptick in trade towards the late afternoon and Joy assumed people going to the Launch would be wanting to be seen in what was still apparently on-trend, although it bothered her selling clothes knowing that there was a certainty this status would change in twenty-four hours, whatever the outcome of Cupidity's efforts.

Close to 5pm, Cupidity returned with a large bag, looking exhausted and stressed and entirely flustered. Her cheeks were bright red and she flung the bag onto the nearest counter. Inside were folded clothing items and a canvas money bag.

"I need you to take this in to Avaritia's offices," she said to Joy without so much as a hello. "We're out of time and I'm too tired to go myself."

"Sure," Joy said soothingly, "but are you *certain* this is what you want to do? We had a good day today. If we keep that momentum..."

"Just *do* it, please?!" snapped Cupidity, tired of this conversation repeating and collapsing onto a chair. Chastened, Joy dutifully took the bag and left the store. Fear was waiting outside and started walking with her as soon as she emerged from the door.

"Well," he said as she hurried through the streets down to the tram stop, "at least we get to ride the light rail again!"

Joy said nothing, waiting for the I-told-you-so that had no doubt been brewing for days.

"Still a very pleasant evening," Fear observed, as they headed down the cobbled street sections and around the corner to the view towards Stadia, where the evening sky opened up and sunset painted vivid colours right as the street lights started to come on. "Say what you like about the city, but the view is good."

Joy remained silent.

"Soooooooo…" Fear continued amiably, "telling your friend she was making a mistake went well, I see."

"Shut up."

"The wise counsel of a good friend is a balm on troubled times."

"Shut up."

"Yes, an observation from a trusted confidante will guarantee-"

"Shut *up!* Cupidity didn't listen to anything I said, okay?" Joy said, exasperated. Fear just grinned at her.

"Who said anything about Cupidity? *I* was talking about *you,* and my very smart advice which has been entirely ignored."

"She's going to lose everything!" Joy protested. Fear just nodded.

"Possibly," he conceded, "maybe even probably. But what are you going to do? Make it your fault? It happens one way or the other; she's put her head in the jaws of the lion, do you really think you're fast enough to pull it out without losing an arm yourself?"

"So what do *you* think I should do, O Wise One?" Joy replied sarcastically. Fear just shrugged.

"Hey, you made this bed. I guess you can only do what you said you would. Or, y'know, we can leave? Your joy isn't here, you know that. You were meant for more than working in a clothing shop."

"I enjoy it!"

"Do you?"

"I have a friend, she needs me, and I don't have time to listen to your nonsense!"

Fear just shrugged. "Ah, it's always good giving considered suggestions to a friend when they're in the middle making a mistake."

"*Your* answer is to run away," Joy retorted as they boarded the tram. "I'm not my mother, you know."

"A strategic withdrawal isn't running away," Fear protested calmly, but Joy went on the attack.

"Oh really?" she retorted aggressively. "You're the personification of fear. All you *do* is make people run away from things. And now you're trying to get me to run away from someone who needs me. Well, my dad stayed, and he suffered through things to give me a chance at finding my purpose, and so *I'm* going to stay and help Cupidity."

She knew it was harsh, but Fear just shrugged at her.

"Anthropomorphisation," he corrected. "Also, you're not here to find your purpose, you're here to find your joy."

"They're the same thing!"

"No. They're not."

Joy fumed until she reached the requisite stop; the Stadia still was an imposing structure, but it was strangely hollow without the crowds surging through it. There was signage towards the administration areas and a large concrete set of stairs that went up through the bowels of the building and eventually deposited Joy outside a pair of beautiful walnut doors with ornate gold-coloured handles. Joy wasn't sure if this was just polished brass or actual, real-life gold; given the money that changed hands within, she wouldn't put the latter out of the realms of possibility. She took a deep breath as she grasped the handle.

"I'm going to do this alone, thank you," she said to Fear primly. "I don't need distractions in an important meeting. Stay out back, please."

"Out back? Whatever you say," Fear replied over her shoulder as she stepped inside. "I wouldn't want to cramp your style while someone's ripping your friend off."

There was an ornately patterned carpet beyond the doors, with deep reds and oranges and a thick pile that was incredibly soft, deadened the sound within the room compared to the concrete exterior and made you feel like you were about to see royalty with each silent footfall.

There was an antechamber that was decorated beautifully, tastefully lit with glass display shelving encased in oak cabinetry around the room, displaying a variety of products that had been acquired over the years. There was a gold inscription on the wood panelling above which proclaimed "A History of Luxoria's Greatest Innovations" but given the volume of goods that came through for promotion, Joy presumed these were in fact products of the major sponsors only. Near the rear wall, before another pair of doors which presumably went into the inner sanctum, there was a hardwood reception desk and, to Joy's surprise and delight, it was currently staffed by Tom. She had been worried that the horrible lady who had delivered the demands to Cupidity would be her first point of contact.

Tom looked up from the paperwork he was attending to, and smiled brightly.

"Well, well, if it isn't our favourite shining star!" he said warmly. "How is the queen of the spotlight?"

"Oh, shush," she said, blushing, "it was one very strange moment. You're not going to make fun of me every time now, are you?"

"Hey, you rocked Avaritia's boat for a moment, and that's enough for me," Tom replied with a smile. "I'll call you whatever you want after that!"

"Joy's fine," she said, returning his smile, hooking her hair back over her ear and still blushing deeply.

"Well, Joy, you did pique my curiosity. You said the other week that you were a recent arrival."

"You remember that?"

"Sure. In a world of people desperate to be the next Avaritia, it's always memorable to meet someone doing their own thing. And washing their own clothes, even."

Joy blushed again. "It seems just such a *waste* to throw everything away. We didn't have a lot of money when I was growing up and we always had to make things last. But here... everyone has so much *stuff.* And I mean, how much do you really need?"

"It's a fair argument," Tom said, "but where abouts did you grow up? One of the other cities?"

Joy gave him a cliff-notes version of her background story; Pleasant lane, growing up with her dad, Fear, finding a flying boat, arriving in Frieland. A part of her was surprised at herself, because hearing herself talk about an invisible friend and rowing through storm clouds did sound like the ramblings of a madwoman. Maybe it was the trustworthy face, or the way her heart seemed to flutter when they made eye contact, that made her so open. Tom, however, gave undivided attention and, aside from a few three-word clarification questions, offered no interruptions.

"So, to be clear," he said once she had finished, "you went on this whole adventure with absolutely no plan and no preparation and on your first day here in Luxoria, you managed to wind up at the centre of the biggest stage in the city, having stolen the spotlight from the most dangerous woman you could meet?"

"Well, when you put it like *that...*" Joy conceded. "It does sound a bit far-fetched."

"And is your friend with us in the room right now?"

"Fear? No, I made him stay out back."

"So, the personification of fear itself does what you tell it to do?"

"Well, *he* says he's an anthropomorphisation, and he doesn't do *everything* I say, but I mean, I guess, he does a lot for me. Mostly he annoys me. I mean, on purpose. I think he just likes to hang around because I can see him, honestly."

Tom looked astounded. "Well," he said at last, "that's the most amazing thing I've ever heard. And you're trying to find...?"

"Joy."

"You didn't have a mirror?" he said with a grin.

"Ha, ha," Joy said sarcastically. "Nobody's *ever* made that joke before. And lived."

Tom just smiled and then his eye caught the clock on the wall and he shook himself.

"Well, Joy, fascinating though this has been, what can I do for you today to help you on this journey?" Tom asked.

"I've brought Cupidity Cooper's clothing and sponsorship payment for Avaritia," she replied, snapping back to the reality of the task and hauling the bag up onto the counter. Tom pulled it towards him and opened it up. "It's always best to check the goods first," he said as he rummaged through the bag, "ordinarily the rule is for you to drop off and walk away, but I just think it would be a terrible thing for a sponsorship to go to waste. Avaritia's terms are pretty clear: she does not alter products submitted, and payments are not refundable."

He took out the sack containing the payment and set it on the desk, then pulled out the clothing. It was clear that Cupidity had put her heart and soul in; the fabrics were beautiful, in a variety of colours and options that she thought would complement Avaritia. Blouses, skirts, pants, and a few jacket and coat options were all included, given the colder weather of late. There was a beautiful, bright red full-length waterproof coat, something that would stand out in a storm on a rainy day, lined with white piping and sporting oversized buttons, which would stand out like a sore thumb on that stage set amongst the concrete of the stadium. From a design perspective, Cupidity had shot for the moon.

Joy couldn't see anything obviously wrong, until Tom started shaking each one out.

On one blouse, a button was missing. Worse, a blazer's sleeve had been sewn to the body of the jacket at the pocket. A pant leg had been hemmed slightly higher than the other; barely noticeable, really, especially if they were being worn, but it was apparent that the time pressures and lack of sleep had led to a few issues. Tom shook his head.

"Look, I shouldn't be telling you this, but Avaritia won't accept this. It's too good an opportunity for her to double the sponsorships; she'll take the payment, say the clothes weren't up to standard, then take *another* sponsorship from someone else at the last minute, and make the original designer pay again the following week."

"But that'll ruin my friend's store!" Joy protested.

Tom looked sympathetic, checked around the room conspiratorially, and started folding the items back into the bag before carefully placed the money back on top. He pushed the bag across the counter and lowered his voice.

"Look, I could get in trouble for this, but Avaritia isn't here right at the moment. She doesn't need to know you came in. Take this all and go back to your friend. She might be able to get in on another week if she's lucky. Or, she might not, but at least she isn't going to be broke at the same time."

"Oh my gosh, thank you so much!" Joy enthused, genuinely moved. "That's so kind of you!"

"I don't know if it's kind, but I'm sick of seeing people get taken for a ride. Maybe it's time I did something about it."

"Will you get in trouble?"

"That depends if Avaritia finds out. But hey, she isn't paying me, what's the worst she can do?"

"Aren't you scared of her?" Joy asked, a little incredulous. Tom thought about this.

"Everyone is scared of her," he said after a beat, "but... if I'm honest, right now I'm more concerned about what *you* think of me than what she does." Joy blushed again, and looked down at the counter and back up at Tom.

"Well... I mean, I'd better... you know, this needs to go back to the shop and..." she stammered, but Tom stood up, took her hands, and placed them on the bag.

"It would have been nice to see you, Joy," he said with a wink. "What a shame you were never here."

Joy took the bag and walked back to the main doors. Fear was leaning against the wall on the other side as she left, a huge grin on his face and, for some reason known only to him, an Akubra hat with corks dangling down. She was not sure where he got such things, or where they went when he was finished with them.

"Croikey," he said with a mock Australian accent, thick and brash, "I was just here in the outback and wouldja look at that? Someone's got the *hots* for you big time, luv. You sure you didn't wanna grab a quick pash out the back of the servo?"

"What are you *on* about?"

"Look, luv, you're a sheila and he's a bloke. Youse would be a match made in Bunnings."

"What's a Bunnings?"

"It's a hardware store that Australians consider to be the closest thing to heaven."

"Why?"

"Probably because it's so hot there they assume they're already in hell."

"What's your point?"

"You liiiiiiiiiiike him," Fear said whilst clasping his hands to his chin and battering his eyelashes, which made his makeshift hat bob back and forth into his eyes. "Ow! Stupid corks. Wait. *Why* do you still have that bag?"

"I thought you knew everything," Joy replied sullenly.

"You asked me to stay out back. Then I had to go find this hat. Explain."

"There was a problem with the clothes. Tom said that they'd keep the money and not wear the garments. He let me take the bag back to save Cupidity's shop."

"Oh? A gentleman to the core. I approve. And your friend, whose future is riding on you having completed the task, will think...?"

"I'm sure she'll be grateful!"

"Oh, yes. That will definitely, one hundred per cent be the case."

It was not, in fact, the case. When Joy returned with the bag, Cupidity looked ashen. Her lack of sleep already had her eyes looking sunken and her face pale, but whatever colour was left drained entirely as soon as she saw Joy bearing anything other than good news. Joy tried to explain the situation, but nothing was talking Cupidity off her ledge.

"I ask you for *one thing!*" Cupidity yelled, after asking for something every day for the past fortnight. "One thing and you can't even support me!"

"Look, *this* one has a sleeve sewed to the body and *this* one has a shorter leg and *this* one is missing a button," Joy protested, holding up the offending clothing. "I was told that Avaritia would take the money and wouldn't wear the clothes if they weren't up to snuff."

"Avaritia wouldn't do that! She's helping me make my dream come true! She'd have let me come down and fix these if you'd told her! I can't believe you would do this to me!"

"I'm sorry! I didn't want you to lose the promotion *and* the money-"

"*Stop lying about Avaritia!*" Cupidity screamed. "She wouldn't do that! You've ruined everything!"

They stood there, Cupidity panting, Joy looking taken aback. Fear leaned in and whispered "you can lead a horse to the astrophysics table but you can't make it do advanced calculus."

After a few tense moments passed, Joy tried to be conciliatory and said "maybe we'll still be OK."

"*We* won't," snapped Cupidity. She was right.

The following Launch had no mention of She's The Man. Someone new was the darling of the moment, the Vision of Now, and whatever other moniker Avaritia used to convince people there was no other place they could buy from. Foot traffic fell to virtually nothing. There was the odd person who had their curiosity piqued when Joy had first taken the stage who still popped a head in here or there, but they came through like a tumbleweed through an empty Western town. Avaritia's representative didn't return to offer a further sponsorship.

Cupidity had said nothing further to Joy all week. Joy had tried cooking for them both in the evening and asking preferential questions for drinks and accompaniments, but Cupidity only made "mmmf" noises or got items herself.

Joy was devastated at the sudden change in their relationship. She had never quite felt at home with Cupidity's vision, but she had enjoyed feeling helpful and purposeful and Cupidity's enthusiasm had always, if nothing else, made her feel appreciated. Try as she might, however, her interactions only seemed to inflame the tensions. Joy began to wonder if she had broken the friendship completely; she and Fear talked when it felt safe to do so, and

Joy had voiced her concerns about leaving while things were bad between them and putting Cupidity in an awkward position. Fear pointed out that the friendship itself hadn't taken her any closer to finding joy, and the purpose of the journey was more than just finding someone to connect with. Whilst Joy knew Fear was right, the thought of just walking away from things galled her. She felt acutely that such a move would put her in the category of being an abandoner, and this picked at childhood scabs that she had thought were scars but clearly still had the capacity to open into the old wounds of her younger self. It was an intense feeling of being trapped by the pressure of both options, neither of them seeming good. However, Joy had also started feeling the restlessness in her feet, and Fear had noted that this couldn't be ignored forever.

At the end of the fourth week after she had been at her first Launch event, however, there came a knock at the door, after hours. Cupidity had gone out, but as she wasn't speaking to Joy at that time, Joy was unaware of her destination or return time. Joy had been downstairs finishing some new arrangements of the clothing and giving the store a dust to fill the time. Hearing the knocking, she checked the peep-hole and was surprised to see that it was Tom.

Joy was aware of her heart rate quickening and her palms becoming clammy. Fear hovered nearby and said "well, he doesn't seem to have an axe or anything, so the odds that he's here for some kind of murder-suicide plot are pretty thin. You may as well let him in."

"Oh, shut up, you just *love* making everything seem terrible!" she hissed back. "What if he's here on Avaritia's behalf?"

Fear stuck his head through the door, and then pulled it back.

"I doubt that very much," he said.

"Why?"

"Because he's carrying a suitcase."

Joy opened the door and, sure enough, there was Tom with a large tan suitcase beside him, still dressed neatly but with a few concessions towards the casual; no tie, a long coat instead of a suit jacket, and sensible walking shoes rather than dress shoes. He was holding a cardboard tray with three cups in it.

"Hi," he said a little nervously, "could I come in? I'd like to have a word with you. And your friend too, but... mainly you. I brought coffee. I don't know if you drink it."

"Uh, sure, come through," Joy replied uncertainly. "I don't really drink much coffee but I appreciate the thought."

He entered, and they both stood in the middle of the room in an awkward silence, not knowing who was supposed to speak first.

"I've been thinking about you," he said at last, breaking the silence. "I haven't seen you since you came into the office."

"Yeah, well, Cupidity didn't get the promotion and so we've been pretty quiet here. She blames me. Maybe she should."

Tom nodded, though not to Joy's self-blame. "I thought that might have been the case," he said. "I don't think your friend should do another sponsorship. But if it's what she *really* wants, I got her another shot."

He pulled a small bundle of papers from his pocket.

"There's a space in this week's programme," he continued, "and it's up to her if she wants to fill it. The fee is always the fee, but this revised contract at least guarantees promotion, if she can get down there by the end of the week. I added a few paragraphs in and put it in with the other offers going out to vendors; Avaritia signed it and didn't read it through first, but at least if she changes her mind about promoting, your friend can get her money back."

"Oh my gosh, thank you!" Joy gushed, overwhelmed with gratitude. "But won't that get you in trouble?"

"Well, I don't see how I could. I'm leaving," he replied, looking nervous. Joy tried to remain calm and play things cool, although her heart had started racing again.

"Oh, really?" she tried to ask nonchalantly. "You quit your job?"

"I did that too. I left my resignation on the desk and went home and packed a bag."

"You're leaving your *house?*"

"I'm leaving this city. With you. I mean, if you don't mind me coming along for a bit. See, after you came in the other day, I couldn't stop thinking about how you packed up and left everything on a whim. I think it's the bravest thing I'd ever heard, and then I started thinking about what I was doing, and I realised *I* was afraid; afraid of not being able to blame my unhappiness on my job, or on Avaritia. Afraid of change where responsibility could be put at my feet. I realised that I'd just given up control because I liked the perks and I could put the negatives at the feet of someone else. But you... you just left, in a boat you found in passing, and flew. I mean, it's the stuff of madness, really, but it's profoundly brave. Maybe the only difference between madness and bravery is success. So, I finally thought: I want to be someone like that."

"Really?"

"Well, no. I actually thought: I want to be *with* someone like that." It was Tom's turn to blush now, and he put his hands up and stammered "I mean, I want to go with someone like and and learn something. Have my own adventure. Be fearless. Except, you know, you bring Fear with you."

"I don't bring him," Joy replied with a smile, "he brings himself."

"Well, I took a chance anyway," Tom continued. "I don't suppose you're looking for a travelling companion?"

"*Another* travelling companion," sniffed Fear haughtily. "It's like he doesn't even see me."

"He *doesn't* see you, Fear. He can't," Joy replied.

Tom raised an eyebrow.

"Oh," Joy said, embarrassed, "Fear was just saying it would be another travelling companion. Because he's here too."

"My apologies," Tom said, looking over Joy's shoulder at where he thought Fear was, incorrectly as it turned out.

"Can I sit down to think about this for a moment?" Joy asked, gesturing to a couple of single ottomans near the change rooms. Tom nodded, and they moved across to the stools. Fear leaned up against the wall over Tom's shoulder, arms folded across his chest. Joy took a deep breath.

"I want Cupidity to be my friend again," she said to Tom. "I'm not sure if she will, but the contract is a huge help and I really appreciate it."

"You're welcome," said Tom. "Go on."

"Fear said the other day that I need to follow my feet and I think he's right. I guess, Tom, I'm not as brave as you thought; I've been scared of letting go of something I didn't know how to fix."

"Hey," Fear soothed, "this hasn't been your fault, Sparky."

"I don't think this is your fault," said Tom, who could not hear Fear, "but everyone here wants to be told what to do, what they should want, what they *need*, and they all want a moment in the spotlight. I mean, that's what *I* thought I wanted, until you made the point: it's all just stuff. We're so attached to it that we never ask what we actually need and when I packed my suitcase, I was surprised at how much I *didn't* need. Not everyone is going to see it that way, though, and your friend might not be ready for that."

Joy nodded.

"I think..." she said after a few seconds of thought, "that you're both right. I do need to go. But I don't want to leave without at least saying goodbye."

"When is she coming back?" Tom asked.

"I don't know."

Tom left a gap in the conversation to allow her to think, and Joy appreciated that there wasn't any pressure put on her in that moment.

"Let me go and start packing some things," she concluded, "and we'll see if Cupidity comes back in between."

It felt strangely final and also strangely freeing as Joy packed up her room. Her bag couldn't hold much and it was clear that the overflow of clothes where Joy's frugality clashed with Cupidity's insistence on new items daily would mean tough decisions would need to be made. For pragmatism, Joy packed a long coat, to double as a pillow if worse came to worst, along with several pairs of the pants/blouse combination that had become her uniform of sorts at the store. She still hadn't been told by Cupidity how much the clothes cost, but she also hadn't been paid for working, and although she felt there might have been a small gap between the living allowances, clothes, and wages she had no idea how much it would be. This weighed on her mind as she packed up the rest of the room, changed the sheets and made the bed presentable. Finally, she took a pair of practice walking shoes, and put these on.

As she did so, she was aware of a sudden sense of relief. The weight of the fractured friendship had come to the point where it had pinned her in place, and it was as if the act of doing up the shoes had finally thrown that off and her feet had again discovered their purpose; she felt a pull in them, an excitement and energy that already led away from the town. A part of her realised that these two components had been fighting each other these past few weeks and the resolution of that inner turmoil was significant. Another part of her whispered that it was also interested in finding more about her new travelling companion, and she felt some guilt in hearing these whispers, as if she were a treasure hunter knocking one statue off a scale and replacing it with replica, hoping nobody would notice. Her frustrations as Cupidity's responses, silence, and the unfairness of the situation had eroded more than Joy had been willing to admit to herself, but the internal whispers continued that perhaps *this* new person had real possibilities.

About half an hour had passed before Joy returned downstairs, bag in hand and ready to go. Cupidity had still not returned. Tom was sitting on the same chair as before, relaxed but expectant. He looked up at her and smiled as she came down the last few steps.

"You look great," he said, half without thinking, and then blushed. "I mean, you look really organised. But also... you look great. Say what you want but your friend knows how to dress you. She deserves that spot on the stage."

It was a very awkward compliment for Joy, and she shifted uneasily whilst also blushing in return. "Thanks, I think," she said.

Fear rolled his eyes. "This kid's more awkward than walking in on your parents havin-"

"*And* since Cupidity isn't back," Joy continued sharply, glaring at Fear "I think it's a good time to leave, or we're going to lose daylight before we reach the next town. I guess all I can do is write a note."

She felt hypocritical about this, but also a sense of relief; it was easier to say things to someone when they weren't there. She took a piece of paper from behind the counter, and an envelope.

Dear Cupidity,

I'm sorry to leave like this. I'm sorry that I seem to have caused a problem with your dream, with Avaritia, with all of it. There is a new opportunity for you in an envelope and I don't know if it makes up for the one you've lost because of me, but I hope something comes out of it because you really do love what you do and I really wish I loved anything that much.

Thank you for being my friend. If you want to go after this opportunity, take the contract in the envelope under this and the clothing once it's fixed and give it to whoever is assisting Avaritia. You know what I think about it all, and I really hope that in the end, you prove me wrong.

I've left some money for the clothes.

-Joy.

She took, from her cash reserves, two hundred local dollars. It seemed like a lot, but simultaneously not enough. Both went into the envelope and she put this on the counter along with the contract Tom had brought. Next to this pile of documents, she put the still-warm coffee cup; it would likely be stone cold by the time it was seen, but it was part of the gesture.

She turned around and Tom was standing by the door, his suitcase in one hand, and his elbow proffered towards Joy.

"Shall we?" he asked, hoping to sound debonair and instead sounding like Mr. Darcy had been hit in the head with a croquet ball.

"After *me*," said Fear haughtily, tossing his imaginary hair over his shoulder and brushing past Tom walking out the door. Joy, hesitating for a moment and allowing excitement to build, put her arm inside Tom's.

Joy felt elated. They stopped at the city's outskirts to buy water and some food, and through that journey from Cupidity's store to the little take-away shops, Tom mainly talked about the upcoming Launches and his increasing gratitude to be away from the centre of the town. However, he was also an excellent listener and as they walked away from the town, Joy found herself opening up in ways she hadn't ever imagined. The sun was shining, the air was clear, the day was full of possibilities, and a handsome young man was interested in her. Joy started talking about *everything*; her mother's departure, her worries about her dad's ability to cope without her, her inability to really connect with people at school, Fear's assurances that there was something different about her that she simply couldn't see, the pressure to have a purpose she couldn't identify and to find a joy she wasn't entirely certain truly existed.

It was a lot of topics, but her mother featured heavily. Joy realised that perhaps she was being unkind, but she hadn't had the opportunity to actually voice her anger at the cowardice she perceived behind the departure, at the responsibility left to put the mess back together that neither her father nor she had made, at the *selfishness* behind telling someone that your dreams of the adulation of strangers was more important than their need for you in their life. Hours passed on the road out of the city, over hills and dales, past small farming communities as they made their way to Securis, and Joy didn't want the time to stop. Fear took her aside when they stopped for a brief water break as the afternoon's sun got fairly low in the sky.

"Hey," he said, "about what you said today."

"Yes?"

"I mean I *knew* you felt that way. I knew what you were afraid of. But... I never heard you say it like that before."

"Oh. I thought I had. And you didn't ask."

"You're right. It's one thing to know what someone's thinking, but maybe there's something a bit more... human, about being able to say it yourself. It seems important. I'm sorry."

"For what?"

"For not asking the right questions."

"Tom asks good questions," she conceded. "You weren't to know."

"He does," Fear admitted, "and that worries me a little."

"How so?"

"Is it a good idea to bear your soul, all your history, to someone you just met? If you don't know how they're going to use it? How genuine their intentions are? Mightn't it be worthwhile asking some questions yourself, to see what you can safely share? I mean, you don't even know where this guy is headed."

"Don't be silly, I'm just being polite and he's just taking an interest," Joy said dismissively. "I can't help it if someone finds me fascinating."

"Everything OK?" called Tom from the road. "If we hurry we'll make it to Securis in another hour or so, I reckon, which'll be good because we've probably only got about two hours of visibility."

Joy shot a glare at Fear, annoyed at him, and then looked back to Tom. "Yeah," she said, "I'm ready to go. Fear was just fussing like an old woman and I had to settle him down."

She continued chatting, in defiance of Fear's suggestion, covering her drawings with her father, her longing for freedom and her guilt at what that would mean, abandoning the man who had raised her, in conflict with what she felt towards her mother. Tom took all this in, offering empathetic statements and, at one point, taking her hand and squeezing it while they walked, which Joy found both reassuring and also set off butterflies in her stomach. She was lost in the whole moment until Securis lumbered its way into view.

It was an odd town. It had a wall which surrounded the city, made of steel with a series of glass serving windows extending around the exterior, wherein the businesses could ply their trade. There weren't any obvious access doors; periodically, the wall would somehow open for a resident to hurry through, but the secret to gaining entry appeared to only be known by the denizens and whomever was operating the wall.

The glass serving windows had holes cut to allow sound through, and purchases were put into drawers which then slid out on rollers for the purchasers to collect and enjoy. There was no clear way into the city, nor, it seemed, a clear way out.

Upon querying this phenomenon, a vendor explained that Securis did not take in newcomers readily. It locked itself away from the world and actual acceptance and entry into the city took considerable time and paperwork, but behind the walls, he assured them, people were safe and protected and therefore happy. It seemed odd to Joy that only interacting with the same people, day in and day out, could bring any lasting Joy; Pleasant Lane had managed to do the same activities without needing any walls whatsoever.

Tom asked how strangers could obtain safe accommodation, and was directed further down the wall to a "hotel". Here, the anomaly continued: whole rooms slid out and formed part of the wall itself, with a single bed and a small table, and trapped the guest within it until the time that had been paid expired and it again emerged outside.

Left with no other accommodation choices, Joy asked if the hotel had any reservations.

"I've got plenty of reservations," Fear muttered, "but nobody cares what *I* think."

They paid for the rooms for the night and Joy soon found herself trapped in four very small walls, surrounded by the creak and groans of the steel structure as it cooled and contracted in the evening. Fear said nothing to her that night, and she said nothing further to him. She hated being trapped in enclosed spaces, but following their previous discussion a streak of defiance reared its head and she refused to air this concern and have it taken away. Instead, she drifted into fitful sleep.

The next day, awakened by the *plink plink* noises of metal expanding in the sunlight and eventually released from the rectangular sarcophagi, all parties agreed that Securis was *not* the place for them. They backtracked to Aureus Creek instead.

Tom had clearly been thinking on the revelations from the previous day, and so the journey was filled with more conversations. Well, conversations in *theory*, but Joy was aware that almost the entirety of the talking was coming from her end. Tom expressed admiration for the ability to survive in the midst of the challenges, saw similarities in her father's continued work and his own resignation to the meagre existence afforded to him in his previous role, and probed her thoughts as she had been escaping the confines of her city in Steve the boat. What had she seen? Had she tried to get out? Was it strange to see everything below, her whole world, getting smaller and less significant with each passing stroke of the oar? Or did she feel like she was losing her tether along the way?

Again the day disappeared in the flow of the conversation, with Joy feeling with each passing moment a greater sense of peace and security in Tom's presence than she had before. No, it was more than that. She felt seen, truly prioritised, a desire from someone who seemed to want nothing more than to know more about her and revel in what he found. The more she opened, the closer she felt.

Aureus Creek turned out to be a bust anyway; they arrived in the evening, and were shocked at the ridiculous prices of all the goods. The town, it turned out, had a mission to hoard wealth; they spent little, charged a lot, bargained and haggled over every price, with the ultimate view being that happiness was derived from both confidence of being able to meet one's own material needs at the highest level, both now and in the future, and achieving a bargain at the expense of someone else. Joy found the population furtive, distrustful, and unpleasant. She did not enjoy having to argue over purchases just to have a simple meal or get basic supplies, mundane tasks which now took on a whole additional energetic burden, and Fear commented on the incessant worry within the population around any change to their financial status, positive *or* negative. People were either worried that the money wouldn't come, or when it did, they were terrified it would somehow be taken.

Joy found herself clinging closely to Tom, his outlook providing some positivity and reassurance, and his experience with Avaritia at least rendering him more skilled when it came to negotiations. She marvelled at his ability to deftly manoeuvre through the obstacles presented, to alternate between flexibility and hard stances, and to not feel overwhelmed by the whole thing.

Ultimately, the viability of the town as even a short-term option was clarified when Joy and Tom roomed for a few nights to review the maps and make a plan for further excursions, and Joy got talking to the hotel owner briefly before dinner the next evening. She took the opportunity to break the ice and complement him on his watch.

"Thanks," he said, "my father sold it to me on his deathbed."

So they left the following day; Joy already knew it was not a place of happiness for her, and both she and Tom faced real risks of burning through what money they still had. Fear agreed, commenting negatively on a life lived in constant apprehension about one's financial status, but Joy surprised herself at how little weight she gave to Fear's rationale. She hadn't like the town, and Tom had agreed with her. That was sufficient for her.

This clearly bothered Fear as well; there was no longer the metric of Joy's own purpose involved in the decision-making. As the group journeyed back through forest territory and took a break for lunch in a partial clearing, he caught Joy's eye and beckoned her away from the campfire they had lit to prepare the food.

"Everything OK?" Joy asked, she she reached the tree Fear was leaning against.

"Yyyyyyyyyyes," he said slowly. "And no. I'm worried about you."

"Is there a problem?" Joy asked, aware that she had been deliberately ignoring Fear and well aware of what he was most likely to be concerned about.

"I don't know yet. I think there might be, if you're not careful."

Joy bristled instantly, but she tried- poorly- to hide it.

"Oh really?" she said archly. "What, are you going to go stick your hand in someone's brain again? You're going to tell someone that if they hurt me, they answer to you or something?"

"I mean, look, I see the way you are with Tom," Fear tried to soothe, "and he seems like a really nice guy. I'm happy for you."

"Oh, are you? You're happy for me?" Joy responded both sarcastically and defensively, already feeling a threat and somewhat surprised at how forceful her response was. "Well, that makes everything just *peachy*. I always make my decisions on what makes you happy. And what, pray, are you going to add to this blessing, your lordship?"

Fear held up his hands placatingly.

"Look, I'm sorry, I'm not trying to cause a problem here-" he began, but Joy interrupted.

"Oh my *gosh*, you're jealous aren't you? You're jealous that I'm telling him things you don't know!"

"No," he said firmly, "but I'm your friend and I wouldn't *be* your friend if I didn't tell you that I was worried about you. You had a lot of eggs in one basket back in Luxoria and you're certainly filling them up again here very quickly."

"What would you know," sniffed Joy dismissively. "You aren't even alive."

"You're trying to be hurtful. I'm just saying, there's a lot that can go wrong here. You don't really know each other, and I can see you putting your heart in a pair of hands without even knowing where those hands are going to be in a week's time. Or before you even know if those hands *want* to hold a heart."

"Nobody's forcing him to care for me," Joy retorted angrily. "Tom cares because he wants to. I'm not going to tell him what to do. Gosh, is it so hard for you to see that maybe someone just likes *me?* That they're happy because they're with me? That maybe *I'm* somebody's joy?"

"Hey, I'm just trying to be a friend and warn you-"

"Warn me? All you ever *do* is warn me. Something is *always* going to go wrong. This person isn't good. Someone else won't listen to what I'm going to say. Wolves will eat me. Whatever. Haven't you got anything to say that shows you *trust* me?"

"Of course I trust you, Sparky," Fear tried to say gently but the use of her nickname rubbed lemon into the wounds Joy was feeling and she began seething. "Heartbreak isn't new to you. I'm just here to say I don't want to see it happen ag-"

"You know what? You know *what*?" Joy yelled. "You aren't the custodian of my heart. You come around and take my fear and treat me like a child who can't handle things and you know what? I could handle it. I don't need you. I *never* needed you! You just *invited* yourself into my life and never left and I never had the heart to tell you that you need *me* more than I *ever* needed *you!* "

Fear looked crestfallen as Joy stood there, clenching her fists and breathing heavily.

"If that's how you really feel..." he said, looking downcast.

"How I really feel?!" Joy said incredulously, almost laughing in his face.

"What have you done for me ever? You say you take my fears to protect me but it's from a world I never get the chance to know! And why? Because of a few sparks? Or because it's always been about you? You always saving the little fragile human from herself or the big bad world? Put me in a display cupboard so nothing delicate could get broken and you could have me all to yourself?"

"Joy-"

"You know what?" she snapped. "Why are you even here? What happiness are you going to show me? Just go! Get out of here and leave me alone. I told you: I never needed you!"

Internally, Joy knew she was being irrational and unreasonable. She wasn't sure why she was so prepared to die on this hill when it was threatened, and she knew what she was saying would hurt a friend she cared about. But in that moment, she just couldn't *feel* that care; instead she felt attacked by the suggestion that these blossoming feelings of being truly heard, understood, and welcomed could be dangerous. The questioning was interpreted as a threat that she didn't fully understand, and the only response seemed to hurt that person back.

Fear gave her a long look with his grey eyes, an ocean of sadness washing in each iris. His face looked impassive, and yet his eyes seemed to encompass the end of the world. "If that's how you feel," he said, "what friend would impose themselves when they are unwanted?"

"Good!" Joy said, hating herself as she did so. "You know the way. Anywhere but here, really. Get lost!"

Fear said nothing further. He just nodded, turned, and walked the opposite way down the forest path. Joy stood there panting, fists still clenched, wondering if she should run after him or stand her ground, but feeling oddly satisfied that she had stuck to her guns. Tom came up to her, and put an arm around her shoulder.

"Are you okay?" he asked. "That sounded pretty intense, whatever it was." Joy said nothing, but turned and flung her arms around Tom's waist and buried her head in his chest, holding on tightly. After a few moments, she pulled her head back and looked Tom in the face.

"You feel like home," she said honestly. "And I told Fear that I didn't need him."

Tom's face reddened. "I've never met someone like you, Joy," he said, and held her face in both hands as he leaned down and placed a single kiss on her forehead. "Someone who would tell Fear itself to leave because of how she feels is just about the bravest thing I can ever imagine."

Kiss me, Joy screamed internally. *Kiss me now, on the lips. Kiss me and tell me you love me. Tell me we'll be partners. Tell me this is our journey. Tell me* something, *something true, or something true enough for now. Tell me everything will be okay. Tell me I'm yours.*

Joy only got one part of her wish.

"You're going to be okay," Tom said. "You've flown through a storm and braved Avaritia and slept inside a wall. I'm here. We'll do this together."

He took her hand, and again Joy felt the comfort and the electricity of his touch.

"Come on," he said with a smile, pulling her back towards the campfire, "lunch isn't going to eat itself."

Chapter 8

Under Treacherous Skies

Hoping we meant the things that were spoken, trying to hold on to something that's broken

The next few weeks flashed by in a blur. Tom was an excellent travelling companion and Joy found herself more drawn to him with each passing day. They stopped in a few towns along the way, offering to work in kitchens and clean odd shops for a few days in order to offset the costs of the stay and see what the town had to offer. It was an approach that made absolute financial sense for two young people making their budget stretch, but for Joy, the ulterior motive was to find more reasons to spend time in proximity together.

None of the towns had any particular standout appeal to Joy, but Tom was more and more fascinated as he undertook activities which had been absent in Luxoria. Joy had shown him how to wash clothes, and he'd undertake the task with relish. Put in kitchens to wash dishes, he'd be up to his arms in suds with a smile on his face and his sleeves rolled up almost to his armpits before the first plate even came across. In shops, he swept with gusto and polished windows and any other odd jobs that were given to him. Joy found herself enjoying each activity more herself, just by the presence of Tom's happiness.

In Philosophia, a town fairly which followed the apparent Frieland tradition of identifying the central thesis behind your view of happiness right from the moment of entry, they encountered the notion of happiness arising from knowledge and education. It was a neat and tidy town, but Joy found the population to be arrogant and somewhat combative with each other; every idea was to be tested in heated debate and combat, and whilst this might sound good on paper where the best idea would win, more often than not it devolved into arguments about the relative education and intelligence of the other party in order to justify the superiority and correctness of one's position. It seemed to Joy that it bogged a lot of simple things down that needed to be done, as every task needed to be accompanied by a discussion about who needed to attend to the more menial components and whose approach to the completing the task was superior.

Despite this, there were some engineering marvels behind the building structures, a testament to the times when actual work was able to be completed by the learned residents, and Tom enthusiastically went from site to site, asking questions about the underlying aesthetic and how certain components were able to be pulled off.

Every restaurant had an opinion about food, its production, meaning, purpose, and delivery, and each one was certain that it was the indisputably correct way to approach cuisine. The hotels all had certainty regarding their guests' needs, such that there were no requests that could be made by anyone staying. The public square, the markets, and anywhere that people gathered, each member announced proudly that their approach was superior through their research. Joy found this exhausting; Tom instead seemed to agree with each one. As he enthused about their philosophy, Joy saw some of the arrogance start to slip away from the populace, and she realised that instead of comparative resistance to the ideas the residents would have in their day-to-day interactions with each other, Tom brought a receptiveness to their thought processes that actually made the speaker think through and question the rightness of their position. Simple questions "and why is that the case?" or "so when you did it like *this*, did you see a change in the people coming in?" and "how much time did you spend reflecting in order to reach that conclusion?" seemed to open up passion and enthusiasm, whereas in most discussions there seemed to be a race to contradict the other. Joy liked seeing that; she felt some small pangs of jealousy, as Tom excitedly teased out whole histories from people, much as he had done with her, but at the same time she loved watching it play out, loved watching the lives touched start to open up like a flower being hit by the first rays of the sun. Tom was still as generous with his attention to Joy as he had been before, and their lunches and evenings were spent talking and reflecting and eagerly considering all the possibilities that Frieland had to offer.

She found their conversation style was very different from her interactions with Fear; far less sarcasm and gloom, and it was refreshing to talk to someone who didn't seem to know *everything*. It brought a level of curiosity out of Joy that she had not hitherto been aware of.

"Do you think about love much?" Tom asked her one afternoon as they wandered through the town back to their lodgings. "Man here said to me that love was unbreakable, but then another guy said that it was *very* breakable and that was why it was valuable, and they argued about whether it was strong or fragile for like an hour."

Joy's pulse rate quickened, but she tried to play cool.

"No, I don't think about it very much," she lied casually. "I suppose, with the right person, you'd have to assume it was strong. Why?"

"I saw some of their engineers talking about tempering metal, and how you can make it harder but in doing so it can become more brittle. It's not a perfect analogy but it's interesting, I think, that something can become tougher *and* more fragile at the same time."

"Hmmmm. What do you think it means?" Joy asked.

"I guess the only accurate test of the truth of love is heartbreak. If love is what tempers a heart, only love can break it. But what a tragedy to know it was really love after it was gone."

"You should write that down."

"Nah," Tom replied with a grin, "these guys would probably take it, copyright it, and then argue about measuring the tensile strength of love."

After the best part of a week, they moved on to Deliria, who took a pharmacological approach to happiness. The citizens took a daily dose of tablets which maintained their mood and certainly made for an agreeable town, with very little conflict of any sort. Joy was initially uncomfortable with the notion, but after a day in the town found that the lack of conflict and challenge that she had found in all the other towns, where people seemed to wrestle daily to carve out their individual pursuit of happiness, was incredibly refreshing. People were just... pleasant, all the time, at roughly the same level, wherever you went.

Joy said as much to Tom on the third day as they had dinner, alone together after closing time, having finished their chores which had been bartered in return for accommodation in the residence above. The owners had left them to their own devices once the last table had been cleared.

"I'm not saying it's the solution everywhere, or mandatorily," she began, "but you've got to admit: everyone's happy, and everyone stays happy, and *nobody* is fighting or haggling or trying to ruin someone else's business or locking guests in walls at night. They're not bothered by anything, really. I could see myself staying here for a bit."

"It's not happiness," Tom replied simply. "The guys in the town square at Philosophia said happiness requires input and output of some kind, and I think they're right. You can't talk to these people; they don't *actually* care about anything in particular. They're not happy, they're numb."

"They *seem* happy," Joy said, a little annoyed at the level of detailed observation that she knew was accurate.

"Not feeling sad, or angry, isn't the same as feeling happy," Tom replied earnestly. "I don't think it's a process whereby you can eliminate all other feelings and *only* be left with happiness by default. Back home they said keeping that fleeting high from having something new was the key, and instead it just left everyone anxious about keeping up. I mean, I tried to talk to people, but they just smile at you. Sometimes they give you a couple of word answers and then they just... float off, doing whatever else they're doing."

"Yeah, because nobody can bring them down," Joy argued.

"Nobody can bring them *up*, either," Tom countered.

"There's times when I think about my mother that I would rather feel numb than feel the way I did. I get why they would want to do it, you know?" Joy offered.

"But if you'd never felt that way, would you have ever come to Frieland?" Tom replied. "I mean look, I'm not trying to tell you what your adventure should be. But sitting here, talking to you... that makes me happy. No-one in this town is going to feel like that, ever; they can't be in the moment with someone. Doesn't that make you feel sad?"

"I make you happy, eh?" Joy asked coyly. "Anything *else* you want to share?"

Tom blushed in return. "You make me pretty happy," he said. "Being on an adventure with you... I never thought I'd see these places. Or think this way. I have you to thank for that."

"Well, you certainly know what to say to a girl. *You* made me let go of Fear," Joy replied, looking at him deeply.

"Whoah, now, you did that on your own," Tom said with a smile, holding his hands up placatingly. "But you know, it's funny. We go to these towns, and each one has such a narrow view. You'd think they'd mingle and maybe, for example, the people in Philosophia could encourage the people in Luxoria to spend longer on thoughts about satisfaction rather than buying new things; the people in Luxoria could who Aureus Creek that loosening the purse strings a little gives rise to more options and innovation, and so on. They don't. And nobody seems to ever drive that; they might trade, but nobody *talks* to each other, you know what I mean?"

Joy looked at him, holding her chin in her hand, enraptured by his voice. "I talked to you," she offered.

"But you're not from here," Tom continued, not wanting to lose grip on the thought. "I mean it; why are we all locked away in our cities? Is it just the fear of the unknown? I'd have loved to talk to your friend; I've always wanted to know more about what Fear actually *thinks*."

"Mostly, he thinks about causing trouble, I reckon," Joy replied.

"Maybe he thinks about you?" Tom suggested.

"What, romantically? He's always been just a friend."

"No, I don't mean that. I don't know, but from what you've told me, he's spent a *lot* of his time with you. It sounds like he's wanted to protect you, or help you... or there's something about being near you. I certainly know that being with you makes a world of difference! But I'd love to have known: what makes a being, who lives outside of time and space, take an interest in a single person? Is it just curiosity? Is it just you? How does a timeless entity come to take an interest in any person, really?"

"He said there were sparks," Joy admitted. "He said they come from certain people sometimes, some friction reaction to his nature, and I was one of those. But maybe it was just pity."

Tom paused, thinking for a moment. "I bet he'd have hated it here," he said after some thought. "Feeling nothing at all? It would make his job hard."

"You know, I've never really thought about it," Joy conceded. "He's just been off, doing what he does. He's always seemed happy about it. Maybe that's the secret. It's funny to think that the two of you would have the same issue with the same town, though."

"Did you *want* to stay here?" asked Tom. "I mean, I don't want to push you, this is just my impression of the place."

He put his head down on the table and snored. Joy laughed and playfully hit his hand with the back of her fork.

"I get it!" she said with a smile. "And no... I don't want to stay here. But I do want to enjoy the peace a little longer, even if it's not really real. Anyway, where would *you* go, Mister Insight?"

Tom pulled the map out of his bag and smoothed it out on the table.

"What about Gastropolis?" he asked, pointing on the map. "That seems like a place you can sink your teeth into."

It was indeed. For once, there was an obsession that Joy could truly appreciate and get behind. She and Tom arrived there two days later, and the scent even on the outskirts was heavenly on its own. The smells of spices, baked bread, roasting meats, melting butter, onion and garlic and herbs all melded together into a beautiful wafting aroma. The populace had reached a simple conclusion: time spent with loved ones around a good meal was all the happiness in the world. And *every* meal was a good meal.

This had a certain impact on the citizenry, who were more or less spherical. They were hearty, jolly folks, loud and welcoming and enthusiastic, but gargantuan in their frames. Joy and Tom got to the main square, dedicated to multiple take-away stands, and spent the afternoon sampling the most delicious meals they had ever experienced. Tom got talking to each of the stall holders, fascinated with the stories behind the recipes, the moments the cooks had found in their lives where the joy they experienced was captured in the flavours of each meal. They talked lovingly about where, when, and who they were with; how they had nurtured the recipe afterwards, refining and enhancing it and bringing it to a point where they could serve to see if that same meal would bring that moment of satisfaction, of release and in-the-moment presence, with a stranger.

Joy, ever the sweet tooth, wandered to the candy stalls and left Tom to his own devices.

Tell him you love him, her inner monologue told her. *Tell him you can't stop thinking about him. Tell him that he's your joy, and that you want him to stay in your life.*

"Hush," she whispered to herself and her betraying thoughts.

Tell him you think he's your person. Tell him you want him to kiss you and never stop.

"I don't think that!"

Liar. Why would you lie to yourself? Tell him that nobody has known you the way he's known you. Look at these hard candies.

"What about them?"

They can have individual messages on them in little circles. It would look amazing at a wedding.

Joy was aware that the things her internal monologue was telling her was insanity. It was ludicrous to be thinking about wedding candies, even if you *did* love the person you were exploring with.

Ah, so you are *in love with him.*

Joy gritted her teeth. Betrayed by her own thoughts, she quickly decided to shut them up with chocolate and sugar. "Excuse me," she asked the store holder, a large woman with a warm smile and an apron whose strings were tucked into her pants because it was clear that they could not make it around the equatorial line of her waist, and whose hair still carried traces of flour or icing sugar or some mysterious white baking powder, "may I sample a few things?"

"What would you like to sample, dear?" the woman asked with a smile. "It's all good, you know."

"What do you recommend?" said Joy, happy to drown her nagging heart. "Well, the chocolate strawberries are great. Our hard candies are first rate. I personally can't live without a handful of our soft caramels at the end of the day," the woman said with a wink. "And a few at the start. But, and I say this with all modesty, our nougat is the best in all of Frieland."

She grabbed a small plate, and started grabbing multiple items. She pushed the laden plate across the stand to Joy. "Here, try one of each. And maybe a chocolate honeycomb, and a peanut brittle, and a candy cane..." and the plate got bigger and bigger. Joy was wondering if she'd have any room left after eating the samples to actually eat a purchase she'd made. She bit first into the caramels, and it was like she had dipped a toe into heaven itself; soft, chewy, melty, gooey, not enough to make your teeth stick closed, creamy buttery and rich.

"Oh. My. *Gosh*," she enthused, but her saliva production had gone into overtime and she almost dribbled out her mouth when the *sh* sound was being made. Her hand shot up but she noticed she couldn't help but giggle and smile. "That is *amazing*."

"Food is love, dear," the stallholder said with a warm smile, "if it's done right. But go on. Try a few more."

Joy didn't need to be told twice. The flavours blew her mind; the comparative tartness and sweetness of the chocolate strawberries, the crunch and then meatiness of the honeycomb, it all washed over her in a hyperglycaemic tsunami of delight. But the nougat; she had never been an extraordinary fan previously, but the squares of airy, pillowy delights melted in her mouth and made her question reality itself for a moment.

Food is love, she said to herself, picking a number of caramels and assorted nougat selections. Her last purchase were chocolate-covered strawberries; if *these* didn't convey her feelings, nothing would.

Tom returned with hot bowls of noodles and they found a small retaining wall surrounding a garden in a nearby park just off the main square to sit and eat. The sun shone warmly on the rather still day; small bees buzzed around the flowers, ignoring their spectators, the background noises of the the market square clinked and tinkled their way along and for a moment, there was nothing between Joy and Tom to be said other than sitting and enjoying the happiness of the day as they enjoyed their meals. *He bought you lunch*, Joy's internal voice told her. *Food is love, right?*

"Oh. Oh my," Tom said as they tasted the noodles for the first time. "This is *incredible*. I reckon things like this would bring the people from Securis outside their little pods! I mean, every meal might be a bit much if you wanted to live past thirty, but I really think there's something to this idea of eating with people you love."

Joy pushed ears pricked up immediately and she had to force this down and focus on just feeling the happiness of the moment. They ate the rest of the meal in silence, savouring the taste; occasionally she and Tom caught each other's eyes and shared a slightly embarrassed smile as a noodle was slurped, but Joy was taken aback by how much the stillness of the moment felt like home. So much of the past few months- no, past few *years*- had been a rush from one thing to the next, class or exams or study or home activities or the adventure itself, and even the evenings had been taken with long discussions and exploratory imaginings of the next place to be. In the pleasant, safe silence of the afternoon, she felt herself actually start to relax tension in her neck and shoulders in the warmth of the sun, and with her belly and taste buds satisfied, in the company of someone for whom she held such deep affection and who knew her without words, she felt as if all the reserve tanks of happiness were about to overflow.

They took the opportunity once they'd finished the meal to wander through the park and take a relaxed position under a large fig tree. They half-dozed in the quiet afternoon, as the subdued sounds of the market nearby floated over them. Remembering her purchase, Joy pulled out the tray of chocolate-covered strawberries and placed it between them, leaving a hand in the tray as she idly picked at the stems to select one. Tom, equally taken with the day and looking around the park, reached down at the same moment as Joy to pick up a strawberry and their hands overlapped.
"Oh, sorry!" he said, but Joy left her hand in contact with his and he did not withdraw it. Their fingers hovered for a moment, and then intertwined. They said nothing more, but sat in the sun, holding hands, feeling a perfect moment like a fragile piece of crystal, unwilling to risk breaking it with any careless return to reality while it was busy breaking the light into prismatic colours for them to see. The chocolate on the strawberries began melting in the stalemate, but neither seemed to care.

It is impossible for perfect moments to last forever, and eventually Tom gave Joy's hand two tight squeezes and got to his feet, picking up the empty bowls.

"We'd better give these back," he said with a shy smile.

"I love you," a female voice blurted out, and Joy was fairly shocked to discover that it was her own. Tom stopped and looked at her, as she felt intense heat in her face and a blush that threatened to remove the tops of her ears, her heart suddenly pounding. She took a deep breath.

"I don't think that there's a place I'm going to find joy. I think it's a person," she continued, part of her reasoning that she'd already stepped off the cliff and might as well commit to the fall, and part of her trying to work out if she could scramble back up on thin air and then find a very deep hole in the ground to hide in. "You're my person. When we're together, I feel like I'm home. I don't care where we go, really, as long as we go there together. And... that's it, really. I wanted you to know. I don't think joy comes from something you get. I think it comes from finding the right person to share it with."

Joy could feel her heartbeat in her eardrums, and her stomach felt like she was being blasted into orbit and it was doing its utmost to remain here on earth. Her inner monologue was screaming at her, *it's too late now, the cat's out of the bag! Just kiss him!* but her feet remained obstinately rooted in the current spot.

Tom took this revelation well, although there's nothing like the sudden profession of someone's most intimate feelings to require a brief break in the flow of conversation while one searched for a suitable reply. Joy noticed that although his face was carefully unmoving, behind his eyes there was a whirlwind of activity trying to find the appropriate response.

"Wait here," he said. "Let me drop these back before they close the stall. But there's a lot to talk about."

He leaned in and gave her a shy kiss on the cheek.

"Won't be a moment."

True to his word, Tom wasn't a moment, because he didn't return.

Joy, despite her initial anxiousness following her disclosure, had felt wistful, even optimistic about the likely outcomes. They would share their feelings- he obviously felt *something* for her, the sheer electricity between them when they held hands again confirmed that. Half an hour went by, but she told herself he had probably gotten involved in a random conversation, as was his way, and she didn't want to interrupt. After an hour, Joy went looking for him.

The sun was starting to set in the square but the vendors were still there, preparing for the night time activities or handing the stall over to their spouse for the next shift. Joy's heart faltered. *Liar!* her monologue screamed. *The stall wasn't going to close.*

Maybe it was a mistake, she told herself. Maybe he got distracted, or had been conscripted into preparing meals or washing up or some other activity to offset the cost of their lunch. But for the first time, she started to feel the icy fingers of fear grip her heart, and it was a foreign feeling indeed for a girl whose concerns and worries had barely had enough time to grow beyond a larval stage, historically. *This* was deep, and it made her heart pound like an animal in flight. It was weird to be walking slowly but feel like you were sprinting, as she tried to tell herself that there was no need for this concern and everything was fine, which felt like a lie.

She approached the noodle stall holder, a woman in her early 40s with sun-scorched cheeks, a welcoming smile, and forearms that looked like a couple of uncooked chickens, and asked tentatively, "have you seen a young man, maybe twenty years old, returning a couple of bowls recently?"

The woman's eyes immediately softened with compassion and pity.

"Oh love," she said sympathetically, "he said you'd probably come by. He dropped off the bowls, asked to borrow a pen and paper, and then asked me to give you this. I said to him, I did, I said 'young man, this had better

be something you absolutely can't say in person, because I didn't put food in your belly to fuel cowardice,' but he assured me it was important and the only way he could tell you what he said you needed to know."
The woman looked guilty for a moment.
"I shouldn't have looked, but he seemed like such a nice young man and was so... upset. I only had a peek, mind," she continued, pulling the letter out of a pocket in her apron and proffering it to Joy.
Joy's heart, which had been thumping constantly and had swung wildly between beats of heightened anticipation and chest-pounding anxiousness, now felt as though it had stopped entirely, along with the world around it. It was as if it froze in time, like a sheet hung out on a clothesline in Antarctica right before a blizzard. Joy felt as if she was not in her own body at all. She could almost see her self over her own shoulder, watching her own arm reach out and take the pieces of paper. She could hear herself whisper a monotone "thanks," a tiny voice echoing in what suddenly seemed, to her, to be an empty void.

Her monologue was quiet. It had nothing to add. Without saying anything further, she opened the folded paper sheets.

Dearest Joy,

This is the worst way this can be done to you. I know, and I'm so sorry. I'm honestly scared that if I come and speak to you, I won't have the strength to say what I have to say, because I care for you so very deeply.

Today, I found my purpose, my place. It isn't in one of these towns, but it's a mix of them all, I guess. I learnt on the road with you, as we travelled and my eyes were opened to all these new thoughts and experiences, a lot of things. That life is short, and there is only a small window for adventure. That intellect should be tempered with service and compassion. That a meal can bring people together, out of the walls they build for security. That simple tasks, done well, improve the lives of others. That special people can come into your world and make you see the same thing a whole new way, so that the thing itself is now new. I could never thank you enough.

But you have a journey to complete, and I have one of my own, and I couldn't do mine with you, and it would be wrong to take you off yours.

I'm sorry I didn't have the courage to face you in person. I just honestly feel that if you asked me to stay with you, I would, and that would be wrong for both of us.

Thank you, for everything.

-Tom.

Joy stood there for a few moments while the structure she had built to see the world slowly began to crack and wobble. She felt her lip tremble and the pit in her stomach opened up wider, as if she were falling into herself. The stall operator tapped her on her shoulder, with a look of sympathy and care, and pushed a thermos in a bag across to her.

"Oh, luv," she said with real affection in her voice, "here, this is an old family recipe. A good soup will never heal a broken heart on its own, but you're going to have to eat some time and it might do something for you. He seemed like a nice lad; polite, like, and respectful. I put a extra few napkins in the bag too, in case you need to blow your nose. No charge, luv, you just look after that heart of yours."

As Joy reached out to the counter, the woman leaned across and patted her hand soothingly.

"It hurts now, luv. You poor thing. It'll hurt less eventually. Come by tomorrow, you can have a meal on the house. It's no fun being alone at a time like this. They say we all sail under treacherous skies, you know? Better to find a port in a storm than be all at sea."

Joy managed to murmur her thanks distantly, feeling the metaphorical bricks that comprised her internal structure start to crack and shift and fall. She turned around and left, wandering out of the marketplace and out through the town and only when she managed to reach the forest at the town's edge, just off the road, did the collapse finally happen. Like a crystal chandelier dropping from a great height, her heart tumbled and tumbled before it shattered into a thousand pieces, drawing chest-racking sobs from her as she cried and cried and cried. Each gasping breath seemed to make the next one worse, as if it fuelled the descent, sadness hitting her like successive sledgehammer blows, the enormity of the loss growing by the second as every conclusion she had drawn to start to build a fragile new concept of life and happiness melted and ran through her fingers.

At the same time, fears continued to take root in every crack and crevice of her faltering worldview. *You didn't deserve him. He was never going to love you anyway. You chose wrong. You did this to yourself.* The further they anchored themselves, the deeper they seemed to penetrate the depths psyche, absorbing her inner monologue and transforming it into something monstrous. *Nobody could love you. You're a silly girl who thought she was special. The girl who ruined her mother's life, who left a world of misery for her father to trudge through. Nobody wanted you at home, nobody wanted you at school, so why would anyone want you now? You who sent away your only friend? You who were so certain you'd figured it all out? What are you going to do, crawl back home with your tail between your legs, loveless, friendless, hopeless?*

The afternoon light started to dim and the wind picked up; it became cold in the forest, and Joy shivered. She felt a level of loneliness she hadn't felt since she was ten years old, just before she had met Fear, when the world seemed to be collapsing. It hadn't lasted nearly as long, and she suddenly yearned for the presence of her friend, to take these worries and doubts and tell her that everything was going to be fine. She'd even settle for some brief gloating about his warnings, if it meant some temporary relief from what she was feeling.

As if crushed by the weight of her emotions, she slowly sank to the ground beside a tree. Unlike other moments, there were no words of comfort to be heard from Fear, no soothing hands from Tom, not even a bright bubble of excitement from Cupidity or a calm conversation over the table with her father. It was as if a million tiny hands reached out from all around her and found nothing to grasp. With no other options before her, Joy did the only thing left: drew her legs up, hugged her knees, and wept until she thought her heart would stop completely.

Chapter 9

Anybody Else

Sad to say, but ain't nobody gonna give you your own voice

Joy awoke with a start, not even aware that she had fallen asleep, exhausted by her misery. There were sticks in her hair and her clothes were damp and stained with dirt. Her neck was stiff and her body ached, and the yawning abyss inside her allowed only enough time for her brain to register that the previous day's activity wasn't a horrible dream, and then re-opened to allow her fall to continue. She was vaguely aware of bodily signals like hunger, thirst, and the need to find a bathroom. She was also conscious that despite the extra napkins, her face was still streaked with tears and dirt and crusted reminders of her runny nose, but it was hard to muster up the strength to care.

She hadn't even opened the thermos, but had no appetite, and just used its still-warm exterior to chase the cold from her hands. Empty of the hope and love she had felt, there was a yearning for some form of reassuring contact, and the only friendly face she could think of was that of the stallholder who had given her the uneaten soup. Once the sun was fully risen, she gathered herself, feeling listless and hollow, and started walking back to the market square.

The vendors were still setting up for the day, and smells were already emerging; melted butter, bacon, eggs, mushrooms, spinach, freshly baked bread, pastries. Ordinarily these were aromas she absolutely lived for, when starting the day with Tom, exploring the nooks and crannies of the townships and finding new places and things neither of them had ever tried before. Instead, each smell now was a bitter reminder of the sorrow she felt and just as she was convincing herself that this had all been a terrible mistake, a heavy hand of pudgy fingers came to rest on her shoulder and a voice said "Ah, pet, how are you? I was just thinking about you. Here, you look a right mess."

Joy turned and looked into a familiar face and instantly threw her arms around the woman whose name she didn't even know, the contact with another human becoming enough to make her feel for a moment that there was a bottom to the pit she was descending in. She wasn't sure if the woman was shocked, because she had buried her face into her shoulder, but she felt a strong set of arms wrap around her in turn and pat her firmly on the back as she sobbed.

"There, there, poppet," the woman soothed. "Aunt Becky's here now. Come on, how about I fix you up a plate of something? Maybe rustle up a hot chocolate for you while we're at it? Nothing soothes a broken heart like a warm meal and a bit of chocolate, me mam always said."

Joy sniffed a few times, finding it hard to let go, but nodded her head and managed to say "mmmmhmmm" into Aunt Becky's shoulder. The stallholder managed to extricate herself and led Joy back to the stand, wiping her damp shoulder with a spare dishcloth as she went to work.

A plate was served to Joy, and then another was placed beside it; one was brimming with an enormous full English breakfast, the next with pancakes, a waffle, and some small assorted pastries, with a small set of pots of jam, cream, and maple syrup. Joy tried to take it all in.

"It's not just for you, you know," Aunt Becky said, bringing a third plate with a steak and hashed browns on it as she sat down, "I'm expecting that you're probably not that hungry at the moment. Heartbreak will do that. But pick a few things here, luv, it's good for you, and I'll manage the rest." Joy looked at the trio of plates, somewhat aghast. At the best of times, this could have fed four people, and right now she was pretty certain that she'd be counted as half a person. She managed to scrape a few things across onto a bread-and-butter plate, some bacon, some eggs, half of a waffle, and then Aunt Becky went to work on the rest.

"Have... have *you* ever had your heart broken?" Joy asked nervously, picking at her plate while her host began a strategic demolition of the pile of food normally associated with civil engineering and old skyscrapers.

"Mmmmf," Aunt Becky replied, endeavouring to swallow a large mouthful, "we *all* get our hearts broken some time or other, luv. 'Course I've had mine broken, and more than once at that, though that was quite a few years and even more kilos ago, if you catch my drift."

She gave a glowing smile, which made her hefty cheeks almost envelope her eyes.

"What did you do about it?" Joy asked, her voice small. Aunt Becky shrugged.

"Ate," she said simply, "and then cried a lot. And then my nan came and told me about the first time her heart was broken, and gave me a meal."

"Hadn't you just eaten?"

"So?"

"So then what happened?"

"Well," Aunt Becky said while she wiped her mouth with a serviette and pushed her now-empty plates away from her; Joy's still contained the original food minus a few bites. "Me mam said that the best thing to do was to stay busy, so I got down to our family stall here in the markets and felt absolutely horrible for a good couple of days. But, y'know, funny thing. The fella who broke my heart, well, he was called away, and I never saw him again. Instead, I met people I hadn't known, and they loved my cooking, and I suddenly felt that I had something to offer again and it wasn't only that young bloke who cared about me, so I kept coming back. And eventually, another young fella came by and liked my food enough to ask me out, and then we got married, and here I am, day in and day out, putting love into people's hands. Love I didn't think I had any more, back when I was young and skinny."

She thought for a moment. "Well, skinni*er*," she added.

"That was it?" Joy asked incredulously. "You just worked at a stall until you met a guy you liked?"

"No, luv," Aunt Becky corrected, "I loved on *everyone* until someone gave it back to me. Gave it back in ways I'd never have thought, in quantities more than I'd ever given out. Here, tell you what, hang around the stall for a bit, you'll meet him later on in the day and you might as well make yourself useful in between."

"You want me to work on your stall?"

"Why, have you got something better to do?"

Joy had to admit that she didn't. "All right," she said.

Oddly, Joy felt the experience fill a maternal gap in her life. She stood side-by-side with Aunt Becky, cutting and tasting and serving the grateful regulars who frequented the stall, in awe of the skill of the older woman. It was oddly calming, given the volume of customers, but it kept her hands and mind busy. Having survived the breakfast run, Aunt Becky said she had to run some errands before the lunch run, and Joy was left alone on the stand for a half hour.

The sudden cessation of activity allowed her previously-quietened thoughts to begin creeping over her, and she started noticing them gather like a wave when a shadow fell across the stall and she heard a familiar voice. "I hope you're better at this than you were at running errands," Cupidity said, looking around the town square. "But *what* have you done to my clothes?"

Joy's head snapped up, absolute shock on her face. She wondered if this was a hallucination caused by not enough food, or too much food, or a fever caused by sleeping in a forest on a bed of tears under a blanket of sadness which really did very little to keep the cold out.

"Ummmm," she said, fumbling for words, "I..."

"You left me a note," Cupidity continued, having never really gotten the hang of letting a conversation be two-sided. "I thought you said you hated notes."

"You heard me say that?"

"Of course! I'm *always* ready to listen to a friend!" Cupidity replied defensively. Joy stared at her. "Well..." she added, "*sometimes* ready."

"What are you *doing* here? I thought you'd have been busy at the shop! You know, landing another Launch, doing all that stuff you wanted to do, becoming-"

"Oh that?" Cupidity interrupted dismissively. "No, I changed my mind."

"You... changed your mind?" Joy asked incredulously. "You didn't talk to me for *weeks* and you just changed your mind?"

Cupidity looked guilty.

"Weeeeeeeell," she conceded, "I guess you could say that I learnt something. The hard way. See, at first I was like, this contract is *so great* and everything was going to be chill. It was Boss Babe time! But you got me thinking. Avaritia is an icon but, like, what has she *made*? Did she even really make the town what it is? Or was I just buying stuff in the hopes she'd tell people to buy *my* stuff? And I looked at the contract, and thought about it costing me my money *and* my friend, I realised... it was all a bit silly. Here I was, chasing somebody who never created *anything*, trying to measure up to them so that they could take more from me. So I decided to keep my savings, and I put the shop up for sale, and came out here!"

"You came looking for me?" Joy asked, brightening. "I didn't know you cared!"

"Ummmmm..." Cupidity continued awkwardly, "No. I came looking for advice. Where's that guy from Avaritia's office who dropped off the contract, by the way?"

Joy had been doing so well. The shock had temporarily distracted her from her misery, healing over like a thin sheet of ice over a winter lake, but now a foot had gone straight through it and she immediately burst into tears. Cupidity looked incredibly uncomfortable.

"What?" she asked. "Did he die or something?"

"No, he left me," Joy sobbed, putting her head down to sob on the counter, while Cupidity patted her awkwardly on the back.

"Hey now," she soothed, "you're going to scare away customers, and that isn't great *at all*."

Despite herself, Joy let out a laugh, causing a big snot bubble to burst. She took a number of napkins and wiped her face, and tried to compose herself.

She gave Cupidity the cliff notes of the last twenty-four hours, and to her credit, Cupidity didn't interrupt once.

"Awwww, *babe*," she said to Joy when she was finished, "That's rough. Like, I'm *super* bummed out for you."

"Thanks," Joy replied with a sniffle, "it actually feels good to talk to some-"

"Now let me tell you what *I'm* doing, because I'm *super* pumped. So, I heard that, like, a few weeks after I left, Avaritia had a **total** breakdown, because all of a sudden, nobody was going to the Launches any more. For real, nobody gave her new products, nobody paid her to sponsor, but like, amazement, nobody even turned *up*. It wasn't even like they started hating her. Just... like all of a sudden, nothing she said was great, and nobody cared. It was as if the whole city felt like I did, when I tore up the contract. She tried going out in the street doing events and nobody came to that, and then her staff quit, and she was all alone in that stadium and she just went *off*! I heard she smashed up her office displays and all. She went from icon to, like, *so* last month."

"What happened?" Joy asked.

"No idea!" Cupidity said happily. "It was the weirdest thing; I've never heard of *everyone* doing the same thing at once unless, like, she was telling them to. But forget her, so I was travelling around and trying to figure out: where do I belong, yeah? Where does a fashionista go to, like, really *give* to people? And I mean, give back by making them super stylish and taking money. I'm not running a charity. So I was in this town, I forget the name but they argued like *all the time*, and one of them mentioned this wise old owl who helps give wisdom to weary travellers, named Peregrine."

"You mean a guy who's as wise as an owl?"

"That's what I thought, but no, it was like *literally* an owl. Huge. It took me like *forever* to find him in the forest, and I thought he was going to eat me or something, and I asked him, like, what do I do to make this work so great? And he hit the nail on the head right away. He told me, 'you don't sell clothes. You sell fabric.' And I was like *OMG, you're right.* With my contacts back in Luxoria, I can get fabrics cheaper than anyone outside the city. So where's a place where they need more fabric for the clothes to make people iconic? And it was obvious: get the fatties looking on point! Just because you're carrying a few dozen extra kilos, doesn't mean you shouldn't feel *so great* about your look. And so here I am; I rented a little shop and just started, and it's been the absolute best. *Nobody* else is making fashionable clothes for these people. I said to them, like, if *every* meal is a special occasion, what do you do on an *actual* special occasion? There's anniversaries and birthdays and weddings and sometimes, you know, you just want to feel your power, your confidence, and not just have it on a sandwich."

Cupidity was effortlessly offensive, and it was amazing that her new shop hadn't been firebombed, but it was always done with such obliviousness that people seemed to let it slide.

"*There* you are, luv," boomed Aunt Becky from behind her, startling Joy and making her jump. "Give me a hand with these bags, would you?"

Joy turned and her new acquaintance was standing there with a hefty man, the pair of them holding bags of ingredients to restock the stall. Like Becky, he had kind eyes, set in a large and slightly red face, with some greying brown hair that gave his age as being in the forties. He had many laughter lines and a pleasant demeanour, and as he joined Becky on the stand, they put away the supplies with military precision, some unspoken thing between them allowing them to pass things to each other almost without looking.

"Got yourself a friend, pet?" Becky said, straightening up. "Good for you. This one could use some feeding up anyway. Here, have I seen you around before, miss?"

"I'm Cupidity Cooper, proprietor of She's The- I mean, proprietor of Waist Knot, Want Knot, larger clothes for the larger...personality," Cupidity replied, smiling and extending a hand. She was instead enveloped in a hug.

"Anyone who cares for our girl here is a friend to us. I'm Aunt Becky, and this here is my husband, John, handsome fellow that he is."

She gestured towards Joy. "Here, is *this* one wearing clothes of yours?" she asked.

"Well, she *was*," Cupidity replied, also looking at the state of Joy's apparel. "Now, like, I'd say she was abusing them. Honestly, Joy, what am I going to do with you?"

"Well, I likes what you do," Aunt Becky said, as she move vegetables into chillers and pulled out jars of garlic floating in oil and chilli. "You definitely gave this one a Look! You know, despite her wearing half the forest too."

"I should get her into something clean," Cupidity said. "Do you mind if I pinch her for a moment? Can't have her getting about, looking like something the cat dragged in. You're welcome to come, if you'd like; see the store, you might find something you'd like?"

"Oh, I'd love to, luv, but the stall is getting ready for the lunch run! Maybe another time," Aunt Becky replied, but there was a tinge of disappointment in her voice and her husband cleared his throat.

"My love," he said to Becky as he rustled through the last bag, "I've got those soup bases ready to go in here. You've been working so hard, why don't you let me run the stall this afternoon? If you can give me five minutes of your time to work through the prep, I mean. Nobody dices like you, you know that."

"Lover, I'd love to but people here depend on me," she replied, holding his hands. "You know how I feel about that."

"Indeed I do, my angel," John replied as they both started dicing. "But let's let absence make the heart grow fonder. I may not be as pretty a face, but I can hold down the fort for the rush. I'm sure the regulars will all be back; after all, I've been back so much that it was cheaper to just marry you!" John said with a grin, nudging her with his elbow.

"Oh, you!" she replied with a laugh, giving him a whack with a tea towel. "Well, if you're sure."

"Always, gorgeous. You go have a bit of time to yourself. These young lasses seem lovely, and I reckon they need you more than I do."

"You're certain you don't need me?"

"I'll always need you, you know that. I'm sure I'll survive an hour or two."

"All right," she replied, giving him a peck on the cheek and folding up her apron, which she put under the counter. She turned to the girls. "Shall we, ladies?"

Cupidity's new shop was only a few streets back and it was a ten-minute walk from the stall to the door for the three of them. Joy was enjoying the distraction from her circumstances, and although she still felt glum, the sensation of falling had, for now, stopped. Lo and behold, Cupidity's store came into view, full of bright colours and bulbous text proclaiming its name. Compared to the restrained and refined style of the previous store, Joy was surprised, but the vibrancy seemed to reflect the town.

"I like the name," Aunt Becky said to Cupidity as she opened the lock, "what's it mean?"

"Well, it's supposed to be a bit of a play on some of the designs I was coming up with," Cupidity said. "Because you deserve to be an icon too! And it was better than the other name I thought of."

"Which was?"

"Wide Power."

Aunt Becky gave her a slow look, but there was nothing but gormlessness in Cupidity's face.

"Good choice," she said at last.

There was a completely different vibe within the shop. The clothes were, obviously, larger than what Joy had seen before but were vibrant, bold and eye-catching. Cupidity disappeared in the back, and came out with a package which she proffered to Joy.

"Here," she said, "These are the clothes I was going to give to Avaritia. You're close in size, and I have to say, you've always had the better frame for these. Go on, I have a shower upstairs. And *you,*" she added, turning her attention to Aunt Becky as Joy started towards the stairs, "come with me. It's time you embrace how *fabulous* you could be."

"Luv, if you've had my food, you know I've been fabulous for years," Aunt Becky responded, but Cupidity shook her head.

"Trust me," she said confidently, "you won't know what that means until I've worked my magic to release *yours.*"

Joy was thankful for the running water which eased her aching muscles and left her feeling thoroughly refreshed, and stepped out of the shower into wonderful feel of the new clothes. On top of the beautiful fabrics, patterns, and cuts, the clothes were paired with the stunning, bright red, full-length overcoat that Joy had seen in Avaritia's office with Tom. She remembered looking over it at the reception desk an age ago, while a stranger put his neck on the line to protect these clothes- and her friend's future- from the rubbish heap. Cupidity had certainly been determined to make a visual statement. As always, the work was first-class, and the feel of crisp and clean fabric buoyed her mood enough that she felt ready to think about Tom's departure.

Her sadness was beginning to give way to anger, as she dwelled on the contrast between the person she had fallen in love with and the person who left her the hated letter. How *dare* he leave with just a note? Lie and say he'd be back? Who did he think he was, to come with her, trick him into sharing her secrets, and just walk away? At the same time, she already felt the gaps in the conversations they would have had, the exploration of the towns and the search for the next adventure. He'd wanted adventure, hadn't he?

Had he? her inner monologue accused. *What did he actually say?* Joy found she couldn't recall specifics. In fact, if pressed, she wasn't entirely sure that she had asked him what he wanted, and if he'd said anything, she hadn't heard it. She pushed the thought from her mind and decided to return downstairs.

Cupidity had done amazing work and Aunt Becky looked truly radiant. She was wearing a dress that somehow lit her up completely, compliment-ing her warm expression and joyful eyes, a multi-colour pattern of yellows and reds and oranges and browns. She spun around, making the dress twirl out,

"My word, girls!" she exclaimed. "I haven't felt like this since I was but a little lass myself!"

"It looks *great* on you," Joy enthused.

"*So* great," Cupidity half-added, half-corrected.

Aunt Becky looked at herself in a mirror, half dancing a jig as she watched the dress sway and flow.

"Feels great, darl, but I'd better give it back. It's not for the likes of me."

"What *is* for the likes of you, then?" Cupidity asked. "You deserve it."

"You do!" Joy enthused. "You've been so kind, feeding me and cheering me up! Here, if it's the cost, I'm happy to chi-"

"And since you've been so good to my friend here," Cupidity interrupted, "the dress is free. I owe her, anyway, if she's happy for me to pay it forward."

"Oh, no, I couldn't possibly do that, pet!" Aunt Becky replied. "We've always kept our heads above water, mind."

"No, she paid for clothes that I'd already given her for working for me. Tell you what, tell people where you got the clothes, I'll consider us even."

"I owe you for the food anyway," Joy said in agreement "Please, Aunt Becky. If you want them, I mean."

Aunt Becky continued looking at herself in the mirror, a different demeanour taking her over.

"Weeeeeell," she said as her inner tug-of-war swayed in favour of her true desires, "it'd be a change for the stall. All right, girls, thank you! Now, we'd better get back. Lunch is on me and I won't hear a word otherwise."

So they made their way back to the stall, and Joy was impressed. Cupidity was still giving clothes away, technically, which isn't exactly a sound business practice, but the solution of having her wears displayed at a popular stall made good sense, and Joy was delighted to offer something back to Aunt Becky for all the kindness she'd been shown. It seemed a good solution for everyone.

Whatever Cupidity had learnt, it was smart. Perhaps it was worth pursuing herself, she thought.

"Hey, so tell me about this owl?" she asked casually. Aunt Becky made a noise.

"You don't want to go around disturbin' him, luv," she said. "Ol' Peregrine, he'd just as near eat you as help you. Wisest creature in the land but way I hear it, he's not one for people, and he *is* a carnivore, after all."

"He didn't seem that way to *me*," Cupidity said happily. "All I had to do was refuse to go away until he answered my question."

"That's it?" Aunt Becky asked incredulously.

"No, I was humming too. Like, a *lot*."

"Who *is* he?" Joy asked. "I've never heard of him before."

"Oh, he's a recluse," Aunt Becky replied. "They say he weighs the hearts of the weary traveller and if they are pure, he gives them wisdom, and if they're tainted, well, *skrrrrrrrsh*," and she made a slitting motion across her neck. "He lives in the Dark Forest, the big one just on the town's outskirts, but I've never seen him. *Nobody* has seen him, except sometimes at nights if he's hunting in the fields and they catch a glimpse as he swoops past. I don't know how your friend managed it."

"Oh, everything just seems to work out for me," Cupidity said happily. "I don't know why people find life so *hard*. I just went into the forest and took a nap and then set a fire because I was cold which kind of spread a little bit too far because I didn't have any rocks but there were a heap of bundles of sticks, and then a tree started burning and then this big whooshing happened and put the fire out and there was the bird. And I was, like, *oh my gosh, like, do you know how iconic you look?* And he was all, 'what the hell are you doing burning down my forest?' And then I was like, 'you have to answer my question, that's the rules.' And *he* said, 'what rules, I'm not a genie.' And so then *I* was all, 'nah queen, I found you, you have to answer my question'. And then I was singing, and then his eye started twitching, and then I was like 'you look tense, you should eat some nougat,' and *he* was all 'I don't want your stupid nougat,' but then he ate it, and I told him what I wanted to know, and he gave me an answer and then took off."

This chain of events was not entirely a surprise for Joy, who had spent time with Cupidity before, but Aunt Becky was aghast. Cupidity continued unabashed.

"So yeah, I reckon if you just take some treats, all pets like treats, right? And then he'll probably tell you anything you want to know."

By the time they reached the square, it was absolutely packed for the lunch rush and there was a substantial line of customers at the stall. John was serving feverishly but when he spied the girls coming across through the crowd, with Aunt Becky's new outfit making her stand out like a bouquet of tiger lilies in an all-white hospital room, his face lit up and he excused himself from a customer.

"One moment, sir," he said, "Just gotta see the love of my life."

For a large man, he was surprisingly light on his feet as he weaved his way through the crowd and reached Becky and somehow managed to pick her up and whirl her around. Aunt Becky laughed.

"Oh, John, you bloody fool!" she chuckled, "you'll do yourself a mischief! I'm not the girl I was when I was twenty, you know!"

"Darl, you've never been anything else to me," John said with a wink and a kiss on her cheek. "And *what* an outfit. These lasses have really done it, I haven't seen you so dolled up since our wedding day!"

He sniffed for a moment, a happy tear in his eye. "You've always been gorgeous, luv, but wow. You could knock me over with a feather!"

Becky leaned up and gave him a peck on the cheek in return. "You do go on," she said affectionately, blushing. "You big sop. You really like it that much?"

"If you shone any more, lover, the sun would start gettin' jealous, I reckon." Aunt Becky laughed again, and took his hand. "Come on then, big boy, if you're going to charm a woman then you'd better help her clear these customers! Can't have you all to myself with a queue here now, can I?"

She looked at Joy. "Twenty-three years," she said. "Twenty-three years this man has loved me, lord knows why. And I, him." She winked. "There's something out there for you, luv, and for what it's worth, don't let one heartbreak stop you taking a chance in future. If you find someone who's prepared to keep the game going with you all that time, well, that's a keeper right there. A good man is worth his weight in gold."

"That's a lot of gold in my case!" John chuckled. "Come on now, gorgeous. Can't keep the people waiting! And thank *you*, girls, you gave our Becky a smile I've not seen for a good while. Made her feel as beautiful as she is to me. Good on the pair of you!"

Joy watched them wistfully. In that moment, she truly saw joy radiating from this couple, and her heart suddenly ached with loss. Not just Tom, but the chance to have seen something similar from her parents back at home, depth and affection and playfulness and moments where the familiar still made someone light up like Christmas. Is this what had been missing all along? How far back did her discomfort go? If this had been what her parents had together at one point, how had it been lost? Was it all really so fragile?

Aunt Becky's outfit was causing something of a stir at the stand, and even more people had started milling around, particularly the ladies of the town who had seen her pass by. Whilst she was working feverishly on the stand, Cupidity and Joy could see her answering questions and pointing towards them.

"That was a pretty smart move," Joy said to Cupidity, "getting Aunt Becky to promote you in return for the dress."

"Well, she never asked for it," Cupidity said. "And that's the difference with Avaritia. People actually love Becky, y'know? Plus, I was serious- I owed you, and you owed her, and now everyone is square. It's... kinda nice to see someone really love what I've done. Almost as nice as doing whatever I want. Back home, there was already an expectation of what things had to look like and you're all just trying to do something a tiny bit different, but here? Well, I can really let loose. I can be different."

"I do appreciate these clothes though," Joy said, feeling a little self-conscious. Cupidity shrugged.

"They look good on you. They were always going to look good on you. You're an icon, after all."

"You say everyone's an icon."

"Sure I do. But you are. And that's why you should go get some answers. That owl will hear what you have to say."

"You think?"

"I think even giant owls know when someone's special."

Joy found this genuine- and surprising- moment of kindness from her friend cause an emotional overflow, turned and gave Cupidity a sudden hug. Cupidity, taken aback, froze, and gingerly patted Joy on the shoulder. "Come on, now," she chided gently, "you can't be all emotional *and* iconic. Think of your fans."

She pushed Joy away and straightened her new coat, then brushed her hair back and generally tidied up. In doing so, she hadn't noticed John leave the stall and approach them again, with a paper bag in one hand and a bowl of noodles in the other.

"Here, girls," he said a little hurriedly, "there's a few baguettes we put together for the road for *you*, Miss Joy, and for *you* miss, well, we thought you could use a proper lunch before the rush."

"What rush?" Cupidity asked, taking the bowl gratefully.

"Oh, there's a fair few ladies who are going to be dropping by your shop today, I reckon. Once lunch is done, of course."

"Oh, so I've got a bit of time?"

"There's a good couple of hours. We take lunch seriously."

"Well, I'll bring the bowl back after closing, but thank you!"

"Don't worry too much, miss. We're closing up early tonight; it's time our Becky had a night to herself. You know, she loves that stand, and she loves what she does, and I reckon we sorta... forgot about receiving a bit ourselves. She looked so happy and *new* and I just thought, 'John, put it all down for a moment and take that woman somewhere she can feel...'" he trailed off.

"Like a queen?" Cupidity suggested. John laughed.

"Oh, royalty is a bit too much for the likes of us. Plus, they're aways choppin' off heads, which is the *last* thing I want to be in the middle of! But if she can feel just a *bit* of what I feel when I look at her, well, maybe that's royal enough!"

He put a hand on each shoulder.

"New beginnings for all of us today, I reckon! All the best, girls. Be sure to stop by any time. Miss Joy, I hope you can find what you're looking for. Now I'd better get along!"

And that seemed to be that. The day was wasting away and with an awkward hug, Joy and Cupidity went their separate ways. Joy returned to the lodgings where she and Tom had previously been staying and found her bag had been thoughtfully put just inside the entrance.

She took a moment so sit on a bench out front, and misery took that moment to strike, digging its cold fingers into her chest.

Like a dog with its tail between its legs, here you are, it whispered. *You really think there's an answer out there for you? This is it: nobody wants you. Not really. Not for good. Not forever.*

She cursed at it internally. She could feel an ache in her head, a burrowing, as if working its way in deeper not just into the brain matter but into her innermost thoughts.

Better to be found in the forest. A victim of your choices and a monstrous bird. After all, what have you got left?

"Nothing," she admitted to herself glumly, and stopped. Something occurred to her, a moment of warmth in her chest appearing as the idea formed.

"If I've got nothing left, then I've got nothing to lose," she said.

You've lost everything. You can't paint that as a win.

"It's not a win."

Then the forest will be your tomb. People will come across you, unmarked, unknown, and wonder who this lonely soul was.

"It might be. It might not be. But of all the possibilities, the worst one is an end. Every other one has to be a positive."

Being torn apart by a wild animal, alone and afraid, isn't a positive.

"Yes, but I can't go back, not without Fear or Steve the boat. I can't stay here. And if this owl didn't eat Cupidity, then he can't be as bad as people make out."

As she said this internally, she felt the cold start to battle the spreading warmth, thesis and antithesis clashing in an internal battleground.

"You can't hurt me," she said to herself. "I might be broken-hearted, but I'm not broken. I've made friends."

You've lost friends. You've lost love.

"Yes. But maybe friends come back. And since you're right- I don't know how to fix friends, or find joy, or find love, then at least I can find wisdom while I figure the rest out."

Hmph.

"You're ugly when you sulk. I should know."

Hmph.

The pain in her head began to recede, and the cold grip in her chest lessened. Despite herself, she felt the start of a smile creep over her. All those years arguing with Fear weren't wasted after all; she hadn't realised it, but she had skills to push back against the tide of self-deception and litany of the worst-possible scenarios. She wasn't sure if she should thank him, should she ever see him again, given the constant aggravation and negativity that he'd used to develop this skill, but she couldn't argue with the results.

It wasn't quite a smile that settled on her face, but whatever it was, it was determined. She put her assorted food and sweet items into her bag, and then began the walk out of town.

Two hours later, Joy was completely lost. It seemed fairly straightforward at concept stage: go back to the forest outside of town, begin searching. She realised- far too late- that there may have been missed opportunities to ask for directions, or some kind of markers or landmarks, or really even an exit point, when she was talking to Cupidity. There had been the beginnings of a trail when she had first entered, not far from where she had fallen asleep the day before, but after twenty minutes it had faded to almost nothing and other than leafmould, there wasn't much to see. The forest lived up to its name, with huge trees creating a canopy that only allowed a limited amount of light through. The ground was mossy rather than grassy, and she could hear rustling under the leaves which was far more concerning now that she didn't have Fear with her, and her thoughts drifted to fill the gaps between noise and sight with imaginary horrors featuring mysterious slime and altogether too many legs.

It's a bad idea to lose your train of thought when wandering in an unfamiliar forest, and this became the primary driver of Joy's eventual discovery of her inability to determine where she had come from, as much as where she was now going. She didn't know what homes for giant owls looked like; a nest for something that size would fall out of a tree, surely.

On the other hand, a giant owl wasn't going to be able to build a house, given the lack of opposable thumbs.

Another half hour went by, and Joy started getting worried about the impending sundown. Perhaps she should have listened to herself, because she hadn't thought to consider what other threats this forest might contain, much less the implications of being in a forest you might not be able to get out of. Once again, doubts and worries started to settle in unfamiliar ways and left her feeling cold. There were probably snakes, or bears, or bears who had teamed up with snakes. Despite her bravado when confronting her inner monologue, despite her feelings of pain and loss, despite her aching heart and loneliness, Joy realised that she really didn't *want* to die. She'd have to figure out something soon- either to continue her search or to pick a single direction that would possibly lead to an exit and continue in a straight line until she was out. She was already getting hungry. Her heart thumping loudly with each step, the rustles of the forest floor continued, when her footfall made a rustling sound with a different note than what she had been expecting. She looked down, and saw that she had stepped in a candy wrapper.

Joy's head snapped up and she looked around hurriedly. Yes, there it was- a tree with scorch marks still visible on the trunk, from Cupidity's ill-fated attempt at camping. She felt hope bloom once again, a warmth which fought the coldness of her worries, and strode across.

There were signs of a camp fire attempt still, or, at least, the charred remains of a number of sticks in circle. It didn't look like a camp fire that Joy had ever really seen; it was too large, like you'd almost have to sit in the middle of the thing. She was wondering how long it would have taken Cupidity to gather all these and weave them together when realisation dawned and the hole in her stomach reappeared. This wasn't a campfire. It had been a nest.

There was a sudden *whoomph* of wings and a loud thud that scattered stray leaves far and wide. Joy covered her head instinctively, closing her eyes as she did so. When sudden death didn't present itself, she pulled her arms from her head and looked up gingerly.

Owls can be unnerving at the best of times, given that a large portion of their faces is made up of oversized eyes, and these only become more unsettling when they are the size of dinner plates on a six-foot bird. Joy presumed that there would have to be a minimum of human-sized owls in existence and, given the instructions she had followed, assumed this could only be Peregrine. He had landed on a fallen tree trunk, his talons gripping the wood and gleaning in the meagre light that had made it through the forest canopy. He drew himself up to his full height, looking rather regal as he peered down at Joy.

"Who?" he said, and then made a noise like a difficult toilet being flushed.

"Are you talking to me in Owl Language?" Joy asked. Peregrine's eyes narrowed.

"No, before I had to clear my throat I was going to ask who the *hell* you thought you were, coming into my forest?" he said scornfully. "You're not another one of those groupie people, are you?"

"What do you mean?" Joy asked, confused. The owl ruffled his feathers, and started half-walking, half-hopping in a circle around her.

"I swear not a *day* goes by without someone coming into my forest to bother me and interrupt my day," he said before carrying on in a mocking, sing-song voice. "Oh Peregrine, I need wisdom! Oh Peregrine, why did I chop my arm off? Oh Peregrine, I ate nothing but chocolate for three weeks, why do I have unstoppable diarrhea? The inane ramblings of a population so obsessed with their bloody happiness that they never stop to think about their responsibilities or the consequences beyond their immediate satisfaction."

His body started heading off in the opposite direction before he spun his head around a hundred and eighty degrees and gave Joy a scrutinizing glare.

"*You're* not going to ask me to solve your life problems, are you?"

"Uuuuum..." Joy began.

"Because you *know* owls are nocturnal and right now you're basically waking me up at the equivalent of your three-A-M and you'd *never* be so stupid as to ask for a favour and advice from someone whose sleep you just interrupted, right?"

Joy thought quickly. "*Actually*," she lied, putting a hand into her bag, "I came here because I was told that Peregrine the Wise had a sweet tooth and I just happened to have gotten the best nougat in Frieland."

The owl stopped pacing, then turned and inclined its head slowly towards her, which is unnerving for those whose necks don't have twenty extra joints.

"You heard that an owl, a nocturnal raptor, a predator of the night, would want your *sugar*?" he enquired, hopping closer along the trunk. "And from whom did you hear this folly, this slander, this *nonsense*?!?"

"Well, I, uh," Joy stammered, looking at the ground, "that's a little personal."

"And I suppose, idiot that you are, you *brought* this nougat to an apex predator, a carnivore whose digestive system is unsullied by humanity's prostituting of nature's bounty into bar form?"

"Well, yeah, I mean I have some right here-" Joy began, pulling out a block of nougat which was immediately followed by a blur and her hand was suddenly empty again.

"Mmmmmph, it'ff an infult an it'ff alfo wermph to merpher mer ffafafgef," he said, the stickiness of the nougat making it hard to open his beak.

"What was that?"

"I *said*," the owl continued, swallowing emphatically, "that it's an insult and it's also wrong to offer me sausages."

"I don't have any sausages," Joy said defensively.

"Well, you're not very prepared then, are you? Goodbye."

"Wait!" Joy called, as the owl crouched and extended its wings to fly off. "I... I do have a question."

"You might have a question, but if you don't have a sausage, then you don't have an answer. I'm not a charity."

"I have..." Joy rustled in her bag, pulling out the paper bag of sandwiches that John had given her. "I've got ham and cheese on a baguette?"

The owl's eyes narrowed, which is worth seeing when they start with so much width in the first place.

"How *much* ham?" he asked suspiciously.

"Lots. There's also... let me see... chicken and salad, roast beef, and-" she cut herself off. The fourth sandwich was egg and mayonnaise but perhaps birds took the use of eggs as an insult. "And that's it, pretty much."

"So you're just going to lie about the egg sandwich," Peregrine said severely.

"At least I know what I'm dealing with." There was another blur, and Peregrine's claw was holding the bag of sandwiches. "I guess you're eating egg."

The egg baguette, still wrapped in greaseproof paper, was thrown at her, and Joy managed to catch it. She was feeling annoyed at the rudeness on display. She unwrapped it and took a bite, as Peregrine picked his own ones out, one at a time, held deftly in a claw and brought up to his mouth where they disappeared in a couple of pronounced pecks. It didn't take long for all evidence of the sandwiches' existence to have disappeared except for torn wrappers. Then, leaning down, the owl turned his head ninety degrees and looked at Joy impassively; the effect was entirely unnerving.

"Those," he said, "were worth my time. Who are you?"

"Joy Summerfield," Joy replied, a little nervous.

"What is it you want from me, Joy Summerfield?"

"I need answers. I'm supposed to be here finding my joy, but I've lost my friend, and I don't feel at home anywhere, and I told a boy I loved him and he left me to return bowls and never came back."

The owl gave her a withering gaze. "Is that all?" he asked. "The answer is: you're eighteen. You're welcome."

With that, he started to ready himself to take off, and Joy waved her arms to stop him. "Wait, wait, what do you mean, I'm eighteen?" she asked.

"Look, kid, it doesn't take much to figure you out," Peregrine replied, settling back on the log again. "Nobody comes to ask me things who *really* wants an answer to the question, they're just terrified that what they know is the right answer can't be changed. They're hoping that it isn't really a simple issue that they can control, because when you're powerless against an invisible force, well, nothing's your fault. And you... let me guess, chronically unhappy at home? Missing parent? Feels an itch for a place they can't name? Bit of a loner?"

"Well... I mean, I wouldn't put it like that..."

"I don't care how you'd put it. I'm not here to be your friend. You wanted advice, right? Is what I said an accurate description of you?"

"I... well, you know... I mean, yes, I guess," Joy replied a little sullenly.

"And how long did you know this boy?"

"Well, we travelled together for maybe the last four or five weeks."

"*Okay*. So, the girl who couldn't find her place, met a boy. A boy who took an interest in her, who let her tell him her innermost secrets by doing something as stupid as listening uninterrupted? And then after a month, she thought nobody in the world would understand her like this boy could?"

"Yeah, sure, that's what happened," Joy replied defensively. The reductiveness of this description made her feel embarrassed; the way the owl talked about it made it all seem so *trivial*, and the monumental pain and loss, to her, anything but. "And then he left me, and didn't even have the guts to face me, and tell me he didn't love me."

"Oh, pfffffffft," Peregrine responded dismissively, rolling his head in the kind of wide circle that requires a neck to essentially be made of rubber, which really drove home the disdain. "Of course he did. You'd just made him completely and solely responsible for your happiness. After a *month*. Who's the bigger asshole there? How does that ever end well for this kid? He tells you no, he has to deal with the fallout. You plead or negotiate. He lies and tells you yes, he's trapped making you happy. He says yes and means it, and what happens with you? There's no doubt it's cowardice, but did you ever stop to check if he was a coward before you dumped the entirety of your emotional well-being on his shoulders?"

"What's that got to do with being eighteen?"

He ruffled his feathers. "It has *everything* to do with being eighteen. Here, I'll prove it: you spent the last month of so with him. Tell me four things about *him*, his innermost thoughts, his plans and desires."

Joy paused. A hot feeling of shame now started to overtake her as she racked her brain. Had she ever asked about his family? Had she heard his hopes? When he was listening to people, engaging with them city to city, had she heard what interested him, what was making *him* come alive? How often had he talked about what was missing in each city? She wanted desperately to prove the owl wrong, and list out lots of facts, but to her internal horror she found herself coming up empty.

"He hated his old job," she managed lamely, "And wanted to do right by people."

"Everyone hates their job. I know that I do, right now," sniffed Peregrine. "That's not a revelation. You put all your hopes and dreams for the future on this boy, bore your soul to him, and you never *once* thought to plumb the depths of this person you were trusting beforehand, even for safety, much less offer reciprocity to someone you allegedly love? What about this friend of yours that you lost?"

"What about him?"

"Well, did you ever ask *him* what he wanted?"

"Uuuuuuuuuuh..." Joy trailed off, feeling increasingly ashamed and increasingly angry. Even Tom had asked this question once before, but it had never occurred to her to enquire.

"And let me guess," the owl continued, "I bet the catalyst for the termination of this friendship was that he threatened your oh-so-important love declaration? Nobody throws a friendship away willy-nilly."

Joy didn't answer at all now. She hung her head and looked glum. Peregrine sighed.

"Look, kid, don't feel down about this stuff. It's like I said: you're eighteen. You're not in love, you're obsessed because you're feeling attention, validation, understanding, and it's got you hooked. At your age, everything you do is self-serving; you've gone from a comfortable home into a world you think you know all about, and you've got a list of needs that used to be met back home that now are flapping in the breeze. It's just the reality of things. It doesn't have to be the person you are forever. But how do you expect to find joy if you expect that it's something external that essentially serves you? A place, or a task, or a town that does things all the same way, or a boy? It's all consumption, and if you let it, it's just going to suck the life out of everything and you're still not going to be satisfied. It's not joy, it's vampirism. Heck, this place is *full* of it, every little city and town that gets together and decides to build a wall and encapsulate their obsession because when it's gathered in numbers, it somehow seems more legitimate. They tell themselves that if there's agreement, if there's consensus, then there's truth, and that's not how truth works. The truth is the truth even if nobody knows it, and it remains true despite any level of mass delusion."

"I thought each city had found their happiness?"

"Oh, please. Did they *seem* happy to you? I mean, *really* happy. Actual joy."

"Well... I mean...maybe Aunt Becky and Tom..." Joy began, and then stopped to think. "What is the difference between happiness and actual joy?"

"And *there* it is, kid. That's the question you needed to have asked *before* you got started looking for it."

Peregrine hopped off the branch and started walk around Joy in a circle. "None of these places," he lectured, his head pivoting to maintain eye contact with every circular step, "has the faintest idea about happiness, much less joy. It's a lie, an obfuscation, a distraction. They run like hamsters on a wheel, thinking that activity is the same as progress. That's why they all come to me and hope against hope I'm going to tell them something other than what they already know, because if they admitted to themselves that they'd built their entire lives around their self-satisfaction, or predictability, or living within the worst excesses of their individual nature, their whole world would come tumbling down. And honestly, the *worst* thing is that whatever little thing you make the centrality of your life, well, it means very little to anybody else. You don't have to take much from the craven for them to lose all hope altogether. That's the thing; ultimately, you're trying to plug a hole with anything that fits close enough. You aren't dealing with the hole. You want to find joy? You want a future? You're going to have to deal with your own past first."

"So do you ever tell these people something other than what they already know?"

"No. I pull down their delusions and they confuse facing the truth for wisdom. Waste of my time, really."

"Well, I'm after your wisdom."

"Then we start with the truth. Your problems are entirely of your own making, because you're young, and stupid, and thought you knew everything."

Joy was about to object, defend herself, but stopped. The statement opened up the pit of fear again, but if the owl was right, then it was fear of the truth, and perhaps this fear needed to be exposed rather than covered up with denial. She wondered how many times she had done this without realising before. It was over in a second but Peregrine noticed.

"You're right," she said instead of the defence she had first planned. "I brought myself here. I left my home and my father. I picked my destinations. I sent Fear away. I thought love served me. And I don't know what joy is, so I don't know how to find it."

Peregrine returned her admission with a long look, then took a deep breath. "Well, you fed me, so I don't have to hunt tonight," he said grudgingly, a little surprised that the surliness he had expected hadn't eventuated. "Fear is a friend of yours, you said?"

"He was," Joy replied, a little sadly.

"Tall fellow? Likes long coats and bad hairdos? Not very big on respecting walls as a convention?"

"Yes!" Joy exclaimed, surprised. She looked into two enormous eyes that, for the first time appeared to really focus on her, seeing her fully. Peregrine stopped his pacing, and then gestured to another fallen log for Joy to sit on.

"Then you have my attention," he said. "Start at the beginning."

Chapter 10

More To Life

I'm not my father or my mother

One of Joy's earliest memories- in fact, one of the few memories she was surprised to find she kept and protected- had been one she had been running from, locking it down in her mind and rarely daring to step a foot back in.

It had been mid-summer when Joy was maybe six years old, when the sun went down late and the holidays stretched out and somehow, free time had snuck in early one evening. Dinner was pending and her father was working late and in that gap, Joy had wandered into the living room to find her mother there, sitting on the floor as light streamed through the window, back up against their old threadbare lounge, guitar in hand. She vaguely recalled that there was a performance pending or a studio session due to happen or something small-scale, but even at her young age, there was something different about her mother and the guitar. It wasn't a rehearsal in the real sense of having an intent or a plan; she sensed it as soon as she walked into the room, that there was a state of flow, running like a slow river through a canyon, carving its way out. Rather than interrupt it, as her mother made eye contact with her but never ceased strumming, and smiled, she felt the flow pick her up and buoy her, carrying her along with it. Her mother sang softly, gentle and warm and beautifully melodious, lyrics that were comforting and homely, wrapping around her like a weighted blanket.

It was as if there was a direct connection between her mother and her, as the music flowed and completed a circuit and they looked at each other, audience and performer, snake charmer and cobra, one single entity. The attention provided a feedback component, as if there was nothing but a loop, and rather than disappear into the ether, the songs were amplified back. Joy could *feel* the love in the strings as they were plucked, as the notes were articulated, as her mother lifted her head and closed her eyes on the high parts and sang of love, and of loss, and of redemption, and of home.

She could feel the warmth of the sun's diminishing rays on her back as they shone through the windows and slowly changed colours, her own private stage lighting. One song morphed into the next and before she knew it, the best part of an hour had gone by and the sun was almost gone.

In that moment, for that time, she had *felt* her mother, truly. It wasn't as the amorphous entity that is "mother" to a young child, familiar arms, safety and kindness to run away from until whatever mischief brought you back for skinned knees or bruised shins or bumped heads to be attended to and kissed away. It was a life of its own, bright and dancing and ebbing and flowing, a spark in the dark. For all the subsequent bad choices and pain and suffering, she had found it hard to forget that moment of connection, the sense of the restless flame that flickered and warmed those in its presence.

She didn't want the songs to end, she wanted to be carried by them, surf them, hear the haunting beauty of her mother's voice singing a world into existence, but the cool started to settle into the room and music couldn't last forever. Eventually, her mother put the guitar down and stood up.

"I loved your songs, mama," six-year-old Joy had said.

"Thank you, baby."

"You're *real* good at guitar."

"Thank you, baby."

"Will you teach me one day?"

"When you're bigger."

"How much bigger?"

"When you can hold a guitar on your own, I guess."

"Did you get that guitar when you were big enough to hold one?"

"Funnily enough, no. Your father bought this for me, when we got engaged. He said he thought it would get more use than a ring, and he could only afford one or the other. I had an older, beaten one before but it eventually broke."

"Is that why it sounds so good?"

"Well, any instrument can sound good, if you can put what you feel into the music you make it play. Maybe it sounds a little better when someone loves you with it."

"*I* love you with it."

"Thank you, baby."

And that was it. Even now, she struggled to remember the exact look of her mother's face; she seemed bigger than she could have truly been, as the eyes of a small child don't change the perspective in memories when they grow, but she remembered the golden hair and effortless style, and how much she ached to be in her mother's presence. It was funny, on reflection, thinking about how awkward her mother seemed to be when actually talking to her. There was a context in which she must have felt comfort, flow and relaxation, but it was only when the music was playing. As the performance died out, so too did that person, and the one who returned in its place seemed to be at a loss about what to do next. The answers were short and Joy had felt like she was pestering somehow. She wanted that moment back, she wanted that *person* back. She tried one more compliment, hoping that it would make her mother bring her into that inner space, metaphorically and physically.

"You should be famous."

"Thank you, baby."

"Will you sing me to sleep tonight?"

"No, baby, I have to go out tonight."

"Why?"

"Because that's how you become famous."

A part of Joy had wondered all these years: had this been the catalyst for her mother's departure? Was it because Joy herself had told her to go and be famous somewhere? And how come, after leaving them, after going off to do what Joy worried she had told her to do, had she not even had the decency to achieve her dream? How could she pay a price like that and not even get what she had wanted? There had been years, *years* where Joy had secretly been waiting between songs on the radio to hear the DJ or presenter or whatever the host was called announce her mother's name before playing the latest single, before she hated the very sound of a radio being played for what it represented: the sacrifice of their family for a failed goal, or as Joy saw it, trading gold for sawdust.

In the universe of disappointment and frustration and, if she was honest with herself, a fair degree of hatred, this one memory still operated as the sun that these planetary bodies of negative emotion orbited. Somewhere, once upon a time, there was a moment where she loved her mother, and was loved in return, and from that emerged a deep bitterness attached to a question: why was that not enough to want to hang on to? Why was she, Joy, not worth more than strangers in a dive bar hoping for a cover of a song they half remember and who would never see you again?

She relayed this to Peregrine, a preamble to the subsequent years and all things hence. The whole story had taken some time, and the sun had gone down; she had continued talking while they built a fire properly, bounded with rocks and not made out of Peregrine's former bedding, and Joy had sat down with her hands out for warmth. The owl listened, occasionally asking a clarifying question, and when she was done, he took a deep breath in.

"That's it?" he asked as the fire popped and crackled. "Look, kid, I don't want you to take this the wrong way, but all of this is some kind of desperate cry for mummy, is that it? You came out here, into a forest you didn't know, alone, for that?"

"Well, no, or I mean yeah a bit, but-" Joy stammered, taken aback after baring her soul.

"Right, then, let's get started," he said, rubbing his wing tips together. "First off: let's put yourself in your mother's shoes. You're eighteen now, only a few years younger than she was when you were born. Here she is, trying desperately to add things into her life that will fill some kind of internal pit

she has. A career, and failing that, a husband, and failing that, a child. And
when that didn't pan out, when she didn't feel what she thought she'd feel,
she left to pursue the next thing she'd pinned her hopes on, yes?"

"I don't like the way you're putting this," Joy said with a huff. "I see what
you're doing. It's not even the same thing."

"*How* is it different, kid? You're mad at your mother while you're doing the
exact same thing as her. And that's not a judgement, but my first question's
gotta be: how come you never thought to ask yourself why your mother
wasn't ever happy?"

"I did!"

"No, you asked why you weren't enough for her, why she needed someone
else. Her problems go back before you; they go back before she met your
father, even. It's a crisis of state."

"What do you mean?"

"Look, you're going to have to stop looking at her as your mum, first."

"So how, precisely, should I look at her?" Joy asked archly.

"As a stupid young woman," Peregrine replied with a shrug. "It's what she
was. That doesn't mystically, magically change just because you popped a
kid out."

"Go on," Joy said cautiously, liking the 'stupid' part.

"OK, so, the world is full of stupid people, we're in agreement on that,
yes? But it's a mistake to sit in judgement and allow that history, that
stupidity, to snare you in the same trap that it caught her in. Perhaps she
was one confronting moment away from discovering the truth, but she
never got there. In the absence of that, what you see in her shouldn't be
some sullen point of grievance, but rather the final destination of your own
behaviour. It's broken people doing broken things. You're acting as if she
owed you *something*, or even like she owed you *someone*, that you never got.
Why is that?"

"Well, everyone *else* got a mum. Isn't that the deal?" Joy asked sullenly.

"It's not written anywhere. It's certainly the ideal, but since when is anything ideal? What about the mothers who stay and belittle and destroy their children, or cripple them with neglect while they feed their addictions? The mothers who bring a revolving door of boyfriends, or who are trapped in poverty and unable to scrape together enough food for a meal? The mothers of venom and spite, for whom the children only serve their desires and are otherwise tossed aside? *Where* is it this mystical deal of yours written?"

"You're not being very helpful."

Peregrine rolled his eyes, which is something you can *really* do when each eye is the size of a dinner plate.

"You didn't come here for helpfulness. I'm not here to reinforce your fantasies. You were about to throw yourself at a boy. Find a city you thought could fulfil all your desires for the rest of your life. What, settle down and hope the story didn't repeat itself? If you don't start looking at your mother as a person first, mother second, you won't be able to actually make a different choice to her. You'll just run so hard that you won't realise you're running in the exact same direction, and then *that* will be her fault, too."

Joy felt furious at this; it minimised her pain and trauma, it dismissed very real and very valid blame, and worst of all, she had a horrible feeling that it was correct, which she absolutely did not want to admit.

"So why couldn't my mother be happy?" she asked defiantly.

"Search me, kid. I didn't know her. That's not the question. 'Could' has nothing to do with it. The question was: why *wasn't* she happy."

"Isn't that the same thing?"

"No. When you ask about 'could' it puts the onus on those external things to be satisfying. Like, 'what more would it take'. Or it comes across as an inherent character flaw, which is rarely the case. The question has to put the onus back on the person and their actions, not question circumstances and capacity. You have to deal with what *is*, and what is *not*."

"Ok, so why wasn't she happy?"

"Now we're on the right path. Okay. So, if happiness is a state rather than a capacity or a source, what's the barrier? If we feel happiness in receiving an item that wanes, what is our answer?"

"She wasn't happy because she wasn't famous?"

"Fame's a source. Push further."

"She wasn't happy because we weren't as important as her dream?"

"Then you'd be a source as well. Think harder. This is not about the externality, this is about the person."

Joy's brow furrowed as she thought furiously, and the realisation dawned.

"She wasn't happy, because she felt that her talent deserved more attention and recognition than she got, and she wasn't prepared to accept less than that. No... she wouldn't *let* herself be happy with Dad and I, because that would mean she'd have to admit that her talent had taken her as far as it could go. She wasn't happy, because she didn't want to be."

"Bingo! It was a choice, not a response, and we're responsible for our choices. Do we have a right to expect anything good? Honestly?"

"So what, your solution is to assume that only bad things are going to happen?"

"No, you've been in towns that have tried that. But it *does* start with our expectations. These come from our habits and our routines, and it doesn't take much for us to forget about where those expectations started, once the routine has become the norm. That's just basic selfishness, right there, and no-one's immune. Our expectations turn into entitlements, and that's where the problems take over; 'I would like' becomes 'I should be given'. Give a man something once, he will be grateful. Give a man something twice, he will expect it. Give it to him three times, he will demand it."

"So we're all terrible people?"

"Maybe. You'd have to decide that for yourself. However, we *can* reset those expectations. So our first principle is: what right do we have to expect good? There is no right. This means we must notice good actively. Has the sun risen? Or have the rains finally fallen? Are we sheltered? Are we in good company? Are we fed, or are we looking forward to food? Therein lies our starting point- what good do we have which gives us a positive anchor in the fight against entropy?"

"Ok, so we have to reset our expectations for good and be grateful first. Seems dumb, but let's say you're right. Now what?"

"Well, just because we can now see and be grateful for the good we thought we were entitled to, it doesn't mean we aren't aware of bad. Every beautiful garden has weeds that want to threaten it. We have to take responsibility for tending to that garden, so now we need to face those things, starting with our fears. Which in your case, has been taken away whenever it was a problem for you, up until now."

"I didn't ask for them to be taken away!" Joy protested, knowing that this wasn't strictly true.

"Whether you did or you didn't is irrelevant," Peregrine sighed. "It's a matter of fact: you didn't have them. And so what were you risking with your actions? Look, here you are, miles away from home, with someone who marvelled at your ability to take bold steps- this Tom of yours- and what had it really cost you personally? What did you have on the line? You went through storms and rejection and embarrassment with not so much as a drop of concern."

"Why should that matter?" Joy asked, annoyed that this seemed to again dismiss the significance or her pain.

"Because," replied Peregrine with an exasperated sigh, like he was talking to a toddler, "if there was nothing to fear, there was nothing to overcome, and if there was nothing to overcome, what was the point of all that suffering?"

"Are you saying suffering is good? I should go and find a way to suffer?"

"It absolutely can be good. It absolutely *should* be, if you use it right. But no, you don't go and actively *seek* suffering; lord knows there's enough of it that will find you, from the mundane tasks like cleaning your home to larger obstacles like rejection, hardship, denial, pain, death of those you love. Suffering produces perseverance, perseverance produces character, and character produces hope. And since hope fights fear, our antidote to fear is found in how we face those fears, those obstacles, those parts of ourselves that prevent us from doing what we know to be right because it seems hard, or there's a personal risk, or because we think it will take us from our comfort. Or even, frankly, the risk of actually being wrong, and having the opportunity to learn from that very painful admission."

"So, be grateful, be responsible, face fears, persevere, hope. It sounds like a fortune cookie to me," Joy said, letting her own dismissiveness enter her speech.

"Look kid, you came to *me* here," Peregrine said archly. "I could be doing other things."

"I'm sorry," Joy sighed, "it just seems too simple."

"That's because your thinking is all wrong still," the owl replied firmly. "And look where it's gotten you. Simple doesn't mean easy, and complex doesn't mean valid."

"Well, I'm not sure I'm following," Joy retorted. "You're saying a lot but you aren't getting to the point."

"Fine. Here's the rub: you thought this trip through seas and storms and cities, these years of suffering and sadness, this *holiday* was your grand adventure. But nowhere in this have you realised the adventure, *true* adventure, is journeying to the very heart of yourself. Knowing who you are, inside and out- wholly, honestly, unabashedly, the warts as well as the beauty. You haven't taken opportunities to develop your inmost self, to learn and to grow, to see the opportunity in the hardship or even appreciate the skill in success, and you most certainly have not offered that self in the service of others, because there's been no risk to you and your grievances justify anything you do negatively. Likewise, your mother wasn't happy for the same reason. She couldn't revel and delight in your presence, a product of the love she shared. She couldn't stop and enjoy that love in its own right. She wasn't happy, because she had shaped her entire world around the notion that joy could be found somewhere out there. "

He drew himself up, and stopped his pacing, looking deep into her eyes. "You see," he said in summation, "you can't appreciate the dry until you've been through the tempest. You can't face the tempest without the hope of the safety beyond. You don't *find* joy. You bring it with you. Sure, you can fake it, when things are good, but how can you appreciate the beauty of a flower without being aware of its delicateness and brevity? When you learn to be grateful without expectation, when you learn to relish hardship in the moment whilst you hope for the calm once it has passed, when you can see the people you care for as flawed individuals in their own right, who give to you out of the depth of their feelings towards you and who, in turn, are awaiting your gifts to buoy them, when you consider that you are made and then determine that you will exert all efforts to find out what you were made *for*, well, you won't need to be searching for joy. You'll just be Joy."

Joy struggled with the sudden silence that followed this monologue. Part of her wanted to object or put her own spin and view on things, but a growing part of her held back the inclinations and gently whispered for her to think about what she had heard before she spoke again.

"I... think I understand what you're saying."

"Well, good."

"But *you* enjoy being scary and then telling people things they don't want to hear."

"Hey," the owl replied with a wink, "it makes me happy."

"So how do I find what I'm made for?"

"Well, kid," Peregrine shrugged, "that, I can't tell you. It's your own journey, and I'd start by asking myself an important question: if I'm made for something, who was I made *by*? But let me ask you this: your friend left you, and you had to face your fears alone. How did that feel? Think about it before you speak."

Joy gave it reasonable consideration. "It felt... *awful*," she said. "At first. A part of me told me the most terrible things. I felt like the earth was going to open up and swallow me whole. But, I hate to say it... when I realised I had nothing to lose, I felt free, for the first time. Like *I* was making the decisions for once, *really* making them, not reacting or doing stuff because someone else told me to. I felt excited, and I don't think I've really felt like that before. I felt excited because I was doing what I was telling myself couldn't be done."

"And there you have it," Peregrine replied with a smile. "There's *nothing* good that doesn't have risk, kid. Risk will always bring fear. Be grateful for that fear, let it give you a moment to ask yourself important questions, but don't live in it. You'll become stronger than you thought you could be and, I suspect, you might pick up a bit of wisdom along the way."

"Really?"

"Really. Wisdom is just learning from your mistakes as much as your successes. There's as much joy in failing as there is in conquering, if...?"

"If I bring joy with me?"

"Got it in one!" Peregrine clapped, delighted. "Maybe there's hope for you yet."

Joy allowed the pop and crackle of the fire to continue as she cogitated on all that she had heard.

"And so, Tom?" she asked. "What do I do there?"

"You can appreciate how much it meant to have someone understand you," Peregrine replied. "That's worth rejoicing over. Things that should end, end where they should, and you can choose to see a young man, acting foolishly perhaps, but bringing an end to something that couldn't really have continued. I would suggest that is forgiveable. It's fine to mourn something of value, but that doesn't mean you have to hang onto it forever."

"And... my mum?"

"How about you tell me?"

Joy took a deep breath. "She was immature, and vain, and threw us away. I can be mad about that. But it's not her fault that I wasn't open and honest with Dad; that was me. I thought I needed to keep him together. And maybe... well, maybe I can forgive her for not being truthful, because I wasn't either. If she doesn't deserve forgiveness, then neither do I, really. Although..."

Yes?"

"I guess I haven't asked my Dad for forgiveness. Neither has she."

"And what's stopping you?" the owl enquired, leaning in closer and narrowing his eyes.

"Well... nothing, I guess. Except I'm... feeling worried, feeling afraid of telling him that I knew I was doing things wrong. That I kept him out, you know? Gosh, that I never cared that we kept our home, and could sit down and draw, as if nothing changed. I wanted things from him that I never told him, because I didn't want to be a burden. I didn't tell him I needed something from him, and then I was mad that he never gave me what I'd never asked for. I'd have to tell him all of that, and it scares me."

"And if you told him that, despite your fear?" Peregrine prompted.

Joy smiled.

"I think there would be some joy there. For both of us."

"Would he forgive you?"

"I know he would. But how do I forgive *her*, then, if she isn't sorry?"

"Well," Peregrine replied, hopping back up onto the log again, "that's something you could figure out. You could always go on a manhunt. But since I doubt you're going to go looking for everyone you've ever wronged, let me ask you this: would you want *them* to hold on to a grudge?"

No?"

"There you have it. If you're hoping for some grace amongst a flawed and fallen creation, perhaps you should start showing it first. Otherwise, this will just continue poisoning you, the way it's stolen the memory of your happiest moment. There's more to life than all this... *stuff*, kid."

"Like what?"

"Life itself."

He stretched his wings out wide, twisting his neck from side to side, limbering up as he looked around the forest.

"I think that's more time than I've given anyone of late. This is prime feeding time."

"Here," Joy said, hurriedly reaching into her bag. "I have a few caramels left over if you'd like-"

The owl waved her away. "You've given me plenty," he said, and he gave a warm smile. "So unless there's anything else..."

"Why are you called Peregrine?" she blurted out. "That's a kind of falcon, and you're an owl."

Peregrine looked around conspiratorially, and put a feathered wing to his beak in a *shhhh* motion. "Well, I don't tell people this normally, but I picked the name out because I wanted to seem scarier and more aloof."

"What was your real name?"

"Owlfred."

"I *knew* it."

Joy thought for a few moments more. "Hey," she added, "my friend lit that fire. On her behalf... I'm sorry that it destroyed your nest. I'm sorry that it damaged your tree."

Peregrine waved a wing dismissively.

"Fire's not bad for a forest," he said. "Allow the bushland to be cleared, sometimes, and you can see how things regrow. Just don't take it as an invitation, please," he finished, looking meaningfully towards the campfire. He fixed her with a long final look, and then extended a claw. Joy stood up, walked across to him, and shook it.

"Thank you," she said earnestly. "I needed to hear what you said."

"Just remember: this is the start of your adventure," Peregrine reminded her. "Even when it becomes familiar, and the number of participants dwindles, the adventure will continue, as long as you are open to it, and bring your joy with you. Your heart will heal in time."

"Of course it will," Joy replied with a smile. "I'm eighteen, after all."

Peregrine winked, and then with a *whoomph* he took off into the night, scattering sparks from the campfire as he propelled himself skywards. Joy was left sitting next to her bag, snacking on the remaining treats which were all the food that she had left. She felt differently than she had hours earlier; the storm inside her had settled and an ocean of calm was in its place. She hadn't realised how much energy the whole day had taken from her, but despite feeling drained, she didn't want to lose this moment to reflect on what she had heard.

Very well. If she had to start by stripping her expectations back, where did she begin? It occurred to her that she started with herself; she'd seen herself in the context of her parents, the divorce, and the survival for so long. Until she met Peregrine, her identity had been fiercely tied to her father, as a caregiver and defender but also because she refused to see in herself the inescapable elements of her mother. Following the confrontation, she was now prepared to notice and accept behaviours and instincts that were a blend of both, but even that wasn't satisfying; in truth, she had quashed many of the positive qualities of her mother, suppressed music and poetry and revelry because she associated it with the person who had destroyed her world. At the same time, she had blinded herself to the negative attributes she was in the process of repeating.

She'd thought of herself as her father's daughter, but the truth was she wasn't her father *or* her mother. Whilst she could see the similarities and acknowledge the origins, she would always have to be herself, an entity accountable in its own right, and this revelation lifted an invisible weight. She wasn't bound to repeat mistakes or doomed to a life where existence was eked out in a crushing daily grind. But she could if she wanted to; if she didn't want to take a risk, or if she wanted to find safety in predictability, she was free to do so. It wouldn't be because of what her father did, or because she was following her mother's approach of abandoning everything in pursuit of a dream. It would be because she chose to do it, and would have to wear the consequences herself.

Despite having experienced terrible heartbreak only a day before, here she was, growing anew. That incident had become a catalyst for a discovery she never would have made; within twenty-four hours, her entire world and outlook had changed, and without it, she'd be preparing for a trip to the next town, running down the clock on her time in Frieland and having to either declare her desire to stay and find her joy in Tom, who did not feel the same way, or surrender and return home, so would have lost him anyway. She had leant too much on him, not because he had offered, but because of a place of lack within her that she was using him to fill. As much as she hated the internal voice that had put her in that position of declaring her love, she looked back without expectation and realised that had she not blurted out her feelings, had Tom not had the willingness to write his letter, and had she not risked rejection and then experienced it immediately, she would not have found this new outlook. It hit her for the first time: a sense of gratitude for the pain, an appreciation for a new strength she would otherwise not have found. Heck, she wouldn't have met Aunt Becky, and then wouldn't have been given the sandwiches that Peregrine asked for; she might have missed Cupidity, never to hear of the owl who gave her wisdom. So she felt grateful, for the joy and for the pain, and the hope that she could become more than she was.

From within her, a calm spread out. It didn't remove the ache of loss entirely, but it was a salve that began to flow over her wounds, the ones from Tom, and the ones from her mother. She pulled her bag across and lay down on it as if it were a pillow, then draped her coat over herself. As she allowed herself to drift, her mind recalled the moment of her argument with Fear, and the look on his face as she'd spat her venom. She missed her friend, but she was also aware of Peregrine's warning. What she she missed all those years, never having to face down her worries for herself? Was that his fault, or was it hers?

Equally, the times they had laughed, the mischief they had shared, his friendship in the middle of those terrible times, had carried her through when she thought she would otherwise break. He had given her someone to take out her annoyance on, had seen the times she cried, had poked and prodded her when she needed to, and had kept her from danger. That was worth appreciating.

He'd promised he'd be there if she called. Why hadn't she done so? Was it shame? Was it self-punishment? No... it was because despite herself, facing real fear had pushed her into defiance. Defiance of her inner voice and her circumstances. She hadn't called, because she hadn't wanted to, and she hadn't wanted to, because she was living.

The relationship had been damaged by her actions. As much as she had been mad at Tom, she had to recognise that he had at least made the effort to express his remorse, however feebly it may have been done. She could not condemn her mother's behaviour if she left the friendship to languish where it was, even if she was now willing to take on her fears and temper them with hope.

She watched the fire as it dropped lower and settled into the steady heat of the log which was turning to coals. "Fear," she whispered into the embers, "I need you."

Come the morning, the fire was gone, and Joy sat up a little painfully, stretching out the crick in her neck. She looked around her; this place had been one of revelation, but she hadn't truly needed to come here if she'd had the guts to face herself in the first instance. The giant owl was right: he hadn't told her anything she hadn't really known. She just hadn't wanted to face it. Her journey had only just begun, and it needed to start with restoration. It started back home.

Resolute, she gathered her belongings, and tried to get her bearings. She was still lost, but she figured that the forest couldn't continue forever.

Using the sun peeking through the leaves as a rough guide, she headed east, and after the best part of an hour, noticed the forest starting to thin. She found a track, following its winding path until she emerged fully into the bright sunlight, looking over a field of lush pasture, a river gently winding its way through in the background, a road cutting its way across the landscape not far from where she was. It was still fairly early in the day, and so she paused to feel grateful for the sun on her face, the gentle breeze blowing across, and for having a destination to aim for.

"Very nice out here, don't you think?" Fear asked behind her, sitting on the ground up against a tree with his hands behind his head, and Joy fought hard to avoid an involuntary gasp when she heard his voice.
"Oh yes indeed," he continued. "Quite lovely. Another day in paradise."
He stood up, smiling, and Joy's heart beat faster with nervousness. Would he be upset? Would he be nursing a grudge? However, this was subsumed by the overwhelming relief of seeing her friend again.
"You came," Joy said, her voice cracking slightly.
"You called," Fear replied with a smile.

Chapter 11

Goodbye, My Fear

The time has come to leave, and to live what I believe.

It was a perfect day. The sun was out but the air was fairly crisp; birds tweeted in the nearby trees and the long grass provided a pleasant susurration as the wind blew through.

Joy and Fear were sitting on an old log, partially shaded by a large oak tree, with a vista across the plain. Joy was doing her best to think of a way to start the conversation, and drew a blank. Fear was uncommonly quiet, but not especially morose. It was odd that he would be happy to sit in silence; his usual métier was to rattle off the list of things that could go wrong and what could have been done to avoid them.

After a few quiet minutes had gone by, he looked at Joy for a moment, frowned, reached out and plucked a Worm of Concern that had appeared and was burrowing into her forehead. He inspected it.

"Ah, procrastination," he said with an expert eye.

"You know," Joy said at last, "I wasn't sure you were going to come back."

Fear nodded. "I know."

"Because I was afraid of it, and you know everyone's fears?"

"No, because I'm smart."

Joy swung her legs on the log. "You were right about Tom, of course," she admitted. She was expecting something self-congratulatory from Fear, but instead he said "Well, I'm sorry to hear that."

"You did try to tell me," she continued.

"Perhaps I shouldn't have," he responded with a shrug.

"You're always right."

"Well, as you know, I do love being right."

"Look, I'm trying to say I'm sorry!" Joy exclaimed.

"But you haven't," said Fear matter-of-factly. "Are you?"

Joy paused for a moment here. This wasn't like the Fear she thought she knew so well. He wasn't revelling in her discomfort or making fun of her, and she suddenly felt a yearning for the very irritations that had grated on her only days ago.

Fear didn't seem angry, or upset. His responses were fairly to the point, but weren't curt. His question seemed genuine, so in line with her new resolve, she subjected it to honest reflection and told the truth.

"I don't know," Joy said at last. "I'm definitely sorry that I said I never needed you."

"Hey!" Fear said suddenly, jumping up. "I think I can see a creek down there a short ways. It's a nice day; do you think you'd feel up to a walk with an anthropomorphic personification?"

"Why, what are you planning to *do* at the creek?" Joy asked cautiously.

"Oh ye of little faith," Fear asked, feigning hurt, "it's a nice day and stroll is good for one's constitution, I'm told."

"Hello? 1913 called and it wants its lingo back," Joy shot back.

Fear put on a old-timey, nasally radio announcer voice. "Listen here, schweetness, the day I let a dame tell me what to do on the stock market is the day you can put me to bed with a shovel. It's got nowhere to go but up, I say!"

He laughed at himself. "Well, we used to walk beside the canals back at home. This is eminently more pleasant. For old times' sake?"

Joy smiled. "Well, when you put it like that, how can I refuse?"

It wasn't a long walk. The meadow was only a few hundred metres long before it gave way, via erosion over the years, runoff points and sandy soil that were cut away by the creek itself. They strolled, making small talk and enjoying the sun, reminiscing about the tavern in Gloomhaven and telling each other about things that were *so great*. For a moment, Joy felt like she was at a funeral and was taking part in the most wonderful eulogy, but she wasn't certain what it was that was supposed to have died.

The creek, when they eventually came to it, was far too wide to jump across, and deep enough that it would buoy and sweep away someone incautious enough to attempt to wade across, but wasn't so deep or so wide that it could be considered a river. It was reasonably quick-moving and babbled pleasantly. Fear sat down on the bank and put his feet in the water.

"How come you do that?" Joy asked. "I mean, it just goes through you."

"I suppose it makes me feel a little more human," he said, laying back on the grass and looking up at her.

"So..."
"Tell me about this great discovery of yours."

And there it was. The whole confrontation she'd been avoiding and it was delivered gently at just the right time whilst a pair of intangible legs dangled in water which never deviated from its path. It was classic Fear. So Joy launched into the whole thing, the story almost falling out of her mouth. In some ways, she was finding herself both relieved and excited just to be able to put it into words, as much to share it as to remind herself that it had all really happened.

She talked about Peregrine, née Owlbert, and his short temper, his direct wisdom, and his refusal to allow her to hide the truth from herself as much as others. She talked about feeling like she had met herself for the first time; Fear asked her if she liked that person enough to meet them again, and Joy said she honestly didn't know. She said there were parts of that person who, frankly, was a bit of a bitch.
She talked about letting go of her dreams and fantasies about Tom as well as her anger towards his departure. Her recognition that she had constructed a whole imagined future without so much as a word of his own input, and the unreasonable position it put him in, but also her lingering sadness that the person who knew all about her heart was no longer in her life.
About her longing for closeness from someone who could help shoulder the load, her tiredness with just surviving the day and keeping people going back home, particularly her dad. The fact that many of her interactions consumptive or built around her need to feel a sense of control in a careening world. Her realisation of the importance of mutuality in any form of relationship; that even with Cupidity, whatever the grievances that were valid to hold, part of Joy's drive had been needing to be needed. Her chance

to finally articulate and say that she felt betrayed by her mother, and her anger and grief, but also the oddness of looking at her as a woman not much older than herself, trapped in a circumstance of her own. Her own revelation that she had tried to shoe-horn a relationship into a gap it was not meant to, nor was capable, of filling, and the empathy that came into the woman she imagined her mother to have been trying to do the same with no real means or skills to manage it otherwise.

"He's good value, that Peregrine," Fear said. "Nothing quite like getting a bird's eye view of your life, so to speak."

"There's more," Joy continued, nervously.

"I'd be very surprised if there wasn't," Fear said gently. "Carry on."

Now Joy talked about feeling fear for the first time, *really* feeling it, feeling the worries grow and the overwhelming sensation of a great ocean moving in at high tide, slowly increasing in height because the breadth was so enormous but moving *mass*, and like a kid on the beach, trying to bail that out with a bucket and spade. Her discovery that she could always blame Fear for the things that went wrong, with no accountability. The questions she had been confronted with, and the emptiness she felt when there was no-one to turn to to voice these, much less remove them.

"I felt..." she trailed off

"Terrified?" Fear suggested.

"Alive," Joy replied. "It's something Peregrine said to me: there was no such thing as bravery without fear, and therefore there could be no joy in overcoming it. And for the first time, really, I was scared; I thought I could die. Or worse, that I'd *live*. That somehow, I'd be responsible for... all *this*," gesturing to herself. "It was so easy when things were someone else's fault, or when other people were dumb, or when you could tell me all the things that were going to go wrong. It was so easy when I never had to *worry* about anything because you took all my fears and worries away. But all that really left me with was forward motion, and that's not the same thing as..."

"Living?"

"Right."

"I thought," Fear said slowly, "that you were sorry for saying that you never needed me."

"I am," Joy said earnestly. "I'm sorry. I was wrong, I definitely needed you. I needed you more than *anything*."

"But...?"

"But..." she began, and found that tears were beginning to well up in her eyes, "I don't think that I need you any more."

Joy looked down at her feet, feeling her ears hot with embarrassment and even a touch of shame. This entity had been her best and only friend through the hardest points in her life. He had used all that he had in his power to smoothe her way forward, had protected her, had warned her, had joined her whenever it was needed. He had cheered her up when she hadn't thought it was possible, and knew all of her buttons to push that she now realised had held things together when the world had become overwhelming; her irritable responses and need to prove him wrong had carried her forward at times she would otherwise have stopped under the weight of the challenge before her.

"Not before time," Fear said cheerfully, and Joy raised her head, to see him with his arms behind his head, beaming. "I was beginning to think you'd *never* get there."

"I don't understand," Joy said, perplexed. Fear got to his feet, and put his hands on the place where her shoulders were.

"Look, I didn't want this gig *forever*, you know what I mean? Not that you aren't great, but you know, invisible friends don't exactly make a lot of sense into your twenties and, besides, I don't want anyone auditing my files and seeing a significant period of using my powers to help a high schooler. I mean, the age gap is *millennia* and people do talk. I could get Me Too'd if I'm not careful."

"I mean, Fear, it's not that I don't appreciate everything you've done for me, I mean, I wouldn't-" Joy started babbling, before Fear pressed a finger to her lips. For the first time since she was small, she actually *felt* this, and little sparks shot out around his fingers. He looked surprised for a moment, then smiled warmly.

"Ah, Sparky," he said fondly. "You don't know how hard it's been for me. I saw you, this unique little grain of sand in the mollusc of the world, being coated with all manner of unpleasantness on her way to becoming a pearl. I wanted to help. I... *needed* to, I think."

"Why did you need to?" Joy asked, feeling her eyes moisten.

"I don't know. In all the centuries and centuries of watching you people, growing your fears and hopefully preventing you all from taking the species off a cliff, there would sometimes be this point of resistance. Someone who acted in *spite* of the fear, not because of it. Sometimes small, sometimes large things. It was fascinating to see; how the fears I grew could be trapped, or partitioned, or isolated, and what they would become *afterwards*; a part of the person, a memory, transformed and carried forward in a way that brought out the excitement all over again."

"I don't understand."

"It meant I realised that these fears could be more than just *fear*, you know? They eventually became happiness to people. They became the stories they inspired others with. That fear wasn't just caution and worry, but opportunity and hope and... well, if fear could change into something else, I wondered if Fear could change too."

He took a big sigh. "But..."

"But?"

"But I'm not human. I am what I am. I saw in you the spark about to be overwhelmed by the world, and I couldn't let it happen. I wanted to protect it, to see this turn into a burning flame. Imagine, Fear doing the transforming? But I couldn't help you conquer fear."

He looked downcast for a moment, and Joy suddenly understood.

"You could only take it away," she breathed, a flood of compassion accompanying the revelation.

"I could only take it away," he nodded. "I did it at first to help, and it seemed to. And I loved watching you flourish in its absence, but instead of growing outwards..."

"I grew with you and stayed there?" Joy suggested. Fear snapped his fingers.

"Exactly! And I couldn't be another person who abandoned you, and turn you back over to the wolves, overcome by sadness and left back in your room in Pleasant Lane, until that house became a tomb. But I couldn't continue to leave you feeling nothing either."

"Like Deliria."

"Yes, like Deliria. Nor could I leave you to wallow in self-pity."

"Like Gloomhaven."

"Exactly. And despite my excellent academic coaching, all the knowledge in the world didn't seem to offer any direction outwards-"

"Like Philosophia?"

"Correct. And I realised... this life, it's an adventure for you humans. All of it, not just one little part of the journey. It's learning new things and feeling discouraged and sometimes being honest instead of putting on a happy face and sometimes putting on a happy face because you need to get through a moment. It's all those things because it ends. Even love. Even heartbreak."

"Like Tom?" she asked. Fear nodded.

"Like Tom, and the others that will come after him. Like your mother. Like any manner of things. And by stopping that pain, by managing those moments, I stopped the adventure; *I* was killing the spark. You're human, so you can be *anything*. But I... I will always be Fear. I can't be anything else."

"So, what? You made this place to teach me something?"

"No," he said, gesturing around. "*You* made this place. You and all the others that came before; the flames in the dark, those unique and special characters who transform what I make into achievements and tales passed down to grandchildren. Those destined to carry joy, *true* joy, in front of them like a lamp."

Joy felt overwhelmed by both gratitude for the words and deep affection; these were compliments on a level of sincerity she wasn't used to in the usually sarcastic interactions they typically had. She remembered when Fear said he hadn't heard her talk like this before, back when she was baring her soul to Tom on the second day they had met.

"You know," she said, swallowing the lump in her throat that was threatening her voice, "I never asked you how you were. Or what you felt. Or what you hoped for."

She looked down for a moment. "I wasn't a very good friend, I'm sorry."

"First one I've had," Fear replied with a shrug. "You get to be the worst, but you also get to be the best."

"Did *you* get something out of this? I don't want this all to have been one-way."

Fear smiled. "More than you'll ever really know, I think. It really depends on what you do after this; if you turn my silly little fears into stories that outlive you, that's enough for me. Plus, of course, I got to sort out Avaritia.

That's just a cherry on top, really."

"Yes, what *did* you do to her?" Joy asked, suddenly reminded of the revelations of the fashion empire's demise. "Cupidity said that she'd gone crazy."

Fear grinned, and rubbed his hands together evilly.

"I didn't **do** anything to her. What I did instead, right, was go visit *everyone* in the city, and I took every fear anyone had ever had that had anything to do with Avaritia away. Every little comparison to her style, every niggling desire for her validation, every drive to let her dictate the right way to live."

"That must have taken a while!"

"It took weeks. I may have under-estimated the task."

"Did you take it from Cupidity?"

"Yes. Right at the end. But I didn't know what she'd do; she was so focussed on her dream that I was worried it might not even make a difference."

"It did."

"I'm glad. But back to Avaritia. The change eroded the world from under that horrible woman's feet, and it fed her number one fear: that she didn't matter. She'd created such a culture of fear that in its absence, there was no love to take its place, and she found herself living her own nightmare-knock over the house of cards, and all that was left was indifference. Nobody even bothered to hate her. They just didn't care, at all, about who she was, or what she did. That plunge into ignominy, for someone who had created a whole city around being the centre of attention... let's just say it was a loooooong way to fall."

"All because she threatened me?"

"All because she thought she could bend you to her will," he said, folding his arms across his chest firmly.

Joy's heart sank for a moment as she considered something potentially dreadful.

"Did you take Tom's fears? Is that why he came around to help that day?

Is that why he decided to leave the town?"

Fear smiled warmly.

"Actually, I'm delighted to tell you no. See, I went to do it to him too, one night after you'd gone to sleep, not long after you'd dropped by the offices. I'd *seen* his worries in the past, his fear of life outside the protection of her status. It was shocking, then, when I got there and found that the worries and concerns were nowhere to be found. They'd shrivelled and atrophied. My only conclusion was this: *you* were suddenly more important to him than everything else. Whatever he felt for you, Sparky, was real. You changed him."

Joy was overwhelmed. She began tearing up, the kindness and reassurance of this revelation touching her deeply.

"Will I ever see you again?" she sniffed, with a little desperation, knowing that this was goodbye.

"Who knows? There's a big-"

"You don't have to go. I mean, we can still be friends," Joy started, and then realised something. "I'm sorry," she said, "you were saying something and I cut you off instead of listening. I guess that's my own worries."

"Ah, yes, the fear of letting someone down. I can take this one if you want-" he said as he reached towards her forehead, but she caught his wrist en route and there was a sudden flash of light at the point of contact. For the first time, colour flowed through Fear's arm from his fingers to his elbow and the sparks leapt and danced. Fear's face was priceless- whilst Joy had seen him shocked before, here he had truly been knocked into orbit.

"Thank you," Joy said, looking at him, "but that fear... it's one for me to deal with now." She let go of his wrist, but Fear's arm stayed coloured, and he looked down at it, flexing his fingers back and forth.

He cleared his throat, and dusted his legs off, making a show of movement while he tried to gather his thoughts again.

"Yes, well, very appropriate, very good," he said, his voice a little hoarse all of a sudden and avoiding eye contact. "The student is the master and such. Is it raining? Is someone cutting onions? My, this pollen."

"Oh, shut up," Joy laughed affectionately. Fear sighed.

"Hundreds of thousands of years, and that has *never* happened," he said, watching his arm as the colour finally started fading back to its usual grey, starting at the elbow and moving back towards the wrist. "I was going to say: we both know what all this means. You're one of a kind, Joy. I'm proud to have been your friend. And I'm grateful that you were mine."

"I'm glad."

"Can I still use your Netflix account?"

"Do you even have a TV?"

"I'm afraid not."

"There's probably a worm for that."

"Well played."

"Fear?"

"Yes?"

Joy threw her arms around Fear and hugged him hard, and in that moment, his whole body became fully solid and coloured, his hair still black and but his irises turning an ethereal blue, and for the first time he felt the breeze across his skin, the wind through his hair, the warmth of the sun on his back, and the dampness in the shirt on his chest where Joy's face was buried in a vain attempt to hide her tears. Fear put his arms around Joy in return and hugged her back, but his face was a picture of shock, as if all the breath had suddenly been knocked out of him.

"Thank you," she said. "For everything."

Fear struggled to say anything, his system overwhelmed with the sudden sensory input.

"How?" he eventually managed.

"Don't know," her muffled voice said from his chest. "Don't ask."

She pulled her head back and tried to wipe the tears from her eyes. Fear put a finger up and wiped it away; he held it up to the sun, looking at his finger glisten in the light. The passage of the wind over the tear drop cooled the tip finger, a sensation he had never before experienced.

"All of the thank-you gifts you could have given me," he whispered hoarsely, "and you gave me humanity, if only for a moment."

A tear of its own rolled down his cheek, and he reached up and touched it, surprised and fascinated in equal measure. He frowned for a moment, looking at the finger with their mingled tears together, and his brow furrowed with new-found concern.

"You'll be OK, will you? You finally found joy?" he asked earnestly, noticing that the tip of his finger started to lose colour and revert back to grey.

"I'm finding her," Joy replied. "And I don't think she's far away. She's singing in the rain somewhere."

"I'm worried about you," he said seriously, the discolouration reaching his hand.

"Well..." Joy reached up, and her fingers passed through Fear's forehead, and she plucked out a Worm of Concern. She looked at it closely, and then nodded with a knowing smile. "The fear of letting go of someone you love," she said.

"Actually," he replied, "that one's Public Speaking."

She hit him playfully on the chest and he said "ow!", froze for a second, and then smiled. "Ah, pain. It's a day of firsts. I don't suppose you'd like me to see you off? Back with our good friend in the top hat?"

"I think," Joy said with a smile, "that things that should end, end where they should."

"Wise words."

"From a wise friend."

Fear smiled, nodded, and began stepping back up the embankment, the colour slowly shifting inwards from his extremities to his chest. "A small parting gift," he said, looking over Joy's shoulder. She realised that she had missed, amongst the sound of the stream, the *schlap-schlap-schlap* of water against wood. Steve The Boat, with impeccable timing, had made his way along the creek and had stopped at the shore, bobbing expectantly. Joy's expression lit up. She looked back to Fear, who was still walking backwards up the hill as the last of the colour drained away from him, and then started to fade entirely from view.

"Goodbye, my Joy," he said, and his words whispered along in the wind.

"Goodbye, my Fear."

Chapter 12

I'm Coming Home

I'm dreaming for you, over time and space.

Joy stayed beside the creek for a while. Steve gave no indication of hurry, as far as she could tell from his wooden expression, and after everything that had happened, she felt incredibly free. She could hear the sounds of bees buzzing over flowers, felt the coolness of the breeze contrast with the warmth of the sun, and there was nothing to do but enjoy the moment. So she put her bag on the ground and lay down on the patch of grass where Fear had been, with her legs dangling into the water, feeling cool and warm at the same time. She closed her eyes, shut out the light, and waited for a dream to take her somewhere far away.

For some reason, she was taken back to a peaceful scene, a dining table, drawing with her father. No; he was there alone, but he was drawing the visions from her head. It seemed like forever since she had turned her thoughts to him; she had thought *about* him insofar as reflecting on her circumstances, but within this memory she had realised how much of a treasure those moments together had been, and how she missed them. She could see him clearly in her mind's eye, going about his day in the empty house, and then sitting down at the table, with the canvases and paper, drawing his hopes and dreams, for himself, for her, for the place the moment took him. And if he had no more dreams to draw, well, she would dream for him, because the world was big and strange and full of invisible people, cities in the clouds, and flying boats.

She opened her eyes, sat up and opened her bag. Refilled a water bottle in the creek and hoped against hope that she wasn't going to discover a new, previously-unheard-of strain of bacteria, but such were the risks and she had at least filled it upstream of her dangling legs. She checked the rest of the bag's contents. Her spare clothes from Cupidity were still in there, along with the beautiful red coat, so Joy wrapped the waterproof garment around the clothes to keep them dry in the event of a storm. There were a final assortment of sweets, and her water bottle. Other than that, the bag was fairly light; she was taking a lot from Frieland, but very little needed to be carried.

She stood and laid the bag carefully into the boat, and then looked at it. "You're not going to rock when I get in, right?" she asked cautiously. "I don't want to go back soaked to the skin."
Steve the Boat, of course, said nothing. However, as Joy stepped in from the embankment, he didn't so much as wobble. Joy ran a hand along the edge. "I knew I could trust you," she said. She settled in the back, finding a comfortable place to sit and resting her bag in such a way that she could

use it to sleep but also access its contents when she needed. The boat still hadn't moved.

Joy looked around, patted her pockets, looked at the sky. The weather seemed clear. This would be about as good a time as any. She took one final deep breath.

"Steve?" She said. "Let's go home."

The boat released itself and began floating down the creek. The oars moved in their locks and riggers, and after a few minutes Joy picked them up and gave four firm rows. Just as it had done back in what seemed like a lifetime ago, the boat began to rise above the water and float back towards Frieland Township. It sailed over the square and beyond the walls with the portcullis, straight towards the angry-looking cloud set which sat like a bruise across the horizon just beyond the pier and moorings.

There were ongoing flashes of lightning within. Joy felt her heart quicken as they approached it, alone in a floating boat destined for the tumult of the Unforgiving Pass. She felt her veins chill and the hairs stand up on the back of her neck as fear ran through her body. Her own fear, wholly hers, for the very first time since she could remember, cherished and longed for. Almost as a surprise to herself, she let out a laugh. It was small at first but it built, and soon, as she felt the buzz from her fingertips to the top of her head and the feeling as though her stomach was going to climb up her throat, she was laughing so hard that she thought that she struggled to breathe. She managed to catch her breath, feeling utterly alive. She grabbed both of the oars.

"We've got this, right?" she asked aloud. The boat dipped down and up as if it had gone over a small wave, the first response she had ever had from it. She shrugged.

"Sometimes, I'm told, the only way out of the storm is through it," she said to the open air, and Steve rocked approvingly. "And if we get wet, well, we get wet."

A few moments later, she was swallowed by the clouds, which closed and left no hint that a mysterious boat had just flown through it.

There is an etiquette for taxis, Ubers, rideshares and friends from whom a lift had been swindled, begged, extorted, or otherwise bummed, but the exact process of thanking a flying boat was something that Joy had not been trained on. She wished she could ask Fear, but the thing about being on your own and doing what's right was that you couldn't pass the buck.

So as Joy floated damply back over the city at night, dropping down above the trees, over the highway, and eventually towards the canal, she thought hard about what to do. Her bag now contained soggy clothes, empty wrappers, and an empty water-bottle. Changing into thankfully dry, albeit not especially clean, clothes in a rowboat by moonlight far above the ocean was an experience she was not especially keen on repeating, but it had been done. She hoped Steve had had the chivalry to avert whatever his gaze would have been.

She had shrugged on the long red trenchcoat, just in case, and by the time they had reached the city, was feeling warm and positive.

The boat disappeared down the concrete embankments, and came to rest near the metal maintenance staircase she had originally stepped down on. Joy didn't move for a moment.

"This isn't the end, right?" she half-asked, half-said as a statement. Steve gave no response. Joy smiled to herself.

"All right," she said. "That's fair. I'll tell you what; when the time comes, and my feet tell me where to go, I'll come and see if you're there."

A sudden surge in the channel made Steve bump up and down again, or perhaps he nodded.

"Besides," she said mischievously, "maybe my next ride will be a flying carpet."

The boat bucked sideways and Joy almost fell out. She fell down onto the seat and laughed.

"I'm sorry," she said, still smiling and patting an oar, "I didn't know that was a sore spot."

She reached out and grabbed her bag, and then stepped out onto the landing. She knelt down, feeling awkward, and hugged the boat.

"It's probably weird for him, too," came Fear's voice out of the air. She spun around but couldn't see anyone there. She wondered if she had imagined it; it was the kind of thing he'd say.

"Fear?" She asked out loud. There was no response. She shrugged, and smiled as she realised that it didn't matter. Real or imagined, it was him, and she loved him for it.

Joy picked up the bag and began trudging up the metal staircase. She was almost at the top when a flashlight beam shone in her face, and she put her hand out to shield her eyes from the glare. A gruff male voice boomed angrily "Who are you? What are you doing in there? That's a restricted access area for council staff!"

The beam was removed from her eyes and when they acclimatised she could see the shape of a very irate police officer, whose car was pulled over on the side of the road without its sirens or lights flashing but its hazard lights blinking.

"Oh, uuhh..." she stammered, "I was just..." *coming back from a city in the clouds?* She thought to herself.

The police officer shone their torch down to the bottom of the stairs; Steve the Boat was gone.

"I dropped my bag down there," Joy eventually managed. "I was walking back home and popped it up on the guard rail for a moment, but it fell down into the canal. It got caught down on that platform so I thought I'd just nip down and grab it; sorry, I didn't know I wasn't allowed."

The police officer said *harrumph* and picked up the bag, which was still soaking wet from its passage back through the clouds and storms. The contents, likewise, were inspected: a bundle of wet clothes, wet plastic wrappers, and an empty water bottle. She could see the story play across his face: this checks out.

"Well, miss," he said firmly, "you shouldn't be down in those things. People fall in and there's enough current at the moment that you'd struggle getting out if you did. Next time, let the bag go. Where did you say you lived?"

"Number Seventeen, Pleasant Lane."

"Well, it's not far. I'll offer you a ride; no point walking home with a soaking wet bag."

"Thank you, officer!"

"It's fine. I have to say, you look very happy for someone who just dropped their bag in the canal."

"Well, joy's where you find it," she said with a smile. "I could be sad that I dropped my bag in the canal, or I could be happy that I was able to save it. Or maybe I'm just grateful a kind person was here and I didn't have to walk home with a wet bag."

The policeman blushed but his former scowl had improved to a slight smile. He opened up the car's rear door, and as Joy climbed in, she could see the dark silhouette of a boat just above the trees behind the officers' head. She smiled again, and he spun around to follow her gaze.

"What are you looking at?" He asked, curious.

Joy just looked wistful.

"Probably just a bat," she said. "It's just good to be home."

And so it was that Joy was driven up Pleasant Lane to the house at Number Seventeen.

"Oof," said the policeman conversationally, "they were stretching the truth with the street name, weren't they?"

Joy just smiled.

"It's pleasant enough for me."

"Oh, I didn't mean to-"

"It's fine. You know, I met a lot of people recently who thought that if you didn't expect much, you couldn't be disappointed. And a bunch of others who thought if you kept getting all the things, then life would be *so great*. And I even thought that the right person would make everything perfect. So who knows, maybe someone thought that naming a street how they hoped it would be, would be enough to make it happen."

"And was it?"

"Not always. But I guess if everyone makes it that way, then it will be one day."

"And if they don't, you can always hope."

"So I'm told. It's pleasant enough for me."

"Well then, miss, I *hope* you have a pleasant evening."

As the police car pulled away, Joy trudged up the final stairs to the front door. It was strange as she raised her hand to knock; it seemed familiar and yet entirely new, as if it wasn't truly hers any more whilst simultaneously being very much hers. It was the signifier of home, which was contained *within* the walls, rather than made by them, and which was not forever but was more than enough for now. She could see, through the window, the living room adorned with their drawings, and realised for the first time that it was, in fact, adorned with their history within which her father immersed himself. Those moments with her, that she had thought of as cheap memories, were his buttress against the world.

Her heartbeat quickened with anticipation as she saw the light underneath the door disturbed by shadows, hearing the soft swish of her father's feet in socks on the carpet. The door opened and there was her father. He looked much the same as when she had left, a little thinner perhaps, but seemed lighter, even more so as he registered who it was and his face lit up. She expected him to rush forward, even expected *herself* to rush forward, but neither of them moved.

"Hello," he said at last.

"Hi, Dad," she replied.

"You look good. Very fancy, you know?" he said awkwardly, gesturing to her outfit.

"Thanks, a friend made this."

She could see behind him, lying up against the wall, was an old guitar case, with stickers on them from various cities around the country.

"Is that mum's old guitar?"

"Yeah, I uh, thought I'd put it out here. You know, in case you came back. Might want it for wherever you are now."

"I'm here now, Dad."

"You're home?"

"Home will be with me anywhere I go. *You're* with me anywhere I go. I'm not going to be staying in Pleasant Lane forever, but if you'll have me, I'd like to be here for now."

"I was worried about you," he said.

"I know," Joy replied. "I'm sorry. I was somewhere I couldn't reach you."

"You can always reach me."

Joy thought of her mind's eye, of seeing her father in the kitchen, drawing her dreams.

"I know that now," she said. "There's lots to talk about. But first... I missed you so, so much."

Her father smiled, and then stepped forward and picked her up in a hug. "I thought you were lost," his muffled voice said over her shoulder. She clung to him equally hard, until he set her back down on the landing and took her bag as they walked inside.

"I was," she replied as she stepped through the doorway, "but came back found."

On her way past, she picked up the guitar and carried it with her upstairs. It no longer signalled apprehension or hope; it was just a pleasant thing, a gift gratefully received. Outside the door, her father could hear the case clasps be undone, and after a few minutes, Joy began to play a song that came directly from her heart, resonating through the house, because she was home at last, right at the start of her grand adventure.